MW00423645

Home Place
A Novel

Sally Crosiar

SALLY CROSIAR

This is a work of fiction.
No resemblance to any living person is intended.

DEDICATION

For My Forebears
Simon and Sarah Owen Crosiar
Amasa Owen and Lovina Brown Crosiar
Eli Ives and Mary Malinda Ogan Crosiar
Warren P. and Darlene Bird Crosiar
And the home they built that I still call
Our Home Place

SALLY CROSIAR

ALSO BY SALLY CROSIAR

<u>Fiction</u>

Come Back: A Novel

<u>Nonfiction</u>

Love Builders: Tools to Build Every Relationship

Find the Love of Your Life

<u>Children's</u>

My Uncle Dave

Find all Sally's books at:
<u>https://www.amazon.com/Sally-Crosiar/e/B075SLLGN1</u>

SALLY CROSIAR

Kat

Face down in barnyard slop, I lifted my head and glared at the stupid cow. "You pull this today? For months, you bellow and bawl if I'm one minute late. And now you refuse to go in the barn door? Stupid Odd cow!"

The beast glared back and, as soon as I was on my feet again, dodged and balked for a full fifteen minutes before she sauntered toward the barn like it was her idea the whole time.

"Damn Stupid Odd Cow!" I muttered. "I won't be sorry to see the last of you!" I jerked a rope through her halter, tied her in the stanchion, and tossed some hay in the trough. "Eat. Eat and act like you want to cooperate, dammit!"

I didn't expect it to work, but you've got to have hope, right? And it had to be done. I warmed my hands best I could and began.

For a few minutes, the pings of milk hitting the bucket, the sounds of her chewing, lulled us both. I leaned my head on the cow's flank. "Last time, old girl. Might never milk again." I dashed a tear with my sleeve.

That's when the stupid cow stepped back into the bucket, kicked out with a hind hoof, and whipped her tail at my face. All before I could duck.

"Son of a…" She turned her head with a malicious *gotcha* in her eyes that shook nostalgia and regret from my mind. "Last time, you stupid, stupid cow! Last time!"

An hour later, I turned toward the house for breakfast and a shower when I heard the rumble of a truck and Dutch's warning bark. I glanced down at my filthy barn clothes and shrugged.

Like any farmer, George Shaeffer knew manure. Probably wouldn't think it seemly for a woman to be caked in it, though. Wouldn't catch his prissy wife and prissier daughter in the barn. No doubt he'd spin a tale to the geezers down at the feed store – how they should have seen Kat Patterson up to her elbows in shit. Oh well.

Mr. Shaeffer climbed down from his truck, held a hand to Dutch, nodded to me. I hurried up the hill toward him. And naturally, arrived out of breath.

"Mornin', Kat," Mr. Shaeffer said with a smirk that foretold the geezers' entertainment. "Here to get your cow. Looks like it's high time."

"You got that right. I'll bring her out from the barn."

I hoped she'd take to lead or that the old farmer would look away when she didn't. No such luck. I pulled and slapped. Nothing. Except the growing smirk on Shaeffer's face.

Finally he said, "Give me that thing." One yank and the two of them locked eyes. "Bossy, I'm thinking you and I understand each other." And damned if that Stupid Odd cow didn't toss a smirk at me and follow him out the barn door meek as a kitten.

Getting her into the truck proved not quite so easy. Attagirl, I thought with righteous vindication as she tried to rear and jerk away. Show him your true colors.

Shaeffer spit and delivered an elbow jab to her jaw. By the time she could muster a response, she was up the ramp. "Get that panel down quick before she takes another notion into that fool head of hers." I scrambled to follow instructions.

Back on the ground, he spit again. "Not your fault, lass. Nor hers neither. Your dad's a fine grain farmer, best in the county. But he had no patience for stock. No gift for 'em neither." Another spit. "How's he doing?"

"Not long now."

"Well." He shuffled his feet, looked up at the cow. "She'll do better at our place. And you'll have one less chore to attend to."

I nodded and reached a hand in between the slats to pat the damn cow one last time. "Stupid." I choked on a lump that blocked my throat. "That's her name. Stupid Odd."

He chuckled. "Seems a right apt name. Come on then, Stupid. Let's get you settled into your new home."

I stood in the driveway till he was out of sight, wishing... I shook my head, made a run for the house. A shower. That's what I needed. Hot as love and quick so there'd be time for eggs and coffee before the sheep man got there. And if I cried in the shower, who would know?

I wondered why tears came now. I was well rid of the damn Stupid cow.

WHIP

The place looked much as I expected. Big house with more grace than aerial photos showed. Big lawn and stately trees that must be a century or more old. Perched on a hill above the road, with sloping hills to the south and down to a creek just out of view.

As I came around the sweep of the driveway, the faded grandeur one saw from the road shifted to the ugly utility of a working farm. Not one that worked well. The collection of outbuildings – corncrib, hog lot, shop, a couple of barns – looked as tired as the rusty combine and rickety hayrack in the barnyard.

Like so many farms across the Midwest, this one was likely prosperous in its time. But that time was gone. And in its place? Another client hoping to make new money off old land. Not a client I relished.

For one thing, I was no fan of McMansions for people who say they want to live in the country but turn it into suburbia. For another, it was Paul Patterson, and I expected that was what he'd want. He was a greedy kid, and I doubted he'd changed. I shrugged. Business. And…maybe it would help me close a door. I didn't set my hopes high.

As I stepped out of the truck, I saw a face at a window. Uh-oh. The little sister. Paul said she'd be off to her town job by now, but I should have known he'd miss the mark. Old slapdash Patterson.

The face pulled back, and I glimpsed a bare shoulder and hair the color of a well-worn penny. Like Scott's. Something odd happened in my stomach. Uneasy if-only thinking that dogged me ever since...

I blinked away old images as the back door opened. She said, "You're early. I didn't expect you for another half hour."

"Ma'am?" I took a step toward the porch. Shower fresh hair hung in wet ropes past her shoulders, and eyes of a familiar green did nothing to settle my roiling stomach. Bare toes. No bra.

She squinted, crossed her arms over her chest, shivered. "You've got another truck coming, right? It's not a big flock anymore, but they'll still never fit in that." She nodded to my truck.

"Um...I expect they'll be along shortly." Play along, I thought.

"I need coffee. Breakfast. Before they get here." She turned, laid a hand on the doorknob. "You may as well come in while you wait."

I hesitated. Not a good idea. But curiosity and something else made me follow her inside where a wood stove pumped heat in a wreck of a kitchen.

"Excuse the mess. Use your imagination. See what it will be. Like a rehabber does. Come back a month from now, and this room will be prettier than when my Great-Gremma came here as a bride."

I let my eyes roam. Half a bare floor, old linoleum on the rest, a gaping hole in one wall, a layer of plaster dust on every surface. It would take a lot more than a month to make the room look like anything but a bomb site.

She laughed as she reached to get mugs from a cupboard. "You don't believe me. But it will be gorgeous." She fiddled with a high-tech machine till steam and the heady smell of coffee wafted.

"That doesn't look like something your great-grandmother would have used." I hesitated to venture any opinion, but I felt like I had to say something.

"Not hardly," she laughed again. "But it makes great coffee. How do you take yours?" She glanced toward the fridge. "I've got fresh cream, but no sugar over here. Don't use it. Don't bake. Maybe over in Dad's kitchen…"

"Black is great."

"Good answer. Want some eggs?"

"No thanks."

"Mind if I go ahead? I've been up since four and I am starved!" She wiped dust off the stove and a skillet, chattering all the while. "Give me a man's opinion. Which of those colors do you favor for the lower cabinets?" She pointed to swatches on the wall. "Green's in first place, I think. But would the lighter yellow be more cheerful? I love the name of the other yellow. Buttered sweet corn. Isn't that great? But I think it's too dark for in here. What do you think?"

"Um. The green is good?"

She nodded, considered before she shrugged. "Maybe. Listen, I'm glad you got here early. Can you pass on a request to Lloyd for me? There's this ewe. She's old, not more than one more lambing season in her. Probably pregnant now as I let the ram in with the herd like your boss wanted. Anyway, this ewe – well, my last 4-H lamb gave birth to Fluffy, and I…well, I got attached. She was Fleecy's last lamb, and...Listen, I know those are the dumbest names in the history of sheep, but I was a teenager. Tell me you didn't do things you regret when you were a teenager. Anyway, I was wondering...hoping...that maybe Lloyd would keep Fluffy around for wool after she lambs. Till she...well. She's a good old ewe, easy to spot as she's got an extra notch in her ear. She won't bring in much at market – not as much as her wool." She trailed off. "No harm in asking. Right? You know how it is when you get attached to an animal."

She flipped scrambled eggs onto a plate and brought them to the table where I sat, my fingers cupped around my half-drunk mug of coffee. She took a bite and closed her eyes. "Mmm." Then, "I'm sorry. I've been yammering on, and I never even asked your name. Have you been working for Lloyd long?"

There it was. The reason I should have stayed in the truck. Or never come. "I don't work for Lloyd."

She shot me a puzzled look as she took another bite. "I don't understand."

"I'm not here for the sheep. My name is Whip Tyler." I watched her stiffen, push her plate away.

"Whip?"

I nodded.

"Unusual name. Not many Whips around."

"Look. I'm not going to apologize, and I'm not going to lie. Whip is my name and I am that guy."

Kat

I lost my appetite.

"What are you doing here?"

He hesitated. "You should ask your brother about that."

"You stay away from my brother. Last time you got mixed up with my...family..." I couldn't finish. "I want you to leave. Now."

He set down his mug and headed for the door. And the sheep guys pulled in – behind his shiny black truck.

"I'll tell them to move. So you can get out!"

"I'll go. After I help with your sheep."

"Don't bother!" Too late. He stepped off the porch and crossed the driveway. Where Lloyd Keegan greeted my unwelcome guest with a big bear hug. Dammit. I scrambled back into my boots and grabbed my jacket.

"Right, boy. Not a problem." Lloyd turned to me. "Morning, missy. I hear your dad's not doing so well.

Flock still out to pasture? Me and the boys will round them up. No need for you to trouble yourself. Your dog any use with 'em?" He paused for an answer – to the last question only.

"He's rusty – not worked much lately. I'll get the gate. Take your truck out to the barnyard." I made my voice flat and even. "So Mr. Tyler can be on his way."

"Whip will give us a hand, won't you, boy? You always was a good hand with sheep. Won the county shearing contest three years running, dintcha? You hop in with me. Buster, you get up in back with the dogs."

I swallowed my annoyance. Pick your battles, I thought. I hurried to hop in with Buster and the dogs, hopped back out when we got to the gate. Damned if I'd let them do it without me. Whatever they thought.

The sheep, as sheep do, saw us coming. All it takes is one to sound the alarm and off they go – all of them. In the wrong direction. Chasing sheep has to be one of God's worst jokes, worse even than wrestling with Stupid. It used to take Dad and me hours to get the flock in the barn.

Alone it was impossible. So it would be foolish to turn down extra help. But did we really need Whip Tyler too? For a dozen sheep? We did, dammit, and it galled me to admit it. Or to note that Tyler seemed as tuned into the sheep as Keegan's dogs.

"Never miss a chance to be grateful." It was one of Gram's favorite sayings. I could be grateful for the time saved. I thought about getting the rest of Gram's kitchen floor scraped. I chafed but knew Gram would expect me to say thank you. Even if it was Whip Tyler. Before kicking him off my land.

By the time the sheep were all loaded up, I was glad to see them go. Except for Fluffy. In a panic, I jumped up on the truck wheel to get a last look at my old ovine friend. Where? Not a double-notched ear in sight. No Fluffy.

I jumped down and turned to Lloyd. "There's one missing."

"Nah, we got 'em all." He gestured toward the hog lot. "That one there? That the one you was missing?"

Fluffy munched contentedly in the near corner. I knew her even without seeing her ears. "What's she doing there? Why isn't she in the truck? You gave me a check for a dozen animals. Without her, you only got eleven."

"Well, now, don't you worry none about that. Whip took care of that aforehand."

"Whip?" I looked around. "Whip Tyler?"

"He hightailed it some time ago. Saw we had them handled. Got that one penned up and took off." He waved an arm again to the lone sheep in the hog lot.

"But...why would he..."

"Don't rightly know." Lloyd took off his hat and rubbed a sleeve over his pale swatch of forehead. "Said that one had to stay. Didn't say why." He put his hat back on and whistled for his son and dogs. "Anyhoo, we're all settled up. You say hey to your dad now."

I had to blink hard – to understand what he said and because dammit, I felt like crying. "But what am I going to do with one old ewe? I can't keep her here."

"Don't see why not." He climbed into the cab. "But time comes you don't want her, I expect Whip could haul her over to his brother's farm. Trent's got a good flock. Not Correidales, 'course. But what's one white face going to matter, eh?" He started the truck. "See you around, missy," and he drove off in a chorus of baas, bleats and barks.

Dutch whined at my side, so I put my hand on his head and wandered over to the hog lot, where I leaned on the fence. "They were all supposed to go. What do we do now, fella? Can you tell me that?"

He tilted his head in consideration, gave a bark.

"You're not much help." Tears. Again. "Does one sheep mean it's still a farm?" Dutch tilted his head. "Damn Whip Tyler!" The anger felt good. Strong. "What in hell was he even doing here? How'd he ever have the nerve – after what he did?"

I stuffed my hands in my pockets and let my gaze linger on Fluffy. She ambled toward the fence. "Looking for oats, old girl? Still some in the crib. Enough, I suppose, for a day or two. Maybe then I'll have a clue what I should do with you."

WHIP

I had two things on my mind when I left the Patterson place. Talk to Paul. Need more coffee. A third thing tried to crowd in – her stiff spine when she heard my name – but I tamped it down.

Coffee first. I wondered again why I let myself get involved with Paul Patterson. Hadn't that weasel cost me enough? No question. Smart thing would be to pretend no Pattersons walked the earth. Or ever did.

I knew all the arguments. I needed the work. Business was looking up with that development other side of the river. Another big job would fatten the checking account, maybe let me hire an assistant.

Still, it didn't sit well, not when Patterson first called, less after I met his sister. Or saw the work she'd put into that kitchen – even with all she had left to do. The way she talked about it. Paul said they'd sell, but you don't quibble about paint color when what you want is a purchase offer.

Not that anybody in their right mind would buy that house. Big old drafty barn. I doubted it had an ounce of insulation. Not the way she cozied up to that wood stove. Not my problem, I told myself.

Coffee. I turned into the Firehouse and smelled the bacon as soon as I got out of the truck. The Firehouse wasn't a new building, but it was a new hot spot in town since Luke James turned it from an empty eyesore to a thriving diner. Luke and I started school together – a good guy and a wizard in the kitchen. He set up his grill behind the counter. Said it was good for business. "Folks trust what they see, and I like being out front with them. So I can keep an eye on who's flirting with Darcy," he said.

He grinned when he said it, one of the happiest grins I expect to see in this life. Darcy was good for business too – and good for Luke. She was a firecracker. Short and a little rounded, with a dancing ponytail, she never stood still. She and Luke seemed made for the diner life. Made for each other too.

As I saw again as I stepped in the door. "Um. Should I leave you two alone?"

Luke grinned and waved one hand. "We're open. Can't keep my hands off her is all." Darcy tried to turn, see who the interloper was, but Luke held on tight. "Guess," he told her.

"Ronald Reagan."

"He's dead, you dope."

"Oh right. Mick Jagger."

Luke laughed. "Ding, ding, ding! Give the girl a cookie!"

She pulled free and whirled, as if she half believed Mick would show up in dinky little Oakton. Her smile dimmed, but only a little. "Hey, Whip, how..." She paled, put a hand to her mouth, shot a look at Luke. "Oh no," she muttered as she dashed toward the ladies' room.

I looked at Luke in alarm, but his grin went wide. "Morning sickness." He lowered his voice with an eye toward the geezers in the back booth. "Five weeks. But we're not telling anybody yet, so don't let on you know. Darcy will kill me."

"Congratulations, man!"

"Thanks." He puffed up like one of those bounce-houses for kids. "But no kidding. Keep your voice down. She finds out I told you, I'm a dead man."

"You look happier than most guys facing death."

"Flying high, pal. Flying high."

The bathroom door opened, and Darcy stepped out, two spots of color riding high on her cheeks. She narrowed her eyes, darted a glance between Luke and me.

"Frying. Frying up a big special for my buddy Whip."

"Right," I said, picking up my cue. "Bacon. Extra home fries. Coffee." For the love of God, coffee.

Darcy got the coffee while Luke got busy at the grill. "You don't fool me, Luke James." She inclined her head at me. "He told you, didn't he?"

"Now honey," Luke began, alarm in his voice. "Don't get mad. I couldn't help it. Whip won't spill it. Will you, Whip?" Save me, said his eyes.

I put a finger to my lips, half afraid Darcy might come after me. "Spill what?"

Luke left the grill to circle Darcy's still trim waist with his arms. "You love me enough to barf for my baby. You love me enough to forgive this one little slip, don't you, baby?"

Darcy leaned against him and sighed. To me, she said, "How can I fight when he says something sweet like that? But don't you breathe a word, Whip Tyler. Plenty of time yet before we need to let the cat out of the bag."

"So to speak," I couldn't help saying and earned a Darcy glare.

"Shut up and eat, buddy. It's safer." Luke slid a plate in front of me.

"Good idea," Darcy said as she grabbed the coffee pot and stepped toward the back booth.

Luke came around the counter and took the stool next to mine while I ate. "So. That's our news. Bet you can't top that!"

"Wouldn't even try."

Darcy slid onto the stool on my other side. "Change the subject, Whip."

"Um…"

"You don't come in this late as a rule. What's up?"

I tried jamming toast in my mouth. But when Darcy asks, you might as well answer. She smells a secret, she's on it like a Jack Russell after a rat. "I stopped up at the Patterson place," I said.

"What on earth for?" she demanded.

"Do we have to get into it?" Darcy's look said we did. Sigh. "Paul asked me to have a look around."

"Paul? Paul Patterson? Asked you to have a look? Why?"

I shrugged. "Wants to do something with the place. I guess."

Her eyes went flinty. "Is Kat in on this?"

"I'm guessing no. He told me she'd be at work."

"Not mornings, which he would know if he was ever around to help out."

"Yeah. Found that out."

"So...?"

"Geez, Darcy, what?"

"Give it up, man," Luke muttered. "She wants a blow-by. You might as well give it to her. She'll get it out of you anyway."

"She thought I worked for Lloyd Keegan."

"Today's the day he came for the sheep."

I set down my mug and gave her a stare. "You know everything about everybody in this town?"

"Just about." Darcy grinned. "Kat and I go back. She's been selling off all the stock. Had to. Her dad's in a bad way and she can't keep her job and take care of him and the farm too." She shook her head. "Rough on her..."

Luke leaned forward, looked past me to his wife. "Call her, honey. Take her out...shopping or...you know...whatever you women do."

"Good idea. We'll do a spa day. Take her mind off everything, off losing...Oh my God. Fluffy. Fluffy's gone? That will break Kat's heart."

For half a second, I thought about keeping mum, letting Darcy find out on her own. But what was the point? "Uh, no. Fluffy's still there."

"Oh thank God! She dotes on that old ewe." Darcy narrowed her eyes. "Wait a minute. How come Lloyd didn't take Fluffy with the rest?"

"I...kind of bought her." I took a big slug of coffee and sent Luke the same kind of signal he'd sent me earlier. Help me!

But no. He was as bad as his wife. "You bought Fluffy? What for? Your brother?"

"No. I don't know. She just seemed so…I don't know. She went on about that ewe, how she hoped Lloyd wouldn't send her to market, and she had bare feet, and…"

"Bare feet?" Darcy's eyebrows shot up.

"You've done it now, Whip. Might as well spin the whole tale. She won't be satisfied till you do."

"I thought I'd look around. Didn't think anybody would be there…"

"Hold on. Don't say another word. Not till I'm back." Darcy made another dash for the john.

"Damn, that's like the fifth time so far today. One more puke by noon to beat her record." Luke stood and picked up my empty plate. Back on his side of the counter, he said, "So what's up with you and Patterson? Why would you do anything for that rat?"

"Business." I shrugged. "Guilt maybe." Couldn't admit it to anyone but Luke. Probably because I knew what he'd say.

"You got that turned upside down, pal. If anybody should feel guilty, it's him."

"Yeah, but…if I hadn't…if we…"

"Bull. And you paid the price." He shook his head. "The guy's trouble, Whip."

I shook my head. "You're not wrong. I know it. Still…maybe he's changed. Grew up?"

Luke snorted. "Leopards and spots, man."

I shrugged. "I said I'd take a look. That's all. Probably all it will amount to. So… enough said?" I said the last quiet and quick, hoping to steer the conversation away before Darcy joined us again.

Luke rolled his eyes and was about to say more when his attention focused on the opening bathroom door. He stepped out to meet her, to steer her to a stool. "Baby, that must have been a rough one. You're still a little green. Come sit down. Have a saltine."

Kat

With all the livestock gone, I hoped to spend the rest of the day digging up linoleum. That hope didn't come to much. Before I clomped off my boots, Maggie stuck her head out Dad's door and hollered that he wanted to see me.

"I'll be over," I said. "Tell him to keep his pants on. Five minutes."

"He's fretful. You should know."

I nodded my thanks and went in Gram's door. Mine now. I liked sharing the space with Gram's memory — and having my own rooms on the other side of the house away from Dad.

As I often did, I wondered what the house was like when my great-greats first occupied it with their nine children. They meant it to be a showplace, I was sure, a testament to their newfound wealth and station in the community.

The wealth didn't last, of course, not even long enough to make their vision reality. Maybe I could do it for them.

I washed up, combed my hair, decided my clothes would do as they were. Dad set high standards for me. Looking good was only part of it. I had to get good grades in school, get a good job, take care of him, the farm. No wonder I disappointed him. But then I always had. No use expecting different.

Standards never seemed so high for my brother Paul. All he had to do was carry on the family name. That he was handsome and charming was a bonus and enough to make it not matter that he was never here. I loved my brother. And I wished he'd shoulder some of the load parked on my shoulders.

Old news, I thought as I crossed Gram's sitting room on my way to Dad's side of the house. Of all the rooms in the house – some fifteen or so – it was the most elegant. Certainly it was the largest, spanning the full width of the house. I'd always thought of it as no-man's-land dividing the two halves of the house and the people who lived on either side. Until I made it my workroom and my table saw and tools took center stage and the furniture got shoved to one corner. I navigated around a stack of lumber to the door leading to Dad's side.

He was hunched in the recliner in the corner of his dining room, where the old wall phone hung, where his books and maps were nearby. Where he managed every day to stagger from the bed now steps away in what was once our living room. Where he'd probably live out the rest of his life.

Maggie, the home health aide who made my life bearable four half-days a week, perched on a stool at his feet. It was a daily ritual, massaging cream onto his thorny heels. She wiped her hands on a towel and said, "How about some coffee, honey? I just put on a fresh pot." Another ritual and just as welcome.

I smiled. "That would be great, Maggie. Thanks." I pulled a captain's chair from Mother's maple dining table – a sleek Scandinavian style I never admired – and sat facing Dad. "How you doing today, Dad? You wanted to see me?"

I don't suppose illness looks good on anyone, but with Dad, I had to work not to show how shocking I found his appearance. Part of me still thought of him as bigger, stronger than life. The man who set fence posts, hurled hay bales to the loft, a robust gut hanging over his belt. Ashen now. Concentration camp thin. Barely able to lift his chin from his chest.

But with eyes that pierced, maybe now more than ever, as there was so little of his face that remained familiar. Eyes that snapped with anger. At the illness and his weakness mostly, I tried to remember. But that anger spilled over. On me.

"They're gone?"

The animals. "Yes. They're gone."

His eyes blamed.

"They had to go, Dad. I couldn't keep it up. Not alone."

"I did."

It was an old story. "I know. I'm not you. It's done."

"You had no right."

I felt my own eyes spark. "Seems like the person who does the work, pays the bills, that's who's got the right. I'm that person now."

"Paul."

"Paul's not here, Dad. I'm here. I had to do what makes sense."

"To you. For you."

"Yes. To me. And to Paul. He wanted me to sell the stock six months ago." And then because I saw disappointment drop over him like a blanket and knew that it ran deeper because the tarnish touched his golden boy, the fight went out of me. Almost. "I chose to cut my time back at the museum, stopped taking rehab jobs so we could keep the animals this long. But with winter coming on? I'm sorry, Dad. It was time. Today, it was time."

The fight seemed to go out of him too, leaving bitter loss in its place. Defeat.

"I'm dying."

I swallowed hard. "Yes." No use denying it, as we had over the last year. "I'm sorry, Dad. But yes."

"Not long now."

"We can't know."

"I won't die in the hospital. Right here."

His eyes demanded truth. "We'll try."

"No! Do! Not try." He coughed, a spasm that had him gasping for air. "Here!"

Maggie came at a trot from the kitchen, shoved a hot mug in my hand, and looped the oxygen tube over his head. "Slow and easy, Vernon. Slow and easy."

When had I stood? I didn't know. "I should go."

Even through his struggle to breathe, Dad said, "No."

I sat, waited for him to regain control. It took a while, so I let my eyes wander to the plaster molding at the ceiling, the ugly priscilla curtains left over from Mother's frilly influence, the mid-century modern furniture she'd favored.

I wouldn't call it a sign of disrespect – to Dad's illness or to the taste that Mother and I never shared – that my thoughts turned to how I'd restore this room. It's what I do. I see a space with history, and I start thinking how it used to look, how it might look again. Isn't that another way to respect?

Where we sat was one of three downstairs rooms on Dad's side. South-facing windows caught nice late morning sun this time of year. With the hog lot empty, the dreaded south wind would lose its olfactory punch. And if – when – I dismantled that lot, the view to the hills would be gorgeous.

I shifted in my chair, and with the slight change in angle I saw Fluffy. I stiffened. Why would Whip Tyler arrange for her to stay? And how could I head off the hell to pay if Dad found out? One glance out the window and he'd demand to know how come I kept one old ewe and not the rest. He'd never believe it wasn't my idea – and if he found out Whip Tyler made it happen... First chance I got, Fluffy would have to go in the chicken yard the other side of the house. To keep her out of Dad's sight.

I dragged my eyes back to the recliner. He was breathing easier now, eyes closed. Sleeping? Apparently not.

"Get Paul home," he rasped. "Not much time. I need to...settle things...explain..." He trailed off as if those few words were too much effort.

"I'll call him," I said. Again.

"Good." Dad nodded once, closed his eyes again.

Was I dismissed? Hard to know. I looked to Maggie, who mouthed, "Sit awhile before you go.

WHIP

When I walked out of the Firehouse, a familiar wave of melancholy came with me. I recognized it for what it was – envy. For what Luke and Darcy had. I shrugged it off – or tried. Happy for them, I thought.

As soon as I climbed into my truck, my phone rang. The contractor at my project across the river. "The developer is here. Wants to see you."

"Tell him to sit tight. Five minutes."

Good excuse to put off the Paul Patterson conversation. Give me the choice of an existing client and one that might never materialize? I'd take the one I already had, thank you very much.

Besides, I liked Stevens. He was a good guy, a developer who didn't want to rape the land. He used it – made money from it – but didn't cut environmental corners to pad the bottom line. So far. I speculated why he'd summoned me. I figured I knew.

At the site, I saw Dixon on the backhoe. His crew were unloading the PVC where the utilities would go on the first ten sites. Stevens stood with his back to them like he had nothing better to do than gaze at the river all day. Was his stance real or part of an image he wanted me to see? Whatever he intended, I saw him for what he was – shrewd and canny.

For the second time that morning I blessed the cold weather. The ground wasn't frozen solid, but it was stiff enough to not slide through muck. Stevens hadn't muddied his loafers either. Probably a good thing.

He didn't turn as I came up to him, so I took in the view too. And waited. Let him speak first. It was a trick I learned from my Uncle Jake. "Use silence, boy," he'd say. "Like as not, they're as uncomfortable with the quiet as you. If they fill it first, you gain time to think about your response." Jake was about as canny as they came. And right nine times out of ten.

"Pretty view," Stevens said. So he knew the silence trick too.

"It is that," I agreed. In my greener days, before I took Jake's advice to heart, I might have added how the view helped make fieldwork pleasant on a project like this, how lush it would look in summer. I waited.

"Too bad only a couple of these homeowners will see it when that stand of oaks leaf out."

I was glad I'd waited. "Unless they walk out the trail here to the point." Find something you agree on. Don't argue. Don't explain. More of Jake's advice.

"I suppose we can't take out those trees?"

It was what I suspected. "Some of the saplings. Thin the stand a bit."

"It's those three big ones that really block the view."

"They sure are big. The state arborist guessed a hundred years old at least."

"The state arborist?"

"Yeah. He came by late last week. Spoke about those trees like they were cousins. Imagine. All the trees in this river valley and he knows these three so well, he could pick them out in a police lineup. So he said."

"I suppose that means they're protected or some fool thing?"

I nodded, tried to look resigned and not like I was the one called the state guy to arrange his visit. "That's what he said. Something about how their root system stabilizes the slope over there too. So it makes it easier for Dixon's crew to comply with the state EPA erosion control regs. Cheaper too."

Stevens leveled his eyes on me. I gave him my best what-can-you-do shrug.

"View's worth an extra ten, maybe fifteen grand per lot."

I nodded. "No doubt." Keep agreeing. Then show him another way to use it. "I've been thinking. Can your marketing folks play up the walking trail, the parks? Show folks how all the homeowners can enjoy the view, the woods, the whole deal. It's the only development in the county with such an extensive trail system."

"Did you get that permit to connect to the rails-to-trail-way?"

"They loved it, Stan. Ate it up. Helped us broker a connection with the state park too. Turns out I know the guy at the park. Used to hay on his dad's farm. So that's in the works. One or two dots and t's before it's a done deal."

"Good." He gave me a knowing stare. He knew I'd had a hand in saving those trees, and I didn't presume otherwise. But he grinned a little and slapped my back, so I knew he liked my work well enough. "The area's growing, Whip, my boy. New jobs, new families needing a place to live. I'm on the lookout for more sites like this one. You keep your eyes peeled, it'll be good for both of us."

Of course, I thought about the Patterson place. What I saw that morning, what I remembered, it was the kind of spot Stevens had in mind. An answer to Paul Patterson's fondest dreams. Mine too, maybe. It was no small risk starting out on my own and I wasn't yet at the place I could turn down opportunity.

But a big old house and the girl with plaster dust in her eggs kept me quiet. No hurry, I thought. Or maybe it was Jake's voice I heard. Wait.

"I'll keep my ear to the ground, Stan. If or when I hear of somebody looking to sell, you'll be the first one I tell."

Kat

Why can't all of life be as simple as ripping out linoleum? Messy and sweaty, sure. But with a clear end and progress easy to see right in front of your eyes. Sure beats dying, I thought. Or watching someone die.

Or calling my phantom brother home. I promised Dad so I placed the call. As I expected, Paul was in a meeting, couldn't be disturbed. I left a message he should call me. That it was urgent. Texted him too. Did I expect him to follow through and call me back? He was many things, my much-loved brother, but reliable wasn't one of them.

Find the positives, Gram would say. Paul was busy – important job I didn't understand, jumping through wedding-planning hoops of Chrissy's making. Better him than me.

But if – when – Dad died? He'd show up then, wouldn't he? To collect? "Sorry, Gram, but you know it's true. Paul has a thing for money." And was eager for his inheritance. "I wish you'd..." No use talking to Gram about that. Or at all since she'd been dead four years

28

already. But why not? I heard Gram-isms in my head all the time. If she talked to me, why shouldn't I talk back?

I shook my head, like I had when she was alive. "You put me in a tough spot, Gram, having to keep your secret. He'll be mad. Spitting mad. I tried to tell you…"

Worry's pointless. Do what's next. There she was again.

"Right. Next up, linoleum." As an outlet for filial frustration, the sweaty, messy job sufficed. For the moment.

Wide planks peeked through spots I'd already scraped and had me panting to get the abstract black and gold triangles on speckled white into the dumpster. "Height of fashion, Gram? In what? The sixties? Great-Gremma's choice? I'd bet on it. Oh, to be a fly on the wall to hear that debate!"

Gram came to the house like Great-Gremma did – as a new bride. With her mother-in-law in residence. On the other side, but the way Gram told it, no-man's-land wasn't big enough for her. Later, once Gram stood up for herself, she liked the older woman. But in those early days, Great-Gremma ran the ship.

Hence the faded modern look throughout so much of the house. Great-Gremma, like my own mother, had a penchant for new-new-new where Gram's style was traditional, more in fitting with the old-fashioned house. "So Great-Gremma won this battle? Or did you decide a floor wasn't worth fighting about?"

Would I have fought? It was butt-ugly, this old linoleum, and I couldn't believe it started its long life any different. But if it were Dad and me, say? Would I fight him on it, or give in? Hard to say.

I'd fought him on a lot. If Dad had his way, I'd have gone to nursing school instead of college and I'd be married to Ronnie Semple, who stood to inherit the adjoining farm. Boo, hiss, and a pox on a man who imagined such a fate for his only begotten daughter!

Still, I gave in at least as much as I fought. Like when I moved back home when he got sick. I loved my apartment in Oakton, the independence, not having to answer to him. He needed someone here, to work the farm, to tend to his needs, but would never have seen it as the sacrifice I did. At the time.

It didn't take long for me to wonder why I ever left. It didn't just feel familiar when I came back. It was home, refuge. Partly, I didn't miss Gram so much here. I liked having her things about, liked how they helped me feel her with me. I felt Great-Gremma, Grandpa Eli, and the whole family tree too – and my place in the scheme of history. It was my place – where I felt safe, most like me.

"It's my linoleum now, Gram. And I do not want it here another day!" I paused to examine my progress before bringing new vigor to my attack. I focused on the warm shine of the floor as it would be. After the jagged hunks of linoleum were in the dumpster. After I got it sanded and oiled. When it could finally breathe after years of being smothered under ugly petroleum-based triangles.

I felt my phone buzz in my pocket and fumbled to get it free. Darcy. "Hey, Darce, how you doing?"

"In general? Or since lunchtime?"

"Huh?"

"Oh hell. We said we'd wait, but Luke already spilled the beans to Whip this morning so…"

"Whip?" Et tu, Darcy?

"Yeah. I'll get back to that. But listen. I've got big news."

"Big big?"

"The biggest!"

"Oh, Darcy, congratulations! When?"

"Wait a minute! Did that big oaf I married already tell you? I swear I'll kill the rat bastard!"

"No, no." Nobody can make me laugh like Darcy. "Just my own deductive powers, since you've wanted to be a mom your whole life. What could be bigger news?"

She sniffed. "Robert Redford could have stopped in for lunch."

"Now that would be big news."

She snickered and went quiet before I heard a different tone. "Oh, Kat. I'm having a baby!" Happy tears – and contagious.

"Darce. It's so…wonderful! Wait! When? Deets, tell me deets!"

Tears gave way to a bawdy Darcy laugh I knew well. "You want to know how it happened?"

"No, you dope! I want to know when it's going to come out!"

"June. Early June."

"Hot diggety! When should we schedule your baby shower? We'll need invitations…Georgia's good with those – and…"

"Whoa, girl. You can't tell a soul. I mean it. We're keeping it under wraps. Not telling anybody. Just you and Whip. And Doc Hastings."

"My lips are sealed. But…Whip?"

"Yeah. About that." She paused. "Luke and Whip are tight. Have been forever. Like you and me."

"Right. I remember now. In school together? But I thought he moved away. After…"

"He did. And now he's back. A couple months ago." She took in a quick breath. "Don't be mad. We didn't say anything because… Well, you know."

"Yeah. I know."

"He came in this morning. Said he'd been up at your place."

"Yeah. He won't be back."

"Kat…he's not a bad guy. I wish…"

"Look. You know I love you and Luke. You guys can be friends with whoever you want. But don't try to sell me on Whip Tyler."

She sighed. "Okay. But it's a small town, honey. You're bound to run into him."

"Not if I see him first. Now let's get back to important things. When will you find out what gender the stork will bring?"

WHIP

My phone rang two minutes after I got off the Twin Creeks site.

"Whip, old buddy, what'd you think?"

"Paul. How you doing?"

"Top of the world – soon as you tell me what I want to hear."

"Don't think I'll do that. Not today."

"What? Come on. That's prime property. We ought to be able to make a killing, you and me."

"You and me? What about your sister?"

"Kat will go along. Wait and see. So what did you think? With that acreage, we ought to squeeze in three-four hundred houses. Or will we make more with fewer really high-end ones? That's what we need you for, pal. Maybe a golf course? This rich old guy used to bring his scouts down to camp. Always said he'd love to golf the hills, the creek."

"You're getting ahead of yourself, Paul. Way ahead."

"Didn't you go yet?"

"I did. But didn't see much. Your sister thought I was one of Lloyd Keegan's sheep wranglers."

"Son of a bitch. She picked today to sell off the sheep? If she listened to me, they'd have been gone months ago." He paused. "I wanted a plan, something to show her first. But no matter…go over again tomorrow, why don't you? Get a better look. She won't mind."

"I don't think so."

"Oh, come on, Whip. Why the hell not?"

Why not indeed? Didn't I want the business? "Feels like going behind her back. I don't like it."

"Nah. Kat will go along, whatever I say. The farm's gone, thank God. It's high time we get something out of the place. For a change."

I thought of the farmers I knew. Good people who thought they had a good life. Not an easy living maybe, but a darn good life. Didn't surprise me to hear Paul Patterson disparage all they did, what his people had done.

"Look. This is between you and your sister. If both of you want me to look at the property again, draw up some plans, let me know. Till then, I'm out of it."

"I get it. She put up her back, huh?" He laughed. "Class-A grudge holder is Kat. Just like the old man. She'll get over it when she sees what it could mean for me – us. Just needs a coax to shift her loyalties, that's all."

I had my own loyalties, and they weren't likely to shift. But what was the point of saying so? Not that he gave me a chance.

"Kat'll do what I want. And what I want is to move on this thing. Soon as we put the old man in the ground, I want bulldozers on the site."

"Nice."

"Hey, I didn't make him sick. And I didn't make him stay on the place all his miserable life either." His tone scalded like lye. I held the phone away in distaste.

It could have been different. Should have been. If only... No point in going down that road either. "Goodbye, Paul. You and your sister work things out. You know how to find me."

Or maybe I should hide. Steer wide and clear from what was sure to be a bumpy ride.

Kat

"Hey, KP, what's up?"

"Paul. Thanks for calling back."

"Don't I always?"

Not always. Not mostly. But no point saying so. "Dad's fading. Fast. He wants to see you."

"Jesus, Kat. I don't have time to get down there now. I've got big stuff in the works."

"Paul. He's dying."

"He's *been* dying for the last six months. If I dropped everything and came down every time there was a minor crisis, I'd have no business left."

"It's close now." Why did he make me argue? "He's so thin. So weak. There's not much time."

"Thanksgiving. It's soon enough."

"Paul. He wants to see you." I played the ace. "He said he wanted to settle some things."

"His will, you mean?"

"He didn't say. But…I guess. He said he wanted to get things settled. While he still has time."

"Well…" I heard rustling paper. "Maybe I can get down this weekend. Gotta check with Chrissy."

"Try. It…it would mean a lot to him. I think."

"Yeah, well, we'll see. So. While I've got you on the line, what happened with you and Whip today?"

"Whip? Whip Tyler?"

"Yeah. Whip Tyler. I asked him to come look at the place. But you drove him off before he got the chance."

"You asked him to what? Drove him off? You talked to him?"

"Yeah, right before I called you."

"Let's get this straight. You called Whip Tyler, *before* you called me back – even though my message said it was urgent."

"Oh, come on, KP. I don't have time for this. What did you say to drive him away?"

"I told him he wasn't welcome here. For God's sake, Paul, why would he be after what he did?"

"Old news. I asked him to come out – to look over the place."

"You said that before. Why in heaven's name would you do that?"

"He's connected to some high-power developers. He can help us when it comes time to sell. We need to be ready."

I held the phone out, stared in disbelief. Breathe, I thought. Don't say anything you'll regret later. "Paul. The farm is not ours to sell. Dad is not dead yet."

"But he will be soon. That's why you called."

"I called because your father wants to see his son *before* he dies." How could I make it any clearer? "That's what we should focus on now. Dad. His life. What he wants in his last days. Everything else can – should – wait."

"Yeah, yeah. Get off your high horse, KP. I gotta go."

"Wait. This weekend? Can I tell him you'll be down?"

"Tell him anything you want. I'll get there if I can."

Why, I wondered, is it me who disappointed that old man?

WHIP

"Whip, honey, it's me. Mom. Your mother."

"Hi, Mom. What's up?"

"Well, honey, I wondered…I'm making meatloaf today. If you aren't doing anything more important? Maybe you'd like to come home for dinner?"

I looked at the stack of work on my desk and thought about the one can of tomato soup left in the cupboard of my apartment upstairs.

"Okay. Sure."

"Really? Oh, Whip, I'm so glad. I…" She paused and I could almost see her trying to gather words. "I miss you, son. I miss… the closeness we used to have. I know it's my fault we lost that. I want to get it back."

"Aw, Mom. It's not your fault." It was. But I couldn't say so.

"Yes, it is. I know it. When your dad died, I…I was a mess. I wasn't there for you. Couldn't see that you and Travis needed me more than ever." Her voice broke. "It wasn't till you went to Jake's that I realized…" I heard her swallow, wondered if she'd break down like she used to. But she collected herself and went on. "I have a lot to make up for. I know it. I want my boy back." Another breath. "Meatloaf. No pressure. Come eat meatloaf with me tonight? Please?"

"Okay, Mom. Meatloaf tonight."

"Really? Oh that's wonderful. I'll make it how you like it… I remember."

I interrupted before she went into full-gush mode. "Sure. I'll see you. Six?"

"Yes. And Whip? Thank you, son."

"See you then."

I glanced at the time on my monitor. Four o'clock. I rubbed a hand over my chin. I'd have to shave, break out a clean shirt. The can of soup was sounding better. Easier. In a lot of ways. But… Mend your fences. Who said that? Jake? Dad.

Take her some flowers. Another thing Dad used to say. He'd pull them up and send me to the house. Like it was my idea. When did I stop, I wondered. I was likely too cool, too bratty long before he died. After…she wasn't the only mess. Not that anything I did got her attention. Till she got fed up and shipped me out to Dakota.

Jake and Sue paid attention. A lot of attention. How they stood me, I don't know. Couldn't stand myself then. They put up with a lot – and worked the tar out of me, making me fight fence posts and heifers till I used up all my fight.

Mom was right to send me there. I saw that later when I earned back a little self-respect. I even saw the truth about how losing Dad screwed us both up. She didn't have it in her to clean up my mess and her own too.

Understanding didn't take away the hurt. Losing both parents like I did. I tried to put it away, especially since

I moved back. She tried too. We were polite. None of the hard words we used to hurl at each other. But it wasn't easy, not like how she was with Trav and him with her.

Didn't seem likely we'd find easy again. But this was the first I'd seen she wanted to. I asked myself what I wanted. I didn't know.

Meatloaf. Could be a place to start. She did make a good meatloaf. I sighed and climbed the stairs to shave. I'd keep the dinner brief, I thought. And keep my focus on that loaf of beef.

Kat

A week later I woke at four. Long before sunup. Again. Stupid's revenge. Oh well. No point in staring at the ceiling. Again.

Truth was, those early hours meant I made a lot of progress on Gram's kitchen. By mid-week I had sanded off layers of industrial gray, bilious green, and dirty white on the cabinet doors. I tackled the upper cabinets next. Or they tackled me. Solid oak and heavy as an elephant. Gray like an elephant too.

I started demo on the wall as soon as they were down. I figured on another week, maybe more to turn the hole into a wide window to Gram's dining room. But when I saw how good it looked – that open sweep joining the two rooms – I couldn't stop.

Except when I had to. Dad had a rough week, so I was at his side a lot, watching the rise of his chest, wondering if it might be his last. Stepping out to place yet another call to my brother, leave another urgent message he didn't return.

And then Dad rallied. Still weak, but breathing easier, eating a little. Holding his own, Maggie said as she pushed me out the door. "Go. Get out while you can. See if you've still got that job in town."

I wasn't worried. Weeks ago Georgia told me they'd expect me when they saw me, to take whatever time I needed. She knew my plan for a rural schools exhibit, knew I'd been planning even when I didn't make it in, and trusted me to get it done in plenty of time for the spring fundraiser and the onslaught of school groups.

I already had a good start with stuff I found at home. School #285 used to be on our farm. We had a shelf of books from when the school closed – *Billy Goat Gruff*, a picture book of all the presidents up to Lincoln, *Rilla of Ingleside* by Lucy Maud Montgomery, pictures, ledgers.

To find other artifacts I'd need to hunt through the museum's jumble of donations. Where to start? Ask Georgia.

She tapped a finger to her lips as if consulting the treasure map she keeps rolled up in her mind. "Look near the north wall of the haymow. Seems to me I remember…"

"Say no more. I'm on it."

She smiled. "Better you than me. It will be a real archaeology dig."

"Just the way I like it." I looked at Georgia in her trim skirt and ruffled blouse. I waggled my eyebrows and grinned. "You could help."

"No chance of that, dearie! That's why they call me the boss. Off you go."

The museum sat on the canal running from the river to town. It was a stone warehouse once with one cavern of a room on the third floor where they used to store hay. Hence our name for it – the haymow.

My nose twitched when I opened the door. And twitched again after I switched on the three bare bulbs hanging by their cords from the rafters. Dust. And so much clutter. It was a sea of cardboard. Boxes of all sizes and shapes, some stacked in neat rows, most piled anyhow and everywhere between old dress forms, lamps, and bric-a-brac families thought must be valuable but didn't want in their own attics.

I smiled. It was my kind of place. Where treasures might lie undiscovered for years. Some people like waterskiing. I like old stuff.

I threaded my way toward the north wall where Georgia's instincts and the exhaustive catalogue in her mind led me. I squinted at the piles. Light would help, I thought, if the window weren't so filthy. Or if I'd been smart enough to grab a rag on the way up the stairs.

Be grateful there are stairs, I told myself, and I was. Till a few years ago, the only way to get to the haymow was to shimmy up a ladder. I didn't mind heights – once I got there. But climbing gave me the willies. Didn't used to. I'd scramble up trees or to the highest perch in the barns without a thought. No more. Not since the nightmares after Scott died.

I missed him. More in the past week than for a long time – like when I left the university and needed my big brother's take on a bad relationship. Something to do with Dad dying, I imagined. Or Paul not showing up. Or Whip Tyler.

I shook my head and pulled a box off the pile. Get to work, I thought. And get lost in a more distant past. The first box held photographs. So did the next two. Stiff unsmiling faces in stiff clothing. Tintypes, sepia prints, snapshots from old Brownie cameras. People families no longer recognized.

Nothing remarkable. We must have had a hundred boxes filled with similar pictures. Still...I saw a wall of faces. A contest. Identify your ancestor. A way to get folks in the door when the town celebrated its bicentennial in a few years. Georgia would love it. I pulled a pen from my pocket and drew a crude face on each box.

I was less enthusiastic when the next box was more of the same. Until I noticed the small frame building behind the group of children, a pony tied to a rail. A school photo. I flipped it over and squinted at the faded script. Not enough light.

I took the picture to the window and swiped at the glass with my sleeve. Laundry tonight, I thought, come what may. I took another swipe and the roofs of downtown Oakton came into view. Not something you'd see every day. Or ever, unless you pulled up Google Earth. I picked out the easy landmarks – the bank, the church steeples, the library. The bare trees of November revealed the grid of the streets, the homes and yards of people I knew.

A few cars on Main Street, but no people. At home or working, I thought. Unlike me. I lifted the photo, intending to get back to my task. Until I saw a man walk out of the feed store, bag on his shoulder, to a truck that looked familiar. Black. Shiny. He tossed the bag in the back, stood, and ran a hand through a mop of dark hair.

Whip Tyler.

I should have turned away to get on with my own business. I didn't. There's something powerful about watching a person when he can't see you. Spying. Especially when you don't trust that person.

I saw his head go up. Miss Mildred pushed a wire grocery cart down the sidewalk. I grinned. "Serves you right, Whip Tyler." Puffs of vapor rose from their mouths, mostly Miss Mildred's. Then he lifted two bags from her cart and followed her up the walk. Seconds later he was back to fold up the cart and hand it through the door. It didn't take a lot to imagine the conversation. She'd push him to stay for a cup of weak tea and ice-box cookies. He'd decline, say he didn't want to trouble her – and mean he had better things to do. She'd press and he'd spend the next hour and a half listening to stories about her cat.

But no. He shook his head and while I thought Miss Mildred looked disappointed, she smiled and waved while he backed away.

He paused by the door of his truck and angled his head upward. I stepped back. It wouldn't do for him to catch me spying. But his gaze went toward the east. I leaned forward again as if the object of his attention might be visible to me too. It wasn't. But I knew where he looked. The water tower.

WHIP

I was already too far in the door to back out when I stopped at the Firehouse for lunch. Would have if Luke didn't holler out soon as he saw me. "Whip, my man! I wondered when you'd get here!"

Cover blown, I took a seat at the counter, not far from Kat Patterson, who was perched on the stool I thought of as mine.

I hadn't seen her around town. Not since that morning at her place. Not that I'd been looking. Her place. Something clicked in my brain. When did I start thinking of it as her place, I wondered. Not the Patterson place. Not her brother's. Hers.

I filed away the question, saw her back go ramrod stiff, and braced myself. Not unexpected. I couldn't blame a Patterson for not wanting to share my company. I shrugged and told myself to act natural.

"Hey, Luke. Darcy. What's on special today?"

I should have known Darcy would poke at the wound. "Hey, Whip. You know Kat Patterson, don't you?"

47

No point pretending otherwise. "We've met. Ms. Patterson." I tipped my head and offered what passed for a smile.

"Mr. Tyler."

Darcy sent eyes heavenward and poked again. "Get over yourselves. Kat, this is Whip. Whip, Kat. We use first names here. Like civilized people. Or I'll beat you both about the head." Luke raised his eyebrows at me, but I noticed he didn't interrupt his bride. "Soup today is minestrone. And it's good. Whip?"

"Soup. Yeah. And…a reuben?"

"You got it." She could be all business, that Darcy. When she wasn't poking in other people's lives.

Luke called out, "Soup and reuben." Darcy tossed her ponytail at me, picked up the order, and set it down in front of Kat. She sent a wicked grin at the two of us. "Looks like you two have something in common!" Kat's color went up, but she kept her eyes on her plate, on Darcy, anywhere, it seemed, but me.

I didn't expect Darcy would leave it at that. But for the moment, she focused on Kat and left me alone. "So your dad's better and you got a get-out-of-jail card?"

"For today anyway. Yesterday, I'd have said he wouldn't last another twenty-four hours. He rallied." She picked up her mug, then set it down again. "He's hanging on. But…he could go anytime." She shrugged and began to eat.

"Rough deal." Darcy came around the counter and gave Kat a one-armed hug. To three guys coming in the door, she said, "Sit anywhere you like. Coffee to start?" She grabbed mugs and the pot and followed them to a booth.

Luke strolled by. "You're up next, man," as he carried a couple plates to the back booth. It would be a while,

I knew. Those geezers liked to jaw. As did Luke. Just Kat and me at the counter now. So...what the hell.

"I'm sorry about your father." I said it low. Just loud enough for her to hear. "It's tough to lose them. The day mine died? Worst day of my life."

Her eyes cut to mine, full of skepticism and resentment I'd have been smart to leave alone. Never was smart that way.

"One of the worst." I tried not to sigh and didn't succeed. "Anyway. I'm sorry." Sorrier than she'd ever know.

She put her spoon down and I watched a struggle between ill will and manners. "Thank you." Manners one, resentment zero. I didn't figure the score would hold, but she surprised me when she went on in a wistful tone. "You and your father must have been close."

I nodded. "We were. Not so with you and yours?" I never knew the man, but I'd heard plenty. Not much good.

She snorted. And surprised me again. I liked the way that snort looked on her. And the echo of memory it stirred. "Dad and me? Hah!" She shook her head. "Not close. Too much disappointment in the way."

I nodded. Not that I agreed or understood. To let her know I heard maybe? "Is it you or him that's disappointed?" I watched as an expression I couldn't name flickered across her face.

"He's never once shied from all the ways I don't measure up, but..." She spooned in some soup. "Can't say I ever thought about it. But yeah. I'm disappointed too."

"He sounds short-sighted to me." Why would I go out on such a flimsy limb?

49

"How would you know? You don't know me."

I ignored the razor edge in her tone and shrugged. "Right enough. But you take on challenges that aren't for the wimpy-hearted. I've seen that. Rounding up bull-headed sheep, that kitchen of yours." Quit now before the limb breaks, I thought. But didn't. "And you're taking care of your disappointing dad. You've got a good heart or you wouldn't get misty about an old ewe." Shit. Why did I have to bring up the damn sheep?

But I had. And cringed as I watched her eyes narrow.

"I'm glad you reminded me. *Your* ewe is chewing up *my* land even as we speak."

Darcy was back. Thank God, I thought. Until Darcy put her two cents in.

"Oh goody. You two are getting on like a house afire. So Whip, let's have this out. What is up with the whole Fluffy deal?"

Luke set down a plate. "Let the man eat. Then he can spill."

Kat

So much for a pleasant lunch with Darcy and Luke. Why did that damn man have to show up? Worse, why did I speak to him?

I polished off my sandwich and pushed back from the counter. Enough. Even my best friend irritated me, the way she pushed the damn man at me. Why should I care why he bought Fluffy? "Time for me to get home."

"Don't go yet." Darcy pouted. "It's been ages since we've seen you. Have some pie. You're too thin. French. Chocolate. Silk." She waggled her eyebrows.

That's the trouble with friends who knew you when. They know all the buttons to push. "Cookie crust?"

Darcy knew she had me. "Fresh today." She whisked away my lunch plate and set down a clean fork. "Whipped cream?"

"You. Are. The. Devil. Luke, you married the devil!"

"Don't I know it, honey bunch. You best do what I do – whatever Darcy says. Easier that way."

I laughed. There was no denying it. Darcy was a force of nature. "All right, you devil. Bring it on."

"Attagirl! But there's a price. Beyond four ninety-nine, I mean. Talk to me, girl. Tell me things."

I took a bite. "Mm," I said, my mouth full of delicious. "Worth every calorie. What things?"

"For starters, how'd you get so filthy?"

I looked down at my sweatshirt and tried to muster a dignified response. "To what could you possibly be referring?"

"Excuse me, your grubbiness. What could I be thinking? Dust is the new black, perhaps?" She gave my arm a swat and a cloud erupted.

"Haymow," I said, trying not to sound defensive. "We don't all get to hide behind an apron when we work."

"Hah. Which haymow? Home or work?"

"Work. Not much need at home anymore. Except for Fluffy, I might never have to climb up there again." I shot a glare at Whip, who seemed to be eavesdropping on what should have been a private conversation. He wouldn't be the first. If you want privacy, you don't choose the counter at the Firehouse. Still. "Have I mentioned that I hate, hate, hate to climb?" From the corner of my eye, I saw the damn man's ears go red. Good!

Darcy grinned. "I've heard." If she noticed his reaction, she let it pass. "The museum haymow then. What ancient relic warranted such grime?" To Whip, she added, "The place is disgusting. Piles and boxes of old stuff nobody in their right mind would keep. But this one thinks it's treasure."

"Some of it is! If you're smart enough to recognize treasure when you see it."

Darcy rolled her eyes. Not the first time we sparred on this topic. "Pray tell, what treasure did you seek this bright and beautiful morning? Dust?"

"Goes with the territory." I shrugged. "Spring exhibit. Early schools in the county. You know. The one-room jobs, the ones they set up in townships after they passed the…"

"The Land Ordinance of 1785."

In unison, Darcy and I turned to stare.

"What?" Whip raised his hands. "Wasn't that how public schools got started? When they sectioned off the land?"

"You're off by two years. They amended the original law in 1787. But yeah, that's the idea." Who was this guy? "How do you know about the Land Ordinance?"

Luke chimed in. "Mr. Lindenmayer. Sixth grade. Made us memorize dates till I thought my head would explode. Remember, Whip? Of course you remember. You always did." He shook his head. "Not me. Once we got past 1492, I was lost."

Darcy patted his arm. "My birthday and our anniversary, baby. The only dates you have to remember now." Then to me, "Poor dumb Denton boys. We learned that stuff in fifth grade, didn't we, Kat? Mrs. Malone?"

I laughed. "Early in fifth grade. But then Oakton kids have always been ahead of Denton kids. We proved it when we all got to the same high school."

"As if," Luke sputtered. "We don't have to take this, Whip. Tell these bratty girls. We got a darned good education over at Denton. Didn't we?"

"We did. Small as it was – like Oakton – they gave us a strong foundation. Got treated like farm hicks in high school till we outdid those Valley Spring kids."

"Will they keep Oakton and Denton open, do you think?" Darcy rubbed her belly, and I knew she was thinking ahead.

"As long as they keep getting good results, probably. But small schools get expensive to run." I took my last bite of pie. "It's why the one-room schools closed down. One reason anyway."

"Denton and Oakton were consolidated districts, right? From those one-room schools?" Whip asked. "I think my mom was in the first class to go all eight years through Denton. Her sisters talk about going to school up at Lone Tree before Denton opened."

"Lone Tree. That's the name I couldn't remember." I pulled out a napkin and jotted it down. "One of the last to close. Sometime in the fifties. The school on our place closed twenty years earlier. Not enough kids."

"Hey…" Luke pointed at Whip. "Doesn't your mom live in an old school?"

Whip nodded. "Three rooms. One of the bigger schools. Good spot for her. Still on the farm, but not under the same roof with Trav and Tess."

Three rooms. "When did it shut down? The school?"

"No clue. Mom would know. She's got scrapbooks, stuff she dug up."

I narrowed my eyes. First Fluffy, now an early school I had to see. Damn the man. "Would she talk to me? Show me the…her house?"

"Probably. I'll talk to her. Let you know."

WHIP

"Mom, it's me. Whip."

"Whip, honey, I was just thinking about you. I'm making cookies for the kids. Remember how you and Travis wolfed down cookies after school? You'd chatter about your day. Five minutes with your mouths full before you were off to play. I loved those five minutes." She sighed. Then, "I loved having you here for dinner too. You'll come again? Soon?"

"Um…sure." I still had leftover meatloaf from the last time. "Soon."

"Wonderful. Let me know when's good, and I'll make chicken and dumplings. You always liked that. Maybe not as much as my meatloaf, but it was your next best favorite."

"Sounds good. Um…Mom?" How to ask? "You know the old papers you found? The Tyler school stuff?"

"Sure. You want to see it all? Makes me appreciate my little schoolhouse even more. I hope you like it too – that you're comfortable here." She interrupted herself with a nervous laugh. "Listen to me. I'm trying too hard, aren't I? You asked about the school. I'd love to show you what I found out."

No thanks. "Um...sure. But there's this girl. She ...works at the historical museum. You know? In Oakton?"

"Of course. Georgia Jeffries has done wonders with that place." She paused. "But Georgia is no girl..."

"Not her. Somebody else. Don't know what all she does..." Just say it. "Name's Kat...Kat Patterson."

"Patterson. *That* Patterson?"

I expected her reaction. What I didn't expect was how my hackles went up too. Like back in high school. "Yes. That Patterson. Scott's sister. She works at the museum. We got talking at the Firehouse."

"Hm?" She wouldn't make it easy.

"So...Kat mentioned that she's researching early schools in the county. For the museum."

"And you told her I live in a schoolhouse."

"Luke did." Throw him under the bus.

"And I suppose she wants to see it now? My house?"

"Yeah. And the stuff you found out about it."

Silence stretched. Till I had to fill it. "Look, if you don't want to..."

"What's her father think about this? Can't believe he'd like it any more than I do."

"I don't suppose she asked him. Like I don't ask you what clients I should work for." I softened my tone, patted down my hackles. "Mom, it was a long time ago. Nothing to do with Kat."

"You like her. You want this to happen."

"Um...I guess." Did I? Like her? I thought of bare toes, her enthusiasm in that wreck of a kitchen, the banter between her and Darcy. "Yeah. I like her. But that's got nothing to do with it. She was interested. For her work. I said I'd ask. That's all." I took a breath. "I'm sure you can reach her at the museum if you decide to…"

"Oh no, you don't. If she comes to see my house, so do you. Dinner. You set it up. Next week. After I meet her…then I'll decide how much of my schoolhouse history I'll share. Or not."

I rolled my eyes. "Dinner probably won't work. Her dad's sick. Dying, sounds like."

Another silence, but not so long as last time. "Can't say I'm sorry. I never liked that man. The way he took after you? Should have paid more attention to his own kids."

"Mom. Stop."

"Okay. I know. I said it all before. And fat lot of good it did then." I heard a ragged breath, as if the effort to rein herself in took a lot out of her. "But…this girl… I don't like it, Whip. That family…" She sighed. "Vern Patterson is mean as a snake. But you like her?"

"Yeah." I made it sound offhand.

"You do. You like her."

"What should I tell her?"

"All right. You set something up, let me know. Then…we'll see."

"Okay."

"But Whip? Don't get mixed up with those Pattersons again."

"Relax, Mom. We just got talking. About schools. That's all." No need to tell her about Paul's scheme or an old ewe with a stupid name.

"If you say so, son." Her code for, "I don't believe it."

Kat

Maggie called as I left the Firehouse.

"Kat, I think you should come home. Soon."

"Is he worse?"

"No. Your dad's okay. The same. It's... Your brother's here, and... It would be better if you were too."

"I'm on my way."

Four minutes later I walked in Dad's back door. And found Maggie waiting for me, hands on hips, fire in her eyes. I looked past her where Dad hunched in his usual spot, eyes closed. No Paul.

"I just got him settled," she said in a low voice before casting angry eyes toward Gram's sitting room.

"Paul? He upset Dad?" I asked.

Maggie rolled her eyes and huffed. "Keep your brother away from me, Kat. Or I will quit. Honest to God."

I laid my hand on her arm. "Maggie. What did he do?"

"Breezed in here like… Acting like…" She took a breath. "He started giving orders, Kat. Bring him a drink, turn down the heat. Like I… I'm not a servant, Kat. Certainly not his!" She stopped, shook her head. "He riled up your dad. Brought on a bad coughing fit." Her eyes narrowed. "And acted like I caused the problem."

"Oh, Maggie." I looked again toward Dad.

She held up a hand. "He's okay. Now. It took more meds than I liked, but he's breathing steady. He'll sleep a good while."

"Thank you." I wanted to bawl on her shoulder. "And I'm sorry. For Paul."

She closed her eyes, took a deep breath. "I don't want to leave you and Vern in the lurch, Kat. But…"

"No, Maggie. Please. Don't leave. Dad depends on you. I depend on you!"

She heard the panic, nodded. "I know how to help him. Ease the pain."

"You do. And knowing you're here… It helps me more than you know."

"I like to think so."

I gave her a quick hard squeeze, then pulled back to look in her eyes. "Believe me!"

She chuckled. Not the gusty laugh I preferred, but enough to calm me, to show why we needed her steady presence so much. "I got worked up. I'll go sit with Vern. Keep tabs."

"Should I come?"

"No." She gestured toward my side of the house. "I've got this. You deal with that other pain in the butt."

"Right." I watched her head back toward Dad, then said, "Maggie?"

She looked over her shoulder.

"Thank you." She smiled, waved her hand in the air, and slipped to the next room.

I found the other pain pacing between Gram's kitchen and dining room, phone pressed to his ear, talking a mile a minute. He acknowledged my presence with a cocked eyebrow and pointed glances at the half-stripped floor, the half-finished window, the stack of trim waiting to be reinstalled. The narrowed eyes as he looked were at odds with the flattering tone of his phone conversation – a silent burst of angry questions.

I cringed. Paul wouldn't like it, wouldn't understand why I wanted to restore this great old house. Wouldn't think it was worth it. Wouldn't think I had the right. To spend money he thought should be his. I knew it. It's why I never volunteered what I hoped to do here.

I told myself to be strong – a familiar pep talk. So it hadn't worked yet. So Paul was a master at getting his own way and disregarding what anyone else wanted. Not this time, I promised myself. Because I never cared so much before.

I tried to muster my arguments, tried not to care that I still wore haymow dust on my clothes, my hair. Not to care that Paul's suit cost more than I'd earn in three months. I ran my tongue over my lips checking for chocolate pie smears around my mouth, over my teeth in search of stray corned beef. It was a suit, not a weapon. And I was a capable adult, not dirt under his pricey shoes.

I told myself to breathe. He couldn't stop me. Gram fixed that. Stand firm. I sank into Gram's rocker and dressed my face in relaxation. Confident homeowner. Not an earthquake on Jell-O. Not this time.

Was my act convincing? I couldn't tell. He kept the phone conversation going, laughing and chatting while a small matter of life and death – my life, Dad's death – hung in the balance. I knew the call and the what-the-fuck-daggers he kept shooting at me were strategic, designed to make me sweat. I tried to deflect it all. But felt every dagger hit a vital organ.

A century – or minutes – later, I heard him say, "See you around," from the furthest corner of Gram's dining room – where destruction did not yet reign. He stood frozen, looking out the door before a slow-motion pivot in my direction.

It was that piece of showmanship – the gunslinger stance – that shifted my relaxed facade into serene reality. Really? I should be afraid of such fakery? Gun's not loaded, brother mine. I nearly laughed, almost said it out loud.

But maybe it was loaded. He stabbed at his phone and took me off guard with his next words.

WHIP

"Whip, buddy, I'm here at the farm. Come on over, would you?"

"Paul." Too bad I didn't let the call go to voicemail. "Um... I've got a busy afternoon here." A lie, but how was he to know?

"Come on, Whip. I don't get down here every day. Come out and take a look. You know we can make money together. Our land, your magic touch."

"I told you before, Paul. You need to work it out with your sister. And leave me out of it."

"It was her idea to call you."

"You're kidding."

"Not at all, pal. She's sitting right here. Want to talk to her yourself?"

"Not necessary." And not a comfortable thought. I wondered why. It wasn't like I was a nervous teenager asking for a date to the prom.

"So the two of us are on board here. And we want to move. Now. While I'm here. Come on, Whip. I know you're busy. But not too busy for an opportunity like this? Not too busy to help out an old pal?"

I rolled my eyes. The guy was never a pal of mine. I played a red queen on a black king. "All right. I'll be there in half an hour."

"I knew you'd come through for us, Whip. See you soon."

I could have been there in five minutes. But Paul didn't need to know that. Besides, I still had to win my solitaire game. And change into a clean shirt, brush my hair and teeth. Like I'd do for any client.

The minute I got out of my truck I knew I should have saved the clean shirt for another day. Paul stuck out a hand to shake, raised the other to grasp above my elbow. Like Bill Clinton's approach. I'd read they called that handshake the full-Clinton. Intended to build a connection, trust. Paul must have read that article. Not that it worked on me.

My eyes went past him to Kat, who stood on one of the back porches, arms crossed tight, eyes narrowed. On board? Didn't look like it to me.

Paul said in a low voice, "Kat's being a pain in the ass, but she'll lighten up. No worries." He raised his voice. "KP, you met Whip, right? Best site engineer around. Going to help us turn this old wreck of a farm into a gold mine. Right, Whip?"

I looked at Paul, back at his sister. "That depends."

"Well sure." Big laugh. "Timing is everything. That's why we need to start planning now. Get a jump on the competition."

"What competition would that be, Paul?" Kat stepped off the porch to join us in the driveway. She uncrossed her arms, but her eyes were slits, aimed at her brother. Not me, I was relieved to see.

"This isn't the only decrepit farm in the area. Price of land's still good. But it won't stay that way forever. Right, Whip?"

I shrugged and stayed noncommittal. "Hard to say."

"Well, we can't take a chance on it. Not when there's so much at stake. So where do we start?"

Kat turned her slits on me. Oh good. "Look. Maybe you two want to talk this out some more. Think about how you want the land used. If it won't be a working farm anymore."

Paul scoffed. "Never was much of a farm. Not one that made money." Then to Kat, "Even you can't argue with that. So I think we sell off building lots. Good money in housing. Or maybe a country club – swimming pool, golf course. With high-end houses. We build a fabulous model. Attract the big money."

The trouble was I could see it, had seen other old farms turn into suburbia a dozen or more times. Worked on some – enough to pay off student loans, set up my business. Land got developed. And I helped make it happen. But I didn't have to like every result.

The slump in Kat's shoulders showed she could see it too. And didn't like what she saw.

"It could work," I ventured. "But developments – housing, retail, what have you – can fall flat. Do more often than you'd think." True enough. "Takes good planning to use land well."

"That's why you're here, pal! You've got the experience, the know-how. What would you do with it – if it was yours?"

Kat slanted a look at me.

"Don't know. I'd have to see it first. Get a feel for it."

"All of it?" she asked.

"All you want to sell."

"All of it," Paul said. "Three hundred acres, right, Kat?"

"Not quite."

"The timber? How much is that?"

"About half."

"There you go! Three hundred acres. People will pay top dollar. Especially for timber lots. On the bluff. Great views. We do it right, and cha-ching, cha-ching!" Paul seemed ready to drool.

Kat's head went up. "Slow down, Paul. We can't do this. Certainly not yet."

"We can plan. We all know the old man's not going to last long. You said so yourself. Come on, Kat. Think of what we can do with all that cash!"

She slanted another look at me, then down at her toes. She shook her head, almost like she had an argument going on in there. "It won't work out that way."

"So it's a gamble. That's why we got Whip here. Hedging our bets."

She straightened. I was surprised I hadn't noticed her height. She had inches over Paul. "That's not what I mean. I mean it's not going to work out the way you think it will."

"Sure it will! Have a little faith, KP."

"It's not about faith, Paul. And it's not three hundred acres."

"What do you mean?"

"I mean, it's not all for sale."

"Okay fine. You want to keep an acre or two for yourself? No problem. Keep this monstrosity if you want. I can't see why you would. But whatever floats your boat. Meanwhile we develop the rest."

"I can't tell you what to do with what's yours. What will be yours. But mine? That won't be for sale."

Paul looked at me as if to say, "Women. What can you do with them?" Out loud he said, "Look, we're just talking here. Just planning. You don't have to decide now."

"It's already decided."

"Fine. Be like that. We'll get it appraised, divide it up. Fifty-fifty. And when you can't pay the taxes on your half, I'll be the good brother and bail you out. By buying you out."

"It's already been appraised."

"What? Look at you. Ms. We-can't-do-anything-till-the-old-man-croaks. But you went ahead and got the place appraised?"

"It wasn't me."

"What's going on, Kat? What aren't you saying?" Paul's tone slipped from derision into veiled threat.

"It's not mine to tell."

"What the hell are you talking about?" The veil dropped.

And Kat shrank. She studied her boots in a sulky silence, while Paul's stature grew. Like a bear on his hind legs. I took half a step, edged toward Kat – not so much that either of them noticed, but enough so I could get between them if I had to. I didn't bother to wonder why. Not then.

"I shouldn't say more. I wouldn't have said this much, except you pushed and pushed at me." She looked as if she were about to cry, and I wished myself a thousand miles away.

"And I'm going to keep on pushing. What gives? What do you know? Why are you keeping me in the dark? When all I'm trying to do is make money – for both of us?" The threat was still there – even with the softer words at the end.

"I don't want the money." She straightened again as if she realized she had to meet the bear in his own stance. "I don't need more than I have."

"Well I do, and I mean to have it! No matter who gets in my way!" He slammed a fist into his hand and again I edged toward Kat. "So what the hell is going on, Kat? Huh?" This last was quiet, and somehow more menacing.

"I can't. Gram made me promise." Big tears spilled down her cheeks.

"Gram?" Paul went still, paced a few feet, whirled back. "Shit. Is this one of those Patterson ancestor deals? Son of a bitch!" He advanced on Kat. "It is, isn't it?" He reached out as if to grab and shake her, and I put a hand out – as if one hand could stem the rage he spewed.

"Paul." She stopped. Looked at me, back at Paul. "Let's not do this now. Not in front of..."

I nodded. "She's right. This sounds like family stuff. I should go."

"Stay put. We're getting to the bottom of this now – and we're planning what to do. Now!"

"Paul, we can't."

"Why? Spill it, Kat! The place stays in the family? No matter what?"

She looked miserable. "Not all of it. Gram was fair."

"Fair?" He swore, eyes rolling up and around. "Let's hear what dear old Gram thought would be fair, she who thought I got dipped in cow shit while the sun rose and set on you."

"Paul. It's not like that." She crossed and uncrossed her arms.

"Then what is it like? Huh, Kat? What?"

She drew a breath, steadied her tone. "Each of us gets half the land."

"And?"

"And…"

"And what?" Again I felt compelled to edge forward.

"Well…first, it went to Dad for his lifetime."

"No shit. Stop stalling. What about us?"

"Gram portioned it out. You get the farmland."

"And the timber? Where the money is? You get the timber." He swore, raised fists. "So much for fair!"

She rose up again. "The family history is in the timber. The creek. Grandpa Eli's dam. Simon's mill." She glanced over her shoulder. "Amasa and Lovina's house." She raised a hand as if to touch his arm but shoved it in her pocket. A better idea, I thought. "Gram knew I…" She trailed off. Then stronger, "I love it, Paul. It's where we came from. Who we are."

"Who you are, maybe. Not me." He didn't spit, but it felt like he had. His eyes did another three-sixty. "Let me hear the worst. What's the split?"

Strength sapped, she mumbled. "You get everything except…the house. Ten acres around it, the hills, the timber – five acres either side of the creek."

"You conniving little bitch. You talked Gram into this, didn't you?"

"I didn't, Paul. I swear."

"Don't think it's going down like this. Not a chance! I'll break that will."

"I don't think so."

"Who's Gram's lawyer?" He snapped fingers. "Old man Stewart. Right?"

She hesitated, then nodded.

He pulled out his keys and turned to me. "You want to see the place? Get a 'feel' for it?" My turn for his derision. "Little sis here will give you the tour. I've got a lawyer to see."

Kat

And Paul was gone. Leaving a cloud of dust and Whip Tyler and me standing there with our mouths open. Maybe only my mouth.

"I'm...sorry you had to hear all that," I said.

"Me too," Whip replied. "Worse for you."

I nodded. "Well..."

"You don't want to show me the farm."

I sputtered out a laugh. It wasn't much as laughs go, but it steadied me. "No kidding. But...if I want to win the war..." I started across the yard. "I'll get the gate. Bring your truck and meet me over there."

I didn't let myself think. Do what's next. I could show Whip the farmland, what would be Paul's. Do some of my brother's bidding. Keep the peace. Until I had to dig in my heels to protect what would be mine.

Whip pulled through the open gate and reached over to open the passenger door.

"No, Dutch. You stay here."

"Aw...let him come. C'mon, boy."

Dutch never refused a truck ride in his life – unless somebody breathed the word "vet." He leaped up on the seat all wags and wiggles. Et tu, Dutch? But my dog was too busy sniffing Whip up and down to hear my thoughts.

"He smells Juno. My Lab," Whip said.

Satisfied, Dutch settled and draped his chin on my leg. Good dog. I sank my hands into his fur and took the canine comfort he offered.

In the voice I used for school tours at the museum, I said, "This lane leads out to the south forty. Eventually. These fields," I pointed to either side of the lane, "alternate – corn, beans, alfalfa, hogs. There used to be an orchard between here and the road. A couple generations ago. Back when farmers raised everything they ate, before they bought apples in town like everyone else."

"Look. You don't need to talk. Not if you don't want to."

I swallowed hard and stared out the window. Anything to avoid looking at him. I managed to say, "I'm sorry to bore you."

"It's not that." He swore lightly and stopped the truck. "I'm not bored. I'm miles from bored."

I felt his eyes drilling a hole into the back of my head, but I couldn't turn to save my life. Wouldn't.

"I just..." He swore again. "It's got to be hard for you, that's all. I'm sorry to be part of making it hard."

Dutch gave a low whine. He crawled further onto my lap. I dropped my cheek to the head pushing into my chest. A minute, I thought. Give me a minute to get hold of myself.

I swiped at my eyes and aimed my face forward again. "Okay." My breath was still ragged. I stopped, breathed again till I was able to say, "It's not your fault. I'm okay now. Let's get on with it."

"Sure?"

I nodded more firmly than I felt. "Once you get past the gate, turn right. The lane goes up a rise. From there you can see most of the farmland this side of the creek."

"You're in charge."

Sure didn't feel like it. But maybe I could act in charge. Time for my sternest pep talk. Stay in the here and now. Deal with the rest later.

And for once, I was – mostly – able to do it. "Since we sold the hogs, we don't keep these gates shut. Don't know why we still close the first one. Habit, I guess."

"You've got a lot of pens and hog-houses out here. You want to sell them?"

"You think anybody'd want them? They're old. Not worth much."

"Might add up, if you find the right buyer."

"I suppose. That's always the way, right? Finding the right buyer." Whip gave me a quick glance. I kept my eyes straight ahead, wouldn't let tears rise.

He slowed at the top of the rise. "This where you meant?"

I was out the door before the truck came to a complete stop. Dutch squirmed, waiting for his all-clear. "Okay, fella." That dog liked getting in a truck, and he loved getting out. He raced out, back, around the truck twice before rolling on the ground. We humans moved at a more sedate pace to the front of the truck, where Whip leaned against the hood.

I pointed. "The south forty is over there. Not so rocky as west of the creek. But Dad turned up rocks on the whole place." I turned to the northeast. "Our boundary is the blacktop on the east, the hard road to the north."

"The hard road?"

She shrugged. "I know. Like it was paved last week instead of seventy-odd years ago. But that's all we ever called it."

"I get it. First time I turned onto our road after I got back, I thought I was lost. Used to be gravel, blacktop now." He kicked at a cornstalk. "Who's farming the land? You?"

"No. Russ Keyser rents it since a year ago when Dad got too sick. That field was beans. Here it was corn. Harvested two, maybe three weeks ago. He's still got a patch of corn on the other side of the creek. Too wet for the combine. Hopefully this week. If we don't get rain."

He turned in a circle, paused toward the southwest. "What about over there?"

I shook my head. "The hills. The creek." I paused. Not his business. But he already saw our family at its worst. "That will be mine. Not Paul's."

I whistled for Dutch and turned to get back in the truck. "I'll show you west of the creek now."

"Where does your land start over there?"

"East of the old drive-in. Along the road, back to the creek. That little patch where the road used to curve. Fifty acres or so all together."

"You can see it all from the road?"

"All the farmland."

73

"Good enough. You don't have to show me."

I felt relieved. And oddly dismissed. I shrugged and pep-talked. Get over yourself.

Whip put out a hand. "Before we go…Can I ask you something? To do something?"

I braced myself. Wary about what he wanted. "Maybe."

"You don't have to. You've done more than anyone could expect already, bringing me out here. It's just…"

"What?"

"Look, I'll understand if you don't want to. You've had a rough afternoon. Let's call it a day."

I glared at him. "What do you want? Tell me or I'll wonder. What?"

He lifted a hand. "Help me see the place, this land, through your eyes. Not just what's there. I want to see…where you did chores, where you played, where you found…something, a nest, a rock… What makes this place, this land, home for you?"

I looked at him in surprise. "You want to know all that?"

"I do."

"Why?"

"I…want to get a feel for it. To see how you feel about it."

"You do this? You ask people what they feel about a place you're going to bulldoze and change so they'd never recognize it or know they used to live there?"

"Yeah. And they think I'm as nuts as you do." His mouth turned up in a small grin that didn't match the serious look of his eyes. "Land isn't just dirt and space. Not to me. To build something that respects the land, I need to understand how it was used before – the people who made their home or their living there."

I looked at him doubtfully. "That's not…"

"How most developers work? Right. And that's why we get crummy housing tracts and strip malls that lack any personality or charm. You want that here? As a neighbor?"

I shook my head, not trusting my voice.

"Besides. This isn't… This land… Don't ask me to explain. I feel…a connection." His eyes went to the horizon for a long moment before he turned back to meet my stare. "Let's say this. We've got a lot in common, you and I – we're farm kids, same friends…reuben sandwiches. I think how we see land is…not that different." He ran a hand through his hair. "This is your land, Kat. Yours and Paul's. But you can't tell me he feels anything for it. Not like you. I'm interested. I'd like to understand what it…means. For you."

"Even if I convince Paul not to sell and Russ keeps farming it?"

He grinned again – mouth and eyes. "Yeah. Even then." He took my shoulders, turned me toward the fields, gestured toward them. "What do you see when you look out there?"

WHIP

She thought I was up to something, didn't trust my words. I knew from her face and the way her shoulders went stiff under my hands. But she played along. Maybe she saw it as a diversion – from the scene with her brother, from me...being me. Maybe the idea appealed to her, a chance to take the lid off the jar where she kept how she felt about the place all bottled up. I didn't know why. I was just glad I asked.

I nearly didn't. Any fool would see she wanted the tour to be over. But I wanted to know. Because of what I said. Responsible development ought to pay attention to what was. And because...of those other connections I felt. And...I wanted to know her. I said I was interested. I was. Maybe more than was smart.

"I don't know where to start."

"Anywhere," I said. "I bet you learned to drive out here on these lanes, right?"

She shrugged. "Sure. Like any farm kid. The old Ford tractor mostly. Dad never trusted me with the International. His old pickup had the stiffest clutch in the world, so I thought I'd never get the hang of changing gears." She smiled, almost in spite of herself. "Damn thing lurched and bucked till you got it in third. I thought every stick was like that till I drove a car with a clutch that worked right."

"How old were you? When you first learned to drive?"

"I don't know. Nine? Ten maybe?"

About the age she'd have been when... I pushed the thought away. "What else?"

"See that ditch over there? At the tree line?"

"Sure."

"I got stuck in the snow there. No school and my mother got tired of having me around. So she sent me over to Perkins' place – beyond the ditch a hundred yards or so – to bring home eggs. It took me an hour or more to get there, the snow was so deep. Doris Perkins fed me lunch, the kids and I played awhile, and then I set out home. With two dozen eggs. Mostly I stayed in my own tracks, but when I crossed the ditch, I lost my balance and stepped in a hole. Up to my waist in snow. Stuck." She mimed, legs caught tight, one arm braced on the snow, one fist on her fragile package. "I was there a long time. Digging myself out shoving the eggs ahead as I crawled over the snow."

"Your mother sent you out by yourself?"

She shrugged. "I got home. Thought I might end my days in that ditch. But I didn't."

"You remember that day anytime you see the ditch."

I liked the sound of her laugh. "You got that right!"

"Now I'll remember too. Tell me more."

She gave me a puzzled look before pointing toward the far northeast corner of the property. "There was a one-room school over there. The Patterson school. At the corner of the hard road and the blacktop."

"Is that where you got the idea for your exhibit?"

"Some. Other stuff we had. Ledgers. Photos from school picnics in our timber."

"Sounds like the kind of thing my mother has."

"And she has the actual schoolhouse. Ours was moved. Gone now."

I nodded. "Mom said to invite you for dinner, see hers. When you can. I told her your dad's sick."

"Nice of her." She looked at the sun. "It's late. I need to get back so his aide can get home."

Before I dropped her at the house, I reached out a hand, pulled it back at her reaction. "I want to say thanks, Kat. For showing me your land, telling your stories. I liked hearing them."

"You're welcome. I guess." She looked away, then swung back to level her gaze on me. "I like the farm the way it is. Not Paul's ideas."

I nodded. "And if he pushes?"

She turned her gaze to the truck's ceiling as if an answer might be written there.

"Paul gets what he wants. He always has."

Bullies do, I thought. Until you don't let them.

She sighed. "I won't have a say about the farmland." Her voice gained steel. "But the timber. The house. He can't touch that."

I smiled. "Good for you. So you know. I'm no fan of golf. If I can, I'll steer Paul toward less...intrusive plans. You've got my word on it."

With a shrug – as if it was too much to believe of me – she stepped down from the cab. She took one step and turned back with a hint of a smile. "Don't take this the wrong way. Paul put you in a bad spot. And you've been...decent about it. But I saw a lot of you today. I won't mind if that doesn't happen again for a while."

Ouch. But I couldn't blame her. "It's a small town, Kat. Might be hard to ignore each other."

Her smile bloomed and a fist squeezed in my chest. "Let's try."

Kat

Paul didn't come back that night. I decided against calling him. Better to let it lie, I thought.

Gram asked Mr. Stewart to explain her will to me when she had him draw it up. Not a usual will, he'd said, but legal, one that would stick. The only challenge might be about mental competence. He laughed, said that would never fly. He said Gram was sharper than a whole box of tacks and everybody knew it.

While I sat with Dad, I thought about her, Paul, the day. I feared Paul's visit would bring on a tough night, but Dad slept. Maggie's morphine boost worked and gave me lots of time to think. Scenes from earlier kept looping. Maggie, Paul on the phone, in the driveway, Whip Tyler out in the fields. And back through the loop.

How could I make Paul understand my feelings for the land, make him care? Like Whip Tyler seemed to know without being told. Or was that a ploy he used on any easy mark?

When my phone vibrated around eight, I jumped. Darcy. I stepped to Dad's kitchen and kept my voice low. "Hi, Darce. What's up?"

"You okay? Your dad?"

"I'm all right. Dad's sleeping."

"Good, I was worried. I saw Paul in town. So I thought maybe…"

"No. Dad's the same." I stuck my head in the dining room and watched him breathe. To be sure. "He's peaceful tonight. God bless drugs."

"Good. I guess. When the end's so close, it's hard to know what to hope for."

I managed a small laugh. "Yeah. Like with your grandma. Any change there?"

"No. My night to visit or I'd have called sooner." She sighed. "She seemed glad enough to see me – not that she knew who I was."

Darcy's grandmother was in Horizons – the upscale name they called the old County Home. Couldn't blame Dad for wanting to live out his days at his home and not the county's. As places like that go, it was okay. No stink of urine. Just…stale, like the air itself was tired.

"Hard to know what to hope for," I agreed. "So…you saw Paul."

"Across the street from the IGA. He drove off before I could say hello."

I knew she wouldn't have hurried. "Did he look happy? Or mad?"

She breathed out a laugh. "Not happy. How'd you know?"

SALLY CROSIAR

"Guessed. He went to see Mr. Stewart. Must not have liked what he heard."

"Stewart? The lawyer?"

"Gram's lawyer." I didn't want to rehash it, but this was Darcy, my best friend since diapers. "Paul wants to sell the place. Gram fixed it so he can't. Not what she knew I'd want."

"Oh honey. Paul didn't know?"

"No. Gram made me promise not to tell."

"And you'd take that promise to the grave."

"I would have. Tried to. But he made a scene. Upset Maggie so much she almost quit."

"You can't lose Maggie."

"No. I can't. He called Whip Tyler, made a scene with him too. So… I broke my promise." Dammit.

"She'd get it. Your gram."

I swallowed the damn tears that tried to force their way out. "She would. Thanks, Darce."

"I speak truth. So…Paul left mad. And you'll be okay."

I laughed. "Could you sound a little more smug?"

"Maybe. After I savor your rotten brother's disappointment a while longer. But hey, I want to ask you something."

"Okay…" What now?

"You'll be the baby's God-Ma, right?"

"God-Ma?"

"You know. The person she'll go to and say, 'God, Ma won't let me do anything!' And you'll listen and be sympathetic and then make her understand whatever she wanted to do was a terrible idea and I was right all along. God-Ma."

Like Gram, I thought. "I have to say you were right all along?"

"Hell yeah! You're my friend. You're only her God-Ma."

"So you know it's a her?"

"I do."

"You had a sonogram or whatever they call it?"

"No. But I know what I know."

I laughed. "Of course you do. I'd be honored to be her – or his – God-Ma."

"Good." I heard the relief in the single syllable, as if she had any doubt. "Now Luke has to get Whip to agree and my girl will be all set."

"Whip?"

"God-Pa."

"I see."

"What's with the chilly tone? You and Whip seemed to get on okay at lunch."

"That was before…" If I couldn't tell Darcy, who could I tell? "Paul wants Whip to develop our place. To figure out where a million luxury houses will go and make a jillion dollars."

"Uh-oh. And Whip agreed?"

"Seems like it."

WHIP

"God-Pa? You've got to be kidding."

"It's Darcy's idea. So no. Not kidding."

"Geez, Luke, she's been pregnant ten minutes. And you're lining up godparents already?"

"Not godparents. God-Ma, God-Pa."

"Okay. I'll bite. What's the difference?"

"God-Pa is the guy my boy…" A pause. A muffled, "Do you want me to do this or not?" Another pause, a mighty sigh. "God-Pa is the guy my *boy* – and he will be a boy – will go to and say, 'God. Pa won't let me do anything.' And you will listen and sympathize. And then you'll make him understand I was right all along."

"She's standing right beside you, isn't she?"

"Right."

"And listening to everything you say."

"Right again."

"And there will be no peace in Luke-dom until I say yes."

"That's about it, man."

"You'll owe me?"

"Oh yeah."

"All righty then."

"He said he would," Luke said, presumably not to me. And then, "Do I have to?" Also not to me. "Okay, okay. Um, Whip?"

"Yes?" I had a clue what was coming. But why make it easy on my old friend?

"Darcy says she saw Paul Patterson in town today…"

"Really?"

"And that he wants you to…what do you call it…draw up plans for their place?"

"So?"

"So, she wants to know. Dammit, Whip, she wants to know if you're going to do it for the little creep."

"And this would be Darcy's business – or yours – why?"

"Oh hell. It isn't. I told her it wasn't, but you know Darcy."

I laughed. "I do. And I don't envy you one little bit, man. Because I'm not saying a word."

"You're killing me here." I pictured him rubbing his neck like any time he got in a spot. Since we were kids. "Just tell me this. Why would you get mixed up with the bum again?"

Since I knew genuine concern was mixed in with Darcy's nosiness, I relented. "I could use the work, could use another project to get my business on its feet. The Patterson place could make me."

"But for that weasel?"

"Look. I don't have to like every client. And it's not like it's a done deal."

"I gather there's a wrinkle? Kat told Darcy."

"So why are you pumping me for info?"

"We don't know your side of it."

"There are no sides." There would be, I thought. Sides with battle lines drawn deep.

"With Paul Patterson, there are always sides. And there's always blood."

I couldn't argue with that or with the tired tone in my friend's voice. "I don't take sides." Liar, liar, pants on fire, whispered the image of green eyes and windblown hair. To Luke, I said, "I looked at some land. Kat showed me. Land she said would be Paul's. That's all I did. All I will do till the two of them – together – want me to do more. Maybe then, I'll get involved. Maybe not."

"What happens up there could affect a lot of people."

"Could bring more business your way, for one thing."

"Yeah. Or it could make Oakton a crummy suburb instead of a nice little town."

"Could." Especially if Paul got his way.

As if he read my mind, Luke said, "Paul Patterson probably *likes* the suburbs."

I couldn't help the laugh. "As do a lot of the population. Some don't say the word like it's got shit smeared on it. But I'm not one of them. So if I do get involved, maybe I can make a case for a different direction."

"Put it like that and it's hard to know what to hope for."

"Man, you got that right. I couldn't agree more."

Kat

When Darcy and I hung up, I stepped outside. The air, cold and bracing, felt good after the stifling heat on Dad's side of the house.

"Thanks, Gram," I said, looking at the sky. "For separate thermostats, for insulation, for how you protected me." I shoved my fears aside and chuckled. "Darcy says thanks too. For the God-Ma training."

When I went back in, Dad was awake. But not breathing hard — until he tried to speak. I tried to shush him but his eyes blazed.

"Paul wants...to sell."

I shook my head, and his eyes sent a reprimand. If he wanted to talk, I couldn't stop him. I shrugged. "It looks that way."

"Might be best..."

"No."

His eyes cut at me again and I got the message. Let him finish. No more interruptions. "Too much... responsibility...for you."

It was hard to watch and wait while he gasped out every word. "I can handle it, Dad. You and Gram trained me well."

A faint nod. "I...wasn't...easy. On...you."

What was I supposed to say? He never was. But should I rub his nose in it? I let it go with a shrug.

"Ruthie..." He looked past me, as if he saw Mother. It was all I could do not to turn and look. "Loved her...so much..." A corner of his mouth turned up. A smile? His mouth drooped so fast I thought I imagined it. "She...hated...this...place. Weren't...made... for...the country." It cost me to watch as a spasm shook him.

"Dad. Drink." I guided a straw to his lips and waited for him to swallow a droplet of water. "Don't talk more. It wears you out so. I can't give you more medicine for..." I whipped out my phone to check the time. Oh God. Two hours. "...a while yet."

His glare shut me up, as it had all my life. Sick or not, the old man still scared me. And then he closed his eyes and all I could see was the sick. Pity replaced fear.

I sat quietly, hoping he'd drift to sleep. But no. He had more to say. "Ruthie...doted..." A tiny shake of his head. "Too...easy...on...Paul. I...should have..."

"It doesn't matter, Dad." Not now.

"Does!" He spat the word, as angry and forceful as if he weren't weak as a kitten. "Need to...own up...while...I...still can. Made mistakes..." His face crumpled, and I felt my heart break for him. Until his acid-filled eyes stared at me again. Maybe the anger was all that kept him going. "Not...apologizing." He sagged like a three-day-old balloon. "Just...saying...why..."

I kept still. For one thing, I knew better than to try making him stop. And – I'm not proud to admit it – but the chance to hear my tyrant of a father grovel? Who wouldn't want a front-row seat?

"I...let her...do...what she wanted... With...both boys." The spasm that wracked him seemed more emotional than physical. He never spoke Scott's name, wouldn't let anyone else speak it since the night he died. "She...fawned...on them. Especially...Paul. The asthma...was..."

"Terrifying. I thought he'd die. Every time he had an attack."

He nodded, and if I'd seen a wearier gesture, I couldn't remember when. "So...did...she. And...I."

My eyes filled. "Then after, she..."

"Forgot...anybody else... existed."

Our eyes met. Mine went wide as I took in his meaning. He felt cast aside too. While Paul opened shiny packages and ate cupcakes in bed.

He raised a shaky skeletal hand to his eyes. "She...used up...all her love on...the boys. Nothing left...for..." His voice withered. He stayed quiet so long, I caught myself watching for the rise and fall of his breath, so focused I jumped when he raised his eyes and said, "She...didn't expect...to have you. Didn't have...enough left...for...another."

I swallowed hard and swiped at my eyes.

"If I'd...taken...a factory job. Moved her...us...into town?" Was he asking me? No. "But...I was...tied here. And...here...at least...you had my mother."

I found my voice – halting, stilted, sounding not at all like me. "Gram loved me."

He nodded. "Like Ruthie...or...I...couldn't."

"So you stayed here for me?" I couldn't keep the skepticism from my tone, and I saw a spasm like before cross his face.

"Some. Not..." He seemed to search for words. "Enough." His voice strengthened. "Farming was all I knew. All...I...could...do." His mouth took a bitter turn. "And they...trapped me."

"They?"

"Ancestors." Tiny flecks of saliva flew from his mouth. Like venom, I thought. There was enough hate in his eyes to poison our creek and all the rivers it flowed to. "Could...trap...you...too."

I shook my head. "No. Protected. Not trapped. They and Gram protected me."

His eyes searched my face for what seemed an age. He nodded, gave the palest ghost of a smile before a dark cloud of trouble took its place. "And...Paul?"

I shrugged. How much should I say? "Paul won't be happy. Won't make as much money as he'd like." My head filled with images of houses and golf carts crowding the south forty. "He'll make enough."

"He gets...most...of...mine."

Did I hear guilt? Apology? From my father? I might not be able to do much about Paul, but I could set Dad's mind to rest on this. "I know. And it's fine. Fair. Gram took care of me."

He nodded. "Her...investments. Apart from the farm."

"Yes." I smiled. "She was a shrewd one. She left a tidy sum. For Paul too. I can make it stretch a good long while."

His eyes bored into mine, as if he had more to say. But his shoulders moved, and it was like all the muscles in his body – tense for the last fifty years – relaxed at once. He slipped into a quiet sleep while I sat and watched every breath.

WHIP

I wanted to rag on Luke about the whole God-Pa thing, but I didn't get back to the Firehouse till a couple days later. A client in Joliet insisted I come up for a meeting one day, and then I chased down another potential job in Peoria. Too much road time, not enough at my desk.

Too much wading through email and messages, putting out fires to take time for breakfast. That's life for a one-man show. Any day out of my office and the shit hits the fan. By lunchtime I crawled out from the worst of the pile, and the gnawing in my gut signaled hunger instead of stress.

I had my mind set on Luke's Landfill Plate, but soon as I walked in, it was clear something was amiss at the Firehouse. I heard Luke yelling from the back room — something he doesn't do as a rule. It's hard to find a more laid-back human. And I couldn't see him yelling at Darcy. Not if he valued his life.

I sat at the counter and scoped out the crowd. No perky ponytail in sight, and a dozen hat brims angled toward the back room.

"Keep the coffee flowing! That's why guys come here! You pour like some…some coffee-hoarding miser, and I'll be out of business!"

Uh-oh. I glanced down the counter to Otto Simms, a lunch regular. "No Darcy today?"

He shook his head. "Lulu Marsh."

I winced. "Uh-oh."

"Girl don't know her ass from her ankle. Dropped two orders in the last half hour – and sasses the boss. Don't know what this world is coming to."

Before Otto could wax on about the state of the world – which I knew from long experience he was wont to do – Lulu streaked from the back room to the front door bawling with an ear-splitting racket that could wake the dead.

Luke emerged a few seconds later. "Sorry for the drama, gents. I'll get your lunch ready ASAP." His voice was his own again, but his face was red and blotchy. He spied me. "Whip, be a friend. Pour coffee. Now."

I shot off my stool and behind the counter, but before I could grab the pot, Luke hissed, "Wash your hands first, you dolt. Here." He tossed me an apron.

The things you do for your friends. I slipped the apron – plain white and no ruffles, thank God – over my head and scrubbed up. Three minutes later, I had fresh coffee poured in every empty cup. A minute after that, Luke barked directions how to make another pot, and I followed best I could. By the time it began to brew, he had two soup and sandwich orders up.

"Over there." He pointed. I delivered.

Five minutes later, I prayed for no more customers. Seven minutes later – after every damn coffee cup in the place was empty again, I hissed at Luke. "Where's Darcy?"

"Tell you after the lunch rush."

Not that I didn't see the woman's worth before, but Darcy moved a batch of notches up my respect meter. How did she do this every day – and make it look so damned easy?

When the last of the lunch crowd left and I finally sank onto a stool, I stared at Luke. He wasn't yet his laid-back self, but he didn't look as wiped as I felt. He slid a couple plates on the counter and came around to join me. Food. Right. That's why I was here. And yes, I was still hungry, if I could still lift a fork.

"I owe you, man," Luke said with his mouth full.

"Damn straight you do. Double." Chicken salad never tasted so good.

He snorted. "Wuss. Darcy can do it with one hand tied behind her back."

"I know. What I don't understand is how."

He sighed. "Damned if I understand it myself. She says it's a gift." He stuffed more sandwich in his mouth. "Sure as hell, Lulu Marsh was out sick the day they handed out that particular gift." He clapped a big paw on my shoulder. "You didn't do bad, though. For a rookie. Want a part-time job? After the baby comes?"

My turn to snort. "Not on your life or my unborn God-child's either. And don't think a chicken salad sandwich will even the score."

He grinned. "I got pie. Lemon meringue."

"Not enough. It's a start. But not nearly enough." I waited in a comatose stupor while he served up two slabs of pie. Then I had to know. "So where is the woman who makes this place tick?"

"Up at Kat's." He sobered. "Her dad passed last night."

I set the fork – full of lemon meringue and halfway to my mouth – down on my plate. "Oh man." Mild words to cover the odd maelstrom flooding me. I'd have to figure out the reason later.

Luke nodded. "It wasn't a surprise," he said. "Old man slipped into a coma night before last, so... But still."

"Yeah. You're never ready."

Luke got up to pour us more coffee. "So that's why you got pressed into waitress duty." He turned off the coffee maker and grabbed a rag to wipe it down, get it ready for the next morning. "Darcy didn't want her to be alone. And Kat's got this harebrained idea to have folks come back up there after the funeral. Don't see how she can get the place ready in time."

"Christ no. It's a wreck, far as I could see. She had big plans, but..."

"I know. But Darcy says it's what she wants. So she went up to help." He sighed. "Soon as I close up here, I'll go too."

"It's crazy. No way she can..." I paused, remembered how my world spun out of control when Dad died. Remembered, too, how Mom scrubbed on her hands and knees that same afternoon. Nothing she could do to bring Dad back, but she could scrub the kitchen floor.

I shoved off the stool and headed toward the door. "I need half an hour at my desk, an hour tops. Meet you there?"

I saw all manner of questions on Luke's face, but all he said was, "Deal."

Kat

"You can't paint, not with little Christabel in your tummy," I told Darcy. "Think of the fumes."

"Right. You paint. I'll clean over your dad's side. Air it out good. Maggie gathered up the rented equipment, right? How about the meds?"

Tears bubbled too close to the surface. "Darce. You…"

"None of that now. You get on with your painting. I'll call the drugstore and see about the meds – whether any can be returned, what to do with the rest."

She turned on her heel, waving the list she wrote the minute she walked in the door. Which was minutes after I called to tell her Dad died. I didn't ask. She just came. What did I do to deserve such a friend?

It was crazy to hold Dad's funeral reception at the house. Completely nuts, what with all the half-done projects on my side and the old-folks-home smell over on Dad's. We couldn't close his side off, Darcy insisted. We'd need his bathroom as well as mine.

"There won't be that many. Most of Dad's friends are already gone," I argued.

She scoffed. "Soon as folks hear you're opening the house, they'll come out in droves. Hmm... What is a drove? Do you know?"

Bless her. Darcy knew me, knew I had to keep moving, never questioned this impossible task. She rolled up her sleeves and helped, adding more to her list than crossing off.

"Finish one thing, then move to what's next," she said, and I needed to hear it. My brain fizzed with all the jobs ahead but staying focused was hard. Hard to draw a full breath too, with a weight on my chest and my head fuzzed from a string of sleepless nights.

Paint. It wouldn't take long – one wall in the kitchen, around the opening to the dining room. I picked up the brush and let my mind drift to crossed off accomplishments.

My workshop almost looked like Gram's sitting room again. The two of us ferried out the stacks of molding and trim. Darcy wanted to haul the oak boards and table saw too, but I put my foot down. "You're pregnant, idiot. Luke and I can get it later."

Soon as we did, the room was ready to be vacuumed and dusted. After the funeral, I'd add wainscoting, a gas fireplace, more built-in bookshelves. If...

I thought back to the tense conversation with Paul early that morning. The way he snapped when I asked for his input on the funeral foretold our upcoming battle.

"At least tell me what day works for you!" I pushed, past caring that Paul responded better to pulling than pushing.

"I've got a lot to juggle here," he said. "I'll let you know."

I hadn't heard from him since. So I was on hold, the funeral home was on hold, Rev at the church was on hold. I couldn't even send the obituary to the paper till we had a date.

Twenty-four hours, I thought. If I didn't hear from him by then, I'd go ahead. Whether he could be there or not.

I could threaten but I couldn't see me making good on it. Paul was the only family I had left. And I needed family. Especially at the funeral. He'd need me too, admit it or not. How else would either of us come to terms with the loss of our father, find closure? If closure was what the funeral could give us.

The long-term specter, our differing visions for the farm, hung low to the ground. Impossible to walk around. I saw skirmishes ahead, picking my battles, currying favor when I could, standing firm when I had to.

Focus on the now, I told myself and let my eyes take pleasure in the soft mellow green of the paint. Gram would call it easy on the eyes and she'd be right. She'd also say to put my focus on cutting a clean line at the ceiling.

Half an hour later, I stretched kinks where I didn't know I could have kinks. Done. The weight on my chest was not quite so heavy.

"How's it coming in there?"

"Looks gorgeous. But you can't come see till it's dry."

"Then you come here. I need a consult. In your dad's kitchen."

"Two minutes."

By the time I got to the sitting room, I heard Luke's voice.

"Hey, Luke. When did you get here?"

"Couple minutes ago," he said from the kitchen. "Come sit."

"What's this?"

"You've got to eat. And so does my lovely bride. Obviously."

Darcy took a big bite of sandwich and said, "S'good." She chewed. "I started without you. Catch up."

Luke pushed me toward a chair and plopped a plate on the table. "Milk for my growing girls?" He moved to the cupboard for glasses and poured. No answer required.

How long had it been since I thought about food? One day? Two? Once in front of me – like magic it seemed – that sandwich filled every crevice of my brain. I dug in. Mm… "Ambrosia."

"Nope. Didn't bring that. But I have lemon meringue for good girls who clean their plates."

"Gimme!" Darcy made a grab for the pie Luke held just beyond her reach.

"Say please."

She narrowed her eyes. He gave her the pie. I laughed. An honest-to-gosh, belly-busting laugh. How long had it been since I did that? And oh my lord, it felt good. Good to be with friends. Good to bite into the juicy tomato on chicken salad. Good to be laughing and alive.

Darcy gave me a wink. "He's magic. But don't tell him I said so. He'll get a swelled head."

"You're both magic." Damn tears welled up, sudden as the laugh a minute before.

"Now you've done it," Luke said. "See? She's the one with the swelled head. There will be no living with her now. And it's all your fault."

So much for tears. How could they survive among so much good will?

I crunched on my sandwich and the thick homemade chips Luke brought to go with it while they bickered amiably. Those chips deserved focus and got my full and undivided attention. Until another crunch snuck into my awareness. The crunch of tires on gravel.

I looked up quick. Paul, I thought. But Luke, who was closest to the door, smiled. Luke wouldn't smile to see my brother.

"Testosterone backup," he said on his way to the door. "Over here, Whip."

WHIP

Walking into Kat Patterson's house felt a lot like going to a junior high dance. My buddy was glad to see me, but what about the girl?

No welcome with open arms. And no surprise either that after one glance – questions in her eyes – Kat didn't look at me. I was the uninvited guest, the interloper – till Darcy brought out her needs-doing list. It took thirty seconds to see that what she meant was needs-doing-by-lug-headed-men-with-more-muscles-than-brains.

I followed the three of them through a short hallway into a big open room, sheets draped over furniture at one end, a table saw and a stack of hardwood at the other. Darcy pointed. "All that has to go out to Gram's porch." She conferred briefly with Kat, who nodded and disappeared down a hallway. Darcy turned back to us. "Well? What are you waiting for? Heft that saw and follow me."

I looked around, curious, the way you get about any big old house along the road. And more because it was this old house. Tight as Scott and I were, I only ever saw the place from the road. We met in the timber, in town, anywhere but here. He said he hated being home though what we both knew was his folks didn't like me. Even before.

The big room, the hallway where we followed Darcy were what you'd expect. Old-fashioned faded wallpaper, thin old rugs over painted wood floors. Wide woodwork thick with generations showing through chips in the paint.

"I'll get the door," Darcy said as we left the hall and crossed another biggish room to the porch. From there I saw a slice of Route Six. North, I decided, sheltered by trees in winter, shady in summer. Another door at the west end of the porch.

"Lumber, same place. I'll find a tarp to cover it."

When we stepped back in, I saw a ladder and something green through a big opening in the wall.

"How's she doing in there?" Luke asked. "Can we use it by… When's the funeral?"

"Don't know yet. Waiting on Paul." Darcy rolled her eyes before giving her husband's arm a pat. "No worries. She'll get it done."

Luke and I exchanged a skeptical look. "Kitchen?" I asked. What was it, a week, ten days, since I saw it? "No chance." I said it low, for Luke's ears, but Darcy heard.

"Have faith. Buffet on the window counter. Bar over by the stairs."

I felt my eyebrows rise. The room where we stood wasn't as bad as the mess I'd seen in the kitchen. But it was far from what my Aunt Sue would call company-ready. More sheets over furniture, boxes and tools strewn about.

Darcy tapped her list. "It'll come together." She shifted her eyes toward the kitchen and raised her voice.

"Because Kat's been a workaholic hermit these past weeks!"

"At least I wasn't getting knocked up. Paint's not dry yet. Get gone, girl!"

"Going." She stepped toward the hall, turned back to us. "Well? That lumber won't move itself."

By the time we made four more trips, Darcy had all the sheets gone in the big room. "Sofa centered against that wall. This chair there, the wing-back recliner there. I'll get the lamps."

When is it ever that simple? "Six inches that way. Too far. Back an inch." And so forth until Darcy was satisfied. She disappeared for thirty seconds before zipping back with a vacuum cleaner that she shoved into Luke's hands. In mine, she shoved a roll of paper towels and window cleaner. "You like looking out these windows? Good. Wash them. Inside and out. And when you're done in here, move down the hall – get the window and mirror in the bathroom, the office."

I shot a look at Luke, wondering if she was this bossy at home. But as he'd already uncoiled the vacuum cord, I figured I didn't have to ask. I washed windows and watched from the corner of my eye as Darcy pulled a bag from a cupboard. In two shakes, she had the room decked out with doilies and doodads, so it reminded me of Jake and Sue's living room right down to the rug draped over the back of a chair. Likely Navajo where theirs were Lakota. But it had the same feel – for company, not for living.

Too bad. It was a nice room. Big and airy. I got my bearings as I washed a big window with a long leaded windowpane at the top. East. The front porch you saw when you turned in the driveway was like the room – for company. Like most old farmhouses. Save the fancy for strangers. Friends and family come in by way of the twin back porches out the windows at the other end of the room.

Twenty minutes later, I looked at an old-fashioned bathtub. While I tried to focus on the window and mirror instead of bare…toes, I heard a succession of ominous sounds – thud, crash, breaking glass. I abandoned my post and broke into a jog toward Kat's kitchen.

Green. Odd that the color should register even as my eyes trained on the swearing woman in a heap on the floor. "You okay?"

"What the hell do you think?"

I took a step back and raised my hands as if to say, "I'm innocent here!"

She huffed in vicious disgust. "I'm fine. Dammit it all to hell." She shifted, put a hand down to push herself up – into a pile of broken glass. I reached to help and had my hand knocked away. So. Kat had claws.

On her feet again, she bent to lift a cabinet door – with jagged shards instead of a glass pane. "Dammit. That will be another trip to the hardware store." She glanced at me. "Damn thing slipped out of my hands. Knocked me off the ladder. I don't have time for this." She pushed at her hair.

"You're bleeding."

"I'm fine." She held up her hand – her way to say mind your own business. Until she saw blood drip to the floor. Her eyes rolled back in her head. If I'd been a second slower, she'd have tumbled to the floor again.

I looked at the kitchen sink. No place to prop her up. I hoisted and headed back to the bathroom. Likely she had stuff we'd need there. She came to halfway there. It was easier when she was out cold. A lot easier.

"Hold still. You fainted."

"I never fainted in my life! Put me down!"

"In a second. Keep your pants on." I plopped her down on the toilet and pulled her hand to the sink. "Let the water run on that awhile. You got bandages? Peroxide?"

Her eyes went big at all the red splashing in the sink and I thought she might go under again. I rummaged through the medicine cabinet. Only girly stuff.

"Kat. First aid. Where do you keep it?"

She started like she forgot I was there. "Cupboard." She nodded toward a built-in. White like the wall tile. No wonder I missed it. "Second shelf," she said midway through my ransack.

When I turned around again with a jar of antiseptic in my hand, her cheeks were scarlet. Likely mine were too. I don't make a habit of pawing through a woman's tampons. Not before the third date. Or the thirtieth.

"Let me see that hand." The water ran pink and I could see the cut. "Looks worse than it is, I think. I don't see any glass so that's good. Bet it will hurt like hell though."

"It's not ba – dammit!" She tried to pull away, but I had a solid grip on her wrist and continued to pour on the antiseptic.

"That ought to do it."

"Holy crow, I guess. Sadist!"

I grinned. "Get it over quick, my mom always said."

"That explains so much," she said in an acid tone. Claws were out again. I figured that meant no more fainting.

"Too big for a Band-Aid." I shoved aside the box and found some sterile pads and gauze. "These will do."

"No way! I have too much to do. I can't have my hand wrapped up like a mummy."

"Either that or you bleed all over your fresh paint." I resumed my grip and wrapped.

"Dammit. I could have had the place looking great. Now what?"

"I'm handy. Tell me what you want done."

"Why?"

"Excuse me?"

"Why are you here? Why would you help me?"

I hesitated, not knowing what to say. I deflected the question. "Why do you want to restore this old barn of a place?"

She stuck out her chin as if used to defending her choices. "I love it. Pure and simple."

I nodded. "Reason enough."

Her eyes regarded me skeptically. "For me. Why are you here?"

Give it to her true, I thought. "Pure and simple? You."

Kat

"Me?" Why did my voice have to squeak? "What do you mean?"

"You…get to me."

I shook my head and felt my pulse jump under his hand. "That…doesn't make any sense!"

"Why?" He kept wrapping and taping. So damn calm. While I felt like jumping out of my skin.

I yanked my hand back and snarled, "Because."

He mocked me with a smile and a raised eyebrow.

"For one thing, you…you're Whip Tyler, for God's sake. And you…you don't know me!"

"Guilty on the first part. But I thought we already established what I know about you." He cocked his head. "Okay. I'll go through it again. You're smart and resourceful. A good friend, someone who values loyalty enough to care for a dying man who didn't deserve you. Loyal even to a brother who'd like to wrestle this house and everything you love away from you. Loyal enough to love your ancestors, the…ones who went before."

He might have been reciting his grocery list. While I sat there with my mouth open. Trying to think of something to say. Something to stop him saying more. As if.

He leaned, trapping me with one hand braced on the sink and one on the back of the toilet. "And I know your hair smells like lemons and one sight of your bare toes can keep a man awake all night."

I jumped at the sound of loud footsteps in the hall. He turned his head but didn't change his stance when Darcy stuck her head in the door, grinned. "Sorry to interrupt, but I thought you should know. Paul just drove in," she said.

Whip straightened – to keep our heads from colliding as I shot to my feet. I felt the flush on my cheeks flame hotter. I bolted across the hall to my bedroom, Darcy on my heels.

"What did I miss?" She waggled her eyebrows. "Wait. What did you do to your hand?"

"Cabinet door. Broke the glass." I waved away her concern as I peered out the window. "Chrissy."

"Ugh and double ugh. Which way are they heading?"

"Dad's side."

"See you later." She beat a quick retreat in the opposite direction.

"Coward!" Too late. She was already gone.

I got to Dad's porch in time to see Chrissy's mauve high-heeled boots glide from Paul's SUV. She probably practiced for days to perfect that move. I hoped she was as practiced on gravel. The last thing I needed was

Chrissy with a broken ankle. Silly to worry. Chrissy was born in high heels.

"Kat, dear, how *do* you manage out here in the hinterlands? It's so…remote."

I forced a laugh at her dainty shudder. "We call it peaceful, Chrissy," I said while she bestowed fragrant air kisses near my ears.

Paul's greeting was less chummy, perhaps due to a lack of breath after wrestling with a giant suitcase. Its wheels were not up to the gravel. "When's the funeral?"

I saw what he meant – how long till they could leave. I raised my hands. "We've been waiting for you to…"

"For Christ's sake, you expect me to do everything?"

"No…" I let the word stretch like a stick of chewed Juicy Fruit. "I asked what would work best for you. You being so busy and all." He didn't get the sarcasm. "So…when do you want to hold Dad's funeral?"

"Yesterday."

"Paul…"

"Tomorrow then. At the funeral home. Not that fusty old church. For God's sake spare me that."

Not big on irony either, I thought, fishing out my phone. A hand full of gauze didn't make it easy. "I'll see what I can do," I said, pasting my best anything-you-want expression on my face. "If they can take us," I said, knowing they couldn't. "Richard, Kat Patterson here. My brother's wondering if you can host the funeral there tomorrow. Oh dear. Two funerals already? When's your next opening?" I paused. "Not till Sunday? Goodness."

"Jesus. Find another funeral home."

I held up a hand. "Richard, can you hang on a minute?" To Paul, I said, "Dad's already there. At Oakton's only funeral home. So?"

"Tomorrow. At the damn church. No way I'm hanging around till Sunday."

"Oh no, we couldn't… We can't miss the dinner at the club Saturday night. It's the most important dance of the season. And I got the perfect dress. You should see it, Kat…deep, deep blue with the most darling…"

I waved my phone and turned away – to make the arrangements and to quash a rude reply that would surely demolish any fences I might hope to mend. "I guess it will have to be the church, Richard. You can still accommodate us there? Right. Two o'clock? Yes, that should work." I glanced back to see more suitcase wrestling, so I lowered my voice. "Two o'clock it is. Thanks. And Richard? I owe you a cold one." I ended the call but boosted my volume a notch and said, "The graveside service? I'm not sure…Can you hang on again? Paul?" Two heads turned. "What about the cemetery? What kind of service do you want at the graveside?"

"Jesus, do we have to?"

"Well…no…" Again I let the word stretch. "I guess…"

"No! That Godforsaken church is bad enough. Jesus!"

"Well…all right. If that's the way you want it…" I never sounded so pathetic in my life. "Richard," I said, "I guess we'll pass on the graveside service. Yes. I know it's what most people do. But…well… Thanks so much, Richard. Paul and I appreciate your help. Bye now."

I should go on television. After I finished the kitchen cabinets, after hooking up the fireplace in Gram's dining room, after… I shot a look at my watch.

"We'd best get busy. Still lots to do. Now what would you two rather tackle? Cleaning Dad's side or shaking out Gram's dining room rugs? We'll have to hustle. I expected another day to get it all done." I sighed. "But with all of us pitching in tonight and tomorrow morning, we can probably get it all done."

"What the hell are you talking about?"

"Getting ready for the funeral lunch. What did you think?"

"What lunch? Where?"

"Here, of course. Where else?"

I swallowed a laugh at the horror on their faces. Paul found his voice first. "Are you insane? Invite people here? To this wreck of a house?"

"It's not a wreck. It's our home."

"It's a fucking dump! Always was. And what you've done – all your stupid half-finished projects? You've got to be crazy."

I swallowed the insult too. "Not to worry. It will be fine. As long as we don't lollygag. I hope you brought work clothes? No? Well, I expect you could fit into some of Dad's old things. You know where to find them, right, Paul? And sheets for the bed in your old room? Clean towels in the bathroom cupboard. You can make do. It's just the one night after all."

Chrissy blanched. Again I wanted to laugh. It was so easy to pull her chain. Not as easy to pull Paul's though. Through clenched teeth he said, "We'll stay in Gram's room. With the bathroom right across the hall."

My hope was to push them toward a hotel. Out of my hair. But no. I heard a voice say, "Staking a claim." So clearly, I almost jumped. Gram? Dad? My bandaged

111

hand came to my mouth. Whip Tyler? How did he get in my head?

No time to wonder. Or to unclench my teeth all the way. Instead I conjured a conciliatory smile. "Oh dear. I suppose that *could* work. I think the bugs are gone now. Most of them anyway. It's been a challenge, they're such persistent little buggers. Admirable, don't you think, how resilient insects can be?"

As one, they turned toward the stairs to Paul's old room. I waited till the door closed before I bent double in silent laughter. In the space of twenty minutes I lied more than I ever had – to Paul or anyone. I should have felt guilty. Gram always said lying was a sin. So why, I wondered, could I not wipe off this grin?

WHIP

What was I thinking? Dumb move to come on to Kat – in a bathroom, of all places. The day after her father died. She already made it clear she didn't want me around. Dumb.

I sprayed window cleaner on the mirror, gave it a swipe, and was surprised to see a grin. I stared and watched as the grin grew. Maybe it wasn't so dumb. Why not put it out there, let the girl know I was attracted? Even if it did sneak up on me too. Can't win if you don't play, I thought. I was still grinning as I headed back to the kitchen where Kat fell. I figured I'd clean up the mess, earn some points.

Darcy and Luke beat me to it. She stopped sweeping and said, "Lothario himself." She propped a hand on her hip. "So? What's going on?"

I should have expected she'd grill me. I glanced at Luke for support and saw "You're on your own, man," written in his eyes.

I shrugged. "Nothing." But I couldn't suppress the grin and added, "Yet."

"Didn't look like nothing." Darcy narrowed her eyes. She should join the CIA. Sic Darcy James on a prisoner, and we'd know all his secrets in five minutes. No need to waterboard.

"Could have been something. Maybe. If you hadn't barged in."

She hooted and shot a triumphant "Told you!" at Luke.

He grinned back at her. "You did, baby. I thought you'd take longer to make your move, fella."

"Geez Louise. You're taking bets on my love life? Both of you?"

"And I won!" Darcy and the broom did a jig. "Foot massages every night for a week!"

Luke pulled a sad face. "You cost me serious sexual favors, man. Don't think I'll forget."

I held up both hands. "Sorry. Fill me in next time. Meanwhile, I got windows to wash."

"Hold your horses, boy." Darcy swung the broom to block my exit. "Unless you want to subject yourself to Paul and..." Her eyes went horror-show big with full shudder. "...Chrissy."

"I wouldn't, Whip. Trust me on this." Luke echoed her shudder.

"O...kay."

"We got work here. No need to venture into enemy territory." Darcy dumped a pile of shattered glass in the trash. "You two strappy specimens hang these cabinet doors while Whip divulges his plan to woo Kat."

I picked up a door, hoisted it to an upper cabinet in an effort to distract Attila the Darcy. "Hinges don't match up with the holes."

"Where's the drill, babe? We'll make new holes," Luke said.

"Try this one," Darcy said, extending a foot toward the door directly below where we worked. Perfect match. As were all the rest down the line.

"Methodical, isn't she?"

"Meticulous. Just one thing you need to appreciate if you hope to deserve my friend Kat."

"Okay, I'll bite. What else?"

"She's not as tough as she seems."

"Got that already."

Darcy nodded as if I were a good student. "She's been hurt. A lot. Makes her skittish."

"Got that too. The skittish part anyway."

"I'm not going to say who hurt her. Or how. That's for her to do. When — if — she trusts you." Darcy put on her scary face. "But hear me on this, Whip Tyler. You hurt her more and I will hunt you down."

I took a door from Luke and hoisted it into position. "Fair enough. I don't plan on it."

"Darcy, love of my life. Give the man a break. He wants to win the big pot, he's gotta throw in some chips."

She smiled and stroked a hand down Luke's back, as he screwed in the last of the doors. "When he's right, my guy's right." She sobered. "Relationships are big stakes for Kat. Be patient with her."

"But not too patient."

Darcy sent me a grin. "My man is on a streak." She hesitated. "Kat's fearless about so much. She'll dive in way over her head — like with this place. Huge project, tons of work, buckets of money. And she chomped at it like a vegetarian starved for meat. Her job at the museum's the same. What she does there is amazing — the exhibits, the programs."

"But she doesn't trust easy. Right, babe?"

"She makes you earn it. If you do, she's there for life."

"But you've already got strikes against you on that score, pal." Luke's face was heart-attack serious. "It's why I thought you'd move slower. You know. History." He raised his palms. "The farm."

He wasn't wrong. "I can't change the history."

"You could give her a clearer picture about it."

I shook my head while Luke and I exchanged a long look. "No. I can't."

"You never have." Luke sighed. "But it wasn't right that you should take all the blame and no mud splashed on Paul Patterson."

"She never talks about Scott," Darcy said. "Wasn't allowed to. Except maybe with her gram. But...she bristles when your name comes up, Whip."

I nodded. Tried to chase images from that night out of my head. Liked that ever worked.

"So you're swimming upstream, bro." Luke clamped a big hand on my shoulder. "Doesn't mean you should stop swimming."

"If you want her bad enough." Darcy's hand went to her hip again. "And you should. You'll never find better."

"Yeah. Got that too." I let a smile flicker and telegraph a message I hadn't fully understood till then. "History is..." I waved a hand. "What it was. I already gave her my word about the farm, that I'd try to keep Paul from raping the land. Get him to respect her wishes."

"So what's your next move?" Darcy cocked an ear, put a finger to her lips. "In here," she called.

"Whose next move?" asked the woman in question. "To do what?"

"To replace this glass. You two lugs call it. Heads or tails. Which one goes to town? While the other keeps cleaning?" Cool customer, that Darcy. "You get the city mice all settled in, Kat?"

Kat rolled her eyes and put on high breathy voice. "One whole night in the hinterlands." Another eye roll and a return to her own voice. "How will Chrissy stand it?"

Darcy let out a bark of laughter. "Horrors!" Her eyes went wicked. "Will we go to hell if we stage a little woo-woo-woo in the deep dark night?"

Kat's laugh set her eyes to sparkle. Reason enough to brave a swift current. The sparkle fizzed like soda pop as she took in the finished cabinets. "Wow. Look what you did!"

"They're not big on brains, but they take direction well," said our taskmaster.

Kat's wide eyes filled. "Thank you." Her gaze lingered on Darcy and Luke, skimmed me. "You've done so much. Helped so much."

Darcy slipped an arm around Kat's waist, and I wished it was my arm. "We got your back, honey." She grinned. "What's next on the list for the brawny boys? Besides the trip to town."

Kat turned in a circle, smiling – at her kitchen this time. It did look good. Hard to believe how good. "I love it. Love, love, love it!" Her eyes went through the big opening to the next room. "Could we get the fireplace hooked up, do you think? And the light fixture? Those are the only big projects left." Her voice dropped as if embarrassed to ask so much.

"How long have we got?" Practical Darcy. Set her loose on Guantanamo and Capitol Hill.

"Tomorrow. The funeral's tomorrow. At two."

Luke winced. "O...kay." He pulled out his phone. "I'll get Nancy to close so I can get out here and get the food set up by three."

"I'll come out in the morning. Do a final spit and polish," said Darcy.

"Can you get by without her?" I asked Luke. "Didn't what's her name quit in a huff? After you screamed at her?"

"Luke, you didn't."

"I didn't scream. And she deserved it." Luke shot a malevolent glance at me. "Whip can fill in at breakfast. He's trained now. Nancy can handle lunch."

No way was I donning that apron again. "I'll be more use here. I can spit and polish," I said. "Breakfast is Darcy's natural habitat. Not mine."

"That could work," said Darcy. "If Nancy can cover starting mid-morning, I'll change, be here half an hour later." She glanced at the clock on the stove.

"You all act like I'm not here," Kat said. "I can't ask you to..."

"Don't recall you asking," I said.

Darcy reached a hand to pat my arm, her way to say attaboy.

"No need to ask. Hup to, warriors. The finish line is in sight!" Darcy swept an arm to the other room. Luke and I moved as one. She slipped an arm around Kat's shoulders. "I do love it when a plan comes together. And when we can watch hunks do what hunks do best."

I'd have to shift an appointment in the morning, a scheduled lunch date with my mother. Small potatoes. Helping could maybe shift the tide, make my swim a little easier.

Kat

Much as I appreciated their help, I wasn't thrilled with how easily those three plotted to take over my life. Darcy saw the protest coming.

"Save it."

"It's just…" I kept my voice low like hers.

She rolled her eyes. "Too independent for your own good…" A sing-song phrase said to and about generations of Patterson women. She paused while I huffed. Once. "He wants to help. Let him."

"But what is he even doing here?"

"Really? You haven't figured that out yet?"

"It's not funny! And it's never going to happen."

"Okay. Let's say he's trying to make up for…" She paused, rubbed my arm. "…the rotten position your brother put him in." Her head came up. "And here's said brother now."

Paul stood at the door to the dining room. He took in everything, I knew. He always had, collecting each detail like a real estate agent. But did he mention how the floors gleamed, how the new arched window to the kitchen let late afternoon sun light the dining room where Luke and Whip worked? No. Nor did he reveal the bitter acid simmering behind his cocked eyebrow.

You wouldn't know unless you grew up with him. A slight tightening of his jaw told me there was trouble ahead. As did the way he greeted Whip.

"Whip, old pal, I didn't expect to see you here." Paul's suspicious tone didn't match the words. "My baby sister press you into service, did she?"

I mounted a fast offense. "Volunteers, Paul. For whom we both should be grateful, so we can be ready to do Dad proud."

Luke laid his hands on Darcy's shoulders in a show of solidarity. "Friends help each other," he said. "You'd do the same for us, Kat."

Paul turned to Whip as if Luke and Darcy weren't there. "I forgot that you and fry-boy here were tight. Back in the day." He smiled and you'd think it was from the heart unless you could read him like a brother. "I was going to call you so it saves time that you're already here. Join us for dinner tonight. So we can talk about our project."

Was Paul trying to be rude, not including Darcy and Luke in the invitation? Or me? I stepped up my resistance. "Good idea," I said, through clenched teeth. "I planned to order pizza, crack open a twelve-pack. But you're right, brother mine. The only decent thing to do is treat our friends to a great meal. We can afford the time – because they did so much. The Lodge would be good. No doubt you'll want to pick up the tab to show your gratitude. Seems only fair since they put in so much more sweat than you today."

Paul narrowed his eyes at me. He took the bait, but there'd be retribution. "Yeah, sure. Why not?"

"Sorry, Kat," Luke said. "We'll have to take a rain check. We've got things to do tonight." He lobbed back Paul's earlier grenade. "Got to prep for tomorrow's business, make the fat bank deposit for today's."

"Paulie? Where are you? I need…" Chrissy's voice from the other side of the house drifted off.

"Be right there, sweetheart. See you at dinner, Whip." Paul gave a curt nod to my best friends in the world and strode from the room.

All I could do was stare at the floor. Silence hung heavy before a simultaneous exhale, like we'd all held our breath from the moment Paul appeared. Maybe we had.

I closed my eyes and began, "I am so sorry."

Darcy slipped her arm around my waist. "Don't be silly," she said.

"He was so rude! When you've done so much."

"Did we expect different?" She looked to Luke and Whip.

"Not in this life, darlin'." Luke grinned, transforming back to his amiable self.

"Can't change a rattlesnake, honey. Just gotta stay out of its way."

"He's not a snake. Not really." I wished I could sound more confident.

Darcy cocked an eyebrow. "You keep believing that if you have to. But don't forget to look out for his fangs."

I already knew Luke was of the same mind. I looked to Whip. "That's what you think too?"

He shrugged. "I might not put it so strong, but..."

"But you'll work for him? Plan his...projects?" Air quotes seemed appropriate.

The shrug turned into a squirm. "If it's not me, he'll find somebody else. So maybe it's better if it is me." He raised his palms, like he wanted to say more. Like he did earlier.

I turned away to hide my cursed red-head skin. No matter what I said to Paul, I wanted that man out of my house. He made me so uncomfortable. Dammit! I remembered dinner.

"Darce. Come with us tonight. Please."

"No deal, honey." She tucked her hand into the crook of Luke's elbow. "Can't subject little Christabelle to a rattlesnake or the dreaded Chrissy." She clapped one hand to her mouth, the other to her tummy. "New name. She can't be Christabelle. What if she turned out like...argh?" Darcy shuddered.

"Can't chance that," I agreed. "How about Zuleika? Your great-great-aunt's name? Right?"

"Much better!" Darcy beamed and asked her stomach, "What do you think, little one? You like it? Me too. I re-christen you Zuleika!"

WHIP

Luke snorted. "My son's name is Joe," he said.

"Lots of great men with the name of Joe." I said, lending guy support. "DiMaggio. Namath."

"Montana. Cocker...um..."

"Biden...Pesci."

"Little Joe."

"Huh?" Luke and I stared at Kat.

"Cartwright. From *Bonanza*. Remember how we crushed on him, Darce? Those reruns on TV Land?"

"He was dreamy." She sighed. "However, she's a girl. She will be Zuleika."

A good-natured squabble ensued while we worked. By the time the light fixture was up, Kat seemed easier, not so spooked to have me around. I hoped.

A chirp from her phone brought back jitters. "Paul made a reservation. For four. Six o'clock." Her frightened fawn eyes almost made me let her off the hook. But who knew when I'd have another chance like this?

Double-dating with the rattler and his wife was not ideal. But if that's what it took, so be it. With time, maybe she'd come to trust me. I didn't mind flustering her, seeing her pulse jump when I looked too long, or stood too close. Who doesn't like that man-woman fizz? But I wanted her trust too. Trust that I cared about her land – more than some other site guy who might not give a rat's ass. That if it looked like I cozied up to Paul, I was playing it cagey. To let Paul think I was like him – all about the money.

"Time to flip the switch, Kat. See if we got the wires right."

"Looks good." I stepped down from the ladder and gathered tools.

"It does. Old-fashioned fixture, but not frou-frou," said Darcy. "Cross that off the list. Only the fireplace to go."

"Not now," said Kat. She consulted her watch and made a face. "It can wait till morning," she said.

Kat

An extra worker made a big difference. I saw it, appreciated it. But I didn't want to have to count on anybody but me. Didn't want Whip coming back tomorrow. Didn't like the way he crossed the room and looked through the fireplace parts.

"I don't need help," I said. "I can do it myself."

He cocked an eyebrow. "Bet you can. When you've got two good hands."

"So we follow the plan," said Darcy. "Whip will be here in the morning, help you with the fireplace. I'll come later for the last spit and polish." She brushed her hands together. "And now, we'll go home. Let you get ready for dinner."

"Darcy, Luke, I don't know what I'd do without you two. Thank you." I hugged my friends. They got their coats and I hugged them, thanked them again. Did it all again as I saw them out the door. Couldn't do it enough, I thought. "You're so good…to do all this work…being here."

"You can't get weepy with a pregnant woman! Stop already!" Darcy pulled me in for one last hug before she turned with a wave. "See you tomorrow."

I blinked and rested my head on the door a moment. "What did I ever do to deserve such friends?"

"Probably by being such a good friend back."

I whirled, startled. "What... You're...still here." Why was he still here?

"I waited." Whip's hand went through his hair. "Look. Can I show you something? It's on the way to the Lodge. We could go now, while it's still light."

"What? Why?"

"It's a project I'm working on. A development site. Come see how we work. Please?"

"But why?"

"Might help you see..." He lifted his palms. "...how you can develop with respect for the land."

Nothing doing. "Show Paul. I don't have land to develop. He's the one who wants...development." The word tasted bitter on my tongue.

He nodded. "But you want a better outcome. Look at what we do. See for yourself." He stopped, eyes boring into mine. "Look. I get why you don't want your place to change. But you're smart enough to know it will. Around you, if not on your land. Wouldn't it be better if you had a say in those changes?" He reached for my good hand. "I think I can help, Kat. If you let me."

I looked down at my hand, back at his face. "I don't think..." I pulled on my hand only to have him tighten his grasp.

"Come with me, Kat. Just come see. That's all I'm asking."

Did he have to sound so reasonable? I looked down at my jeans. "Now?" I said, and he took it to mean I'd go. It wasn't what I meant, but he persisted.

"How long will it take you to change?"

"Ten minutes." Dammit.

"It will take me five. My place is on the way. That will still give us half an hour before dark." His place? No way. He saw my reaction and persisted. "Five minutes. You can wait in the truck."

"Paul will expect me to go with them."

He raised eyes to the ceiling. "I haven't met Chrissy. But I get the feeling you'd rather not be stuck in a car with her?"

A snort came out before I could suppress it, and his grin went wide. Chrissy cinched the deal. I rolled my eyes and said, "Ten minutes."

WHIP

As she left the room, I congratulated myself. One stroke upstream. Only one, I had to remember. I planned my pitch about the Twin Creeks project, what to show her, what to say, how to get it right while flipping through fireplace instructions.

"You're a quick one." I said as footsteps sounded. "Oh. Hi, Paul. I was expecting your sister."

"Yeah? What's up with that, Whip, old pal? When did you and Kat get so chummy?"

Cagey, round one. "I wouldn't call it chummy. It's a small town. You bump into people."

"So you do grunt work for everybody you bump into?"

I laughed. Casual, easy. "Most folks I bump into are over sixty with a three-day beard. Not so pretty as Kat." But it was time to speak his language. "And since it's obvious you and your sister don't see eye-to-eye about this place, I figured it wouldn't hurt to get on friendlier terms with her. Break down some barriers."

His narrow-eyed stare called up Darcy's reptile description. "You're still working for me, though. Right?"

The loyalty test. And time to wave my own colors. "I'm my own boss, Paul. You want ideas to develop your land. I'm working on those ideas. In my own way. Time comes we agree on a plan, I'll work *with* you – not for. With Kat too, and every owner of neighboring land. For everybody's best interests. Because that's how you get things done right."

The stare continued, so I did too.

"The way I see it you want a big cash payoff. Your sister wants the land to stay as it is. You both dig your heels in, could be neither gets what you want. I've seen it go that way." I shrugged, lifted my hands in a what-are-you-going-to-do gesture. "Lose-lose. Or..." I paused to see if he'd take the bait.

His eyes stayed narrow but focused. "Or what?."

"Or one of you changes your mind. I'm guessing that won't be you."

"You got that right."

"From what I've seen of Kat, might not be her either." I let my eyes wander the room, what she'd made it. "I don't know her well, but she strikes me as...determined?" I made it a question.

"I can get around her."

I nodded. "Likely you can. About a lot of things. This? I'm not so sure. Seems like she's got her heels dug in pretty deep here. So...if I help her out, get her to see me as a good guy, might be I can smooth the way. Some."

"You think you can charm her into selling."

I laughed. "Not a chance in hell. But to listen, to not block everything you want. If the plan is reasonable. If the plan gets you both part of what you want."

"You got that plan?"

I shook my head. "Not yet. But ideas?" I put on my most confident smile. "I'm chewing on some." I put up a hand. "Not ready to lay them out yet so don't get your boxers in a twist. Still figuring." I heard Kat's footsteps, so I raised my voice. "I'm taking Kat over to a project across the river before dinner. Show her the project I'm working on. And here she is." I sent her a smile. "You got some wellies you can bring along? Mud's up to your ankles with yesterday's rain." Paul wouldn't want to wreck his shiny loafers. I hoped.

Kat's eyes shot me a question. She turned to Paul and said, "I don't know why he wants to show me and not you."

"Why didn't I think of that? Come along, Paul. Bring your missus. We can all go on to dinner from there." I made it sound sincere.

"Chrissy hates mud. Tell us about it later."

"Suit yourself. Ready, Kat?"

"Soon as I collect my coat and boots at the door. I'll lock up over here. You'll lock up on Dad's side, Paul?"

He turned to the hall and waved a hand. "Yeah, yeah. See you later."

We watched him go before Kat turned to me and said, "It didn't rain here yesterday."

"Didn't it? I must have my days mixed up."

"You and Paul seemed to have a lot to say."

I took her hand, pulled her toward the kitchen. "Time's wasting. Tell you on the way."

Kat

When I pulled my coat off the hook by the door, Whip reached out to take it.

"My mother taught me to hold a woman's coat."

I considered grabbing it back. But what was the point? I stuck my bandaged hand in first and held out the other arm. It's a simple thing, putting on a coat. So why did he make it seem so…intimate? I reached my hand back to pull my hair out from the collar but froze when I felt his hand already there.

I stepped away, opened the door, took a deep breath of bracing air.

"Don't forget these." He stooped to pick up my boots.

"Will I need them?"

He grinned. "Probably not."

"Then why the pretense?"

"I promised you wouldn't have to share a ride with Chrissy." He grinned. "And I wanted you to myself.

Don't look so suspicious. I'm not going to pounce on you – unless you ask."

I felt my cheeks go hot even as I wanted to wipe that cocky smirk off his face.

"No, look," he said as we stepped off the porch. "I already told you. I'm attracted to you. I'm not going to hide that. Even if it does make you uncomfortable." He grinned again quick as lightning, then sobered. "But this thing with your place – what happens here – that's a different deal. Not separate exactly, because you're you and he's…him. It's all part of the mix." His hand went through his hair. "How I see it anyway."

Good hair. Thick. Good hands too. That spent a lot of time in his hair. When he was at a loss for words? Flustered? Huh. Maybe he wasn't as calm around me as he pretended. Huh. I should have hated that idea. And didn't. My nerves settled, and for once I felt like I could hold my own. I yanked my thoughts up short as he pulled the door to his truck open. Like I was too weak to do it myself. "So what's that mean? For the farm?"

"Get in. I'll tell you on the way – what I told Paul."

I was glad for the few seconds before he climbed in the other door. For the chance to put cool hands to my cheeks. To observe the papers sticking out from the visor, the half-empty bottle of Coke, the travel mug in the cup holder. To stop thinking about his nerves or mine. Or the last time I let a man talk me into a ride.

"Your mobile office?" I asked.

"Pretty much." He turned off the radio, fiddled with the heater. "Warm enough?"

"Fine. You were saying…"

He stopped at the end of the driveway and shot me a glance. There went the hand through his hair. "What I told Paul. Okay, so here's the problem. You two want way different things. Leave it up to him, you'll have a fancy golf course and McMansions on your doorstep – if he leaves you a doorstep at all. You'd hate that."

"But he can't. Gram…"

He waved a hand. "I know. Your gram specified which land each of you gets. But you think he'll sit back and let you have it?"

"What else could he do?"

"I don't know if he can win, but do you think he's stopped fighting? He'll lawyer up if he hasn't already. Who knows what they'll come up with? Accuse you of undue influence – or some other legal mumbo-jumbo."

"How do you know I didn't? Unduly influence Gram?"

"Honey, you're as clear as water. What you're doing in that house? Sure you want it nice for you. But a lot is about paying respect to your gram. Isn't it?"

It was, but how did he know? "But that doesn't mean I didn't…"

"I can see you loved her. Probably took care of her like you did your dad. So maybe some judge would see that as influence. Nobody who knows you would."

I didn't know what to say. How was it Whip Tyler of all people saw so much?

"Suppose Paul fights your gram's will. Even if he doesn't win, you'll be in for a battle. Ugly charges against you, massive legal fees, time, the whole nine yards. You want that? Any of it?"

I couldn't help a shudder. "Of course not. But…"

"But Paul might be a good brother, let it work out the way you want?" He stopped at the one light in Oakton, and I felt his eyes on me. I studied the red reflection on the hood of his truck as if it held the answer to all the questions of the universe.

"You talked to Paul about how to fight me in court?"

I heard him sigh as the light turned green and he eased along Main street. "You're determined to see the worst in me, aren't you?"

"Why shouldn't I?"

"Because I am not the enemy here. I am on your side, Kat Patterson, whether you believe it or not." There went the hand through his hair.

"Why?"

I heard him take a deep breath as if to calm himself, and it seemed to work because in an even voice he said, "What I said to Paul was that I'm working on ideas for both of you to get part of what you want. A compromise that looks out for your interests as much as his."

He pulled over and parked the truck. I looked around, startled.

"My office. I live upstairs. You okay here?"

I nodded.

"Five minutes."

And he was gone, leaving me with more questions than I knew how to think about. And the hood of his truck gave no answers. My mind buzzed like radio static till I asked myself what would Darcy do? I reached into my coat pocket and found my trusty notepad. Who needs a horse? My kingdom for a list.

WHIP

When I opened the truck door, she jumped like a cat on a live wire. "Sorry. I thought you saw me." I glanced down at the notebook in her lap. "I guess you were busy. What you got there?"

"Questions."

"For me?"

"Yes."

"Shoot," I said in a nothing-to-hide tone and started the truck.

"Number one…"

"You numbered your questions?" One look at the defiant slant to her eyes and I swallowed the grin that wanted to split my face. "All righty, then. Number one?"

"How do I know I can trust you?"

No puny weapons for this girl. I had to admire how she went first for the big guns. I let her hear my sigh. "I don't suppose you can." My biggest gun – truth.

Surprise flashed before she clamped down on all expression. "Paul hired you. But you say you want to help me. Which could put you against him. So how do I know what to think?"

"Standing in your shoes, I'd wonder too." I let a moment pass, held tight to calm. "You think I'm playing the two of you against the middle. For some benefit of my own?"

"Well…"

"No, it's okay. I get it." I scrubbed at my hair, worked to relax the white knuckles on the hand that clutched the steering wheel. "You don't know me. And what you do know – or think you know – doesn't give you reason to trust me." I concentrated on the bridge now, like the truck might wander out of its lane and take a nosedive into the river.

Once across, I said, "So maybe you shouldn't trust me. I can say I respect the land like you. I can say I don't like Paul's notions for your land – or what that might do to Oakton. Or you." I tried but didn't manage to swallow another sigh. Give her truth. "But all that – whatever I say? Words. Can't trust words. Mine or…anybody else's." We both knew I meant Paul. "So maybe your best course of action is to stick with your own instincts. To what you want most."

I didn't look at her while I spoke. Might not have found the nerve if I had. When I did look, she'd turned her face away as if the flats and fields absorbed all her interest. I let it be. I said my piece. She didn't want to respond, I couldn't make her. Upstream in a fast current.

I wondered whether there was much point in showing her the Jensen development. But we were there, so I turned in and pulled to a stop. She roused then, peered out the windshield, turned questioning eyes at me.

I'm not sure how, but I kept my voice easy. "I'm guessing one of those questions you wrote down is why I wanted you to see this place I'm working on?"

Her mouth nearly twitched, and I swore inwardly at how much that small sign made me want to dive back into the current. "Number three. Almost," she said.

"What? Two point five?"

Another near twitch. "The question is what do you want me to see?"

It was like running full tilt into a door. And seeing stars. The want pouring through me was that big. That I'm a good guy, I thought. That I am on your side. That I loved him too. And wish I could have saved him instead of Paul.

I took a deep breath and said as lightly as I could manage, "I'll collect your boots. Then we'll take a walk and I'll show you what I do."

Something about the question threw him. I saw it, but I couldn't imagine why. What I did imagine was he'd insist on opening the truck door for me. No way I'd let that happen. I'm a woman who does for herself. Show him.

I was out the door and stepping out in the lot before he was all the way out his door. "I don't need boots."

He grinned and swung into step beside me. "There might be a patch of mud back by the woods." He pointed. "We could dip your boots in it. Enough to convince Paul we didn't make it up – in case he looks."

I shook my head. "He won't. Not the kind of thing he'd notice. So…" I looked around. "Where do we start?"

"This way."

We followed a dirt road through trees till we saw utility pipes sticking up in places, piles of dirt in others.

"Most of the water and sewer lines are in so you can start to see where the houses will sit in among the trees. The street will be about here." He pointed. There were a lot of trees. More than I expected. And a thick covering of fallen leaves and acorns crunching beneath our feet.

"It was Jensen land. Don't know if you knew them? Twin girls? Gabi and Gwen?"

"No."

"They're a couple years older than…" He trailed off, but I knew what he was thinking. He and Scott were in the same class, on the football team together. I knew that much. Number five on my question list. He cleared his throat. "Gabi's a lawyer in Peoria. Gwen's a doctor – finishing up her residency in Chicago. Their dad died a few years ago. Mrs. Jensen moved to assisted living near Gabi last fall."

"So they decided to sell."

"Gwen's keeping their old house. Plans to move back and join the medical group here in Oakton."

"She'll be welcome. They've had a hard time keeping docs."

"So I hear. Gwen will stick. She says she misses home. Sick of city life."

A break in the trees opened ahead framing a view of the river below. "Quite a view."

"It's a big selling point. That's what Clay had in mind, what he told the girls before he died. Seems he bought this plot – forty acres all told – as a kind of insurance. To help the twins get a start. Pay off their student loans."

"They must have whoppers. Takes a lot of school to be a doctor."

"Lawyer too." He jammed his hands in his coat pocket and looked around. "But they're square now. With some to spare. See the lot south of that big oak? That's Gabi's. In case she wants to come back sometime."

"So you wanted me to see how selling helped them."

He shrugged. "Takes money to fix up an old place like yours. But that's not... I thought you might like to talk to them, the twins. Hear what they think."

I was surprised. But it made sense if... "They'll talk to me? Like a...reference?"

"I'll get you their numbers."

"They get along, I take it?"

"Seem to. They were tight back in school. Always together. Cheerleaders, school play, that kind of thing."

"Maybe I do remember them. Blonde? Tall?"

His grin flashed. "Volleyball players. Good looking. And nice enough to let young squirts down easy."

"Paragons of virtue." It came out with more edge than I intended.

"Call. Get them to tell their story. I bet you'll like them."

I turned my back to the river, swept an arm. "So that's it? What you wanted me to see?"

He opened his mouth, closed it again with that same unreadable look from back in the truck. And then it was gone. "I wanted you to see we do it responsibly. Development, I mean."

"You'll take down a lot of trees."

"Some. Thin out saplings, leave a lot of them. See that patch of woods in the middle? Between the streets? That will be a park. Some wild, some groomed. Walking trails through the wild, out to the river, connecting with the state park up behind, the old railway trail."

"It won't be the same."

"No." His hand went through his hair. "But families will build their homes, their lives here. And their kids will grow up with lots of reasons to get outside, appreciate the wildness."

"You think that makes a difference?"

"Hope so. Didn't it for you? Help you learn to love the land? Worked that way for me."

"Sounds nice, but..."

He shrugged. "It doesn't work for everybody."

I turned back toward the river, not wanting him to see my eyes. "Pretty spot. Before the houses." I sighed. "But I suppose it could be a pretty place to live."

"I think so. Sun's almost down. We better go."

We turned back toward the truck. "How many houses did you say?"

"Permit's for up to fifty units. My guess is it will take ten years before that happens. If ever."

I stopped. "Fifty. On forty acres?"

"A third to half will be one-acre lots. Most will be smaller." He chuckled, kicked up leaves in our path. "For folks who don't want to spend all their time raking and mowing."

"Big fancy houses? Like what Paul wants?"

He shook his head. "Not so big. Fifteen hundred to three thousand square feet. The idea is to spend the money on design and quality, not for rooms you never use. Not So Big."

"Like the book. The architect from Minnesota?"

"Sarah Susanka. You know about her?"

"I like houses. So I read, look for ideas. I like hers."

"I'm surprised," he said.

"Because my house *is* so big?"

"Something like that." I saw his grin in the fading light.

"Families were bigger in the 1870s." I tried not to sound defensive. "Generations, hired hands, schoolteachers — they all shared the same roof, needed the space."

"And now?"

"What do you mean?"

"Seems like your place houses a not so big family now."

WHIP

She bristled. Didn't want to talk whether it made sense for her to live in such a big place. I was curious how she thought she'd use all that space. But not now, I thought. Another time when she's not so tender.

We were almost back at the truck when she tripped. A tree root, a rock under the leaves, something. For the second time that day, she'd have fallen without me there. At least this time she was conscious. I took my time righting her, keeping my hands on her arms longer than was strictly necessary. Enjoying the lovely flush that rose in her cheeks, the citrusy scent of her.

She pulled back, of course. Tried to brush off the moment before I let go when our eyes locked and the air sizzled around us. Bring on the fast current, I thought. I am ready to swim.

"I have more questions," she said, trying to open the truck door with her bad hand.

"I'll get that." My hand brushed hers in the process and I heard her breath catch. "I keep forgetting to oil that latch," I said, knowing I'd keep putting it off as long as it gave me an excuse to touch her. I stood at the open door. "Need help with the seatbelt? Since you've only got the one good hand?"

"No!"

I smiled at her fluster and closed the door. By the time I rounded the truck to the driver's side, my head was full of fantasy. Here's how I hoped it would go. I'd tuck a strand of hair behind an ear. Let my hand linger on her cheek. Tug just a little... And we'd be back at my place pulling off clothes before we hit the stairs, dinner be damned.

Yeah. Fantasy. Soon as I opened my door, she said, "It's later than I thought. We have to get to the Lodge."

I put the key in the ignition and glanced at the clock. Twenty after five. "Weren't we supposed to meet them at six?" I asked.

"We'll be late. Hurry."

"The Lodge is ten minutes from here. We've got plenty of time." Time that could be used well.

She shook her head, eyes fixed on the windshield. "I don't want to be late. Paul hates waiting for people. We have to go."

"But..."

"What? Why are you just sitting there? We have to go!" Her voice caught on the last word, and she turned abruptly away.

"Kat? What's up?" I reached a hand to her shoulder, retracted it as she flinched.

"Please! Let's just go."

"O...kay." I started the truck. I snuck glances at the back of her head while I drove. No clues there. Then halfway up Lodge Hill, three deer leaped out in front of me and I had to brake hard. I missed them, but the tires hit gravel and the truck skidded toward the ditch.

I swore as I fought the wheel for control, and it wasn't till we were stopped on the road's shoulder that I realized I'd been steering one-handed. That's when I heard her breath come hard and fast. And noticed the softness of her breasts against my arm. I jerked away like my arm was on fire.

"Sorry." Jesus. My ears burned. "Sorry. Reflex. With Juno. My dog. To keep her from…"

"I know. I do the same thing with Dutch." Her voice was shaky, but at least now she looked at me. "That was close."

"Sorry. Didn't see them in time."

"Me neither. I hate when that happens." And then she giggled. It was a weak, nervy kind of giggle, but it had a friendly feel to it, and I grinned back at her.

"Sorry." The giggle grew to a full-blown laugh. "Sorry. I…always…do… this." The laughs came harder.

"You laugh in the face of danger?" I pulled back onto the road.

"After. Once I know I'll survive. Before…I'm too scared and I get…"

"What? If you laugh after, what do you do during?"

She shot me a hostile look, like I had a bright light aimed at her eyes. But she answered. "I get mad."

"Mad?"

She rolled her eyes. "I don't like feeling scared. So I get mad."

I grinned. "So…back at the site? When you got into an all-fired hurry? You sounded mad. You saying you were scared?"

"No!" Then as my grin widened, her lips twitched too. "Maybe a little."

"Of me." I was liking this.

"Don't be ridiculous!"

I liked it more. "You, um…sound kind of mad again."

"Dammit!" She slid her eyes at me as I began to laugh. "It's not funny!" But couldn't quite squash down a snicker of her own.

I turned into the Lodge and grabbed the first parking spot I saw.

"So now you think the danger's past?"

"Yes, I…"

She stopped when I leaned over, took her chin in my hand, and pulled her in for a kiss.

I'm not a complete lout. I kept it gentle. Just a little kiss – not scary. Or only a little, which was fair. I was a little scared too. At feeling so much so fast. But I'd done no more than lay my lips on hers when I knew it was a mistake. She jerked away and I saw more than nerves as she slammed out of the truck. I saw panic.

Kat

What the hell was wrong with the man? Why couldn't he keep his hands – his mouth – to himself? Holy God!

I ran up the steps hoping I could get inside and…and hide in the ladies' room until…until I turned into a different person.

"Kat. Wait. I…"

At the door, I came up short. There were people inside. At the desk. In the lobby. Maybe someone I knew. I turned on my heel and followed the wide porch around to where a row of rocking chairs invited Lodge guests to take in the view. I sank into one of those chairs and put my hands to hot, hot cheeks.

Light spilled out from the lobby windows. As a hiding spot, it was far from ideal. But it felt a whole lot safer than sitting in that truck. I closed my eyes and cringed. I bolted away like an outraged virgin. Like I thought he'd tear off my clothes and have his way with me. When the truth was, I was the one thinking about…

I shook my head, tried to clear out images I didn't want. What would Gram say? Look at what's in front of you. Not behind. Now. Not then. The Lodge's great view stretched in front of me, an eagle's vista that swept over the tops of hundred-year oaks as far as you could see, interrupted only by a long slice of river. I knew the view. In daylight.

Stupid, stupid, stupid. It boomed inside my brain. Why did I have to be so stupid about men? I crossed my arms over my chest and held on tight – more to grip my emotions than to ward off the evening chill.

But before I got anywhere close to a firm grip, Whip dropped into the chair next to me. Wouldn't you know? He didn't say anything. Not for a solid minute, maybe more. Which was maybe worse. When I couldn't stand the silence another second, I opened my mouth to say something. Who knows what? And then he spoke.

"Nice view." His tone was casual, like you might comment to a stranger on a train. "A tad...dark. But nice."

I snorted. Damn the man. The last thing I wanted was to laugh. Not at something Whip Tyler said. "I like the dark."

"Oh certainly. Dark is way underrated." I heard the smile in his voice. "Needs better PR. Trip Advisor or something." He went into tour guide mode. "Pull up a chair on the Lodge porch and enjoy the silhouettes of hundred-year oaks against the twilight sky."

I let myself play along. "Feast your eyes on the hand in front of your face. If you can see it."

He chuckled and settled deeper in his chair, as if he planned to unpack his bags and stay the night. Meanwhile I clenched my jaw to stop my teeth from chattering. With no escape route in sight. Not without the outraged virgin act again.

The silence dragged. And the chill began to bite. Say something, I thought. Get up. Say we should go inside. Say…Say you're freezing, dammit! But no. It seemed important to outlast him. To show I was tough. If he wanted to sit out here on a frosty November night, then by God I could too. A wintry eddy swept up dry leaves from the forest floor and changed my mind. I stood. "I'm going inside where there's a fire. And central heating."

In a flash, he was up and pulling me by the hand. "I knew you were a smart girl! Let's go!"

Later, I'd resent the easy way he got around me, the way I couldn't help laughing at how ridiculous the pair of us were. That's what I told myself as shivers turned to giggles while we dashed around the porch and into the lobby. We stood just inside the door, catching our breath, still shivering, my hand still in his. Smiling at each other.

"F-f-fireplace?" I nodded as he pulled me through the cozy furniture. "Excuse us," Whip said to a couple seated facing the fire. "We're on an emergency warming mission here." He pulled me as close to the burning logs as we could get. Any closer and we'd need a fire extinguisher.

The man of the couple, a jovial seventy-something who looked like he enjoyed more calories than his svelte wife approved, said, "I'd have thought a strapping young fella like yourself might find another way to keep a pretty girl warm."

Whip tightened his hand around mine as if he feared I might run away. "I tried that, sir. Thing is, the girl's not quite ready, and as she's an important girl, maybe the most important girl, I had to take a different tack. Put the ball in her court, you might say."

My jaw dropped, my face burned – not from the fire – and I wanted to sink through the floor. I tugged on my captive hand to no avail. How dare he! I turned away as far as I could get, which wasn't far enough.

"And now you've embarrassed her, Mike, you big dolt – and you too, young man! The two of you – march right into the bar and order this poor girl a glass of wine. No. Cream sherry." I felt a female arm slip around my waist so that Whip had no choice but to finally let my hand loose. "Go on. Move!" And then to me, "Men. Idiots, every last one of them."

WHIP

The man his wife called Mike stood. "Take it from one who knows, son. Yvonne takes that tone, the smart choice is to do what she says. Come on. I bet you could use a belt too. On me. Since I seem to have landed you in hot water with your girl."

I looked past a smooth blonde head toward Kat whose whole self was hunched small. When would I ever learn to keep my big mouth shut? Mike gestured with his head. I shrugged and stepped with him toward the bar. In a lower tone, he said, "Let Yvonne smooth it over. She's good that way. Let's get your girl that drink."

He downed the half-full glass in his hand and licked his lips. "I'm due for another myself," he said as he approached the bar.

I hung back a step when I saw who was behind the bar. Jerry Townsend. Close to Kat's age if I remembered right, so he might not recognize me. With luck. She wouldn't be happy to have him link my name with hers.

"Another Manhattan, Mike?" Jerry knew who buttered his bread. He kept his eyes trained on the man beside me.

"You're a good man, Jerry." To me, he added, "How about you, son? What'll it be?"

The Manhattan sounded like the kind of stiff drink the occasion called for, but I'd better stay sober. "Coors Light. Thanks." I reached for my wallet.

"No, no. This one's on me. And for your pretty girl?"

I shook my head slightly, mouthed, "No names," when Jerry turned to grab the bourbon.

My new best friend Mike got the message and nodded. "Jerry, would you mind bringing those over to the table by the fire?" He gestured to the pub's wood-burning stove.

"Sure thing, Mike."

At the table, the older man leaned in to ask a quiet question. "You're not stepping out with Jerry's wife, now?" He seemed to imply he didn't object but would appreciate a warning to duck in case a fight broke out.

I couldn't help but grin. "Nothing like that. She just wouldn't like…" I shrugged. "Small town."

Mike nodded. "You're walking on eggs, huh?"

"Swimming upstream. In a fierce current."

I turned my head toward the fire as Jerry came over with the drinks. "Nectar for the Gods, Jerry, my friend. And what did Yvonne say she wanted? Oh yes. A chardonnay and a cream sherry." His eyebrows played elevator. "If I get her tipsy, I might get lucky tonight."

The guy was a master at diversion. From the corner of my eye, I watched. Jerry never gave me a glance. Once he was gone, Mike leaned in again. "So your girl is timid?"

I shrugged and nodded. "But it's more than that." I took a long pull of beer, wiped foam off my lip. "She thinks I'm responsible for her brother's death." I wondered as I spoke, why I'd say it to a guy I never met before.

"But you're not."

I looked at him in surprise. "You say that like you already know the story. Like you believe it. Without knowing a thing about me."

Mike smiled. "Son, I sold insurance for forty years. Tended bar, even dabbled in politics. I can smell a lie three states away. Not a whiff on you. Or you wouldn't have risked upsetting that pretty girl out there by talking to an old geezer like me."

"I wish she saw me the way you do. But that's only one reason she doesn't want me." I looked up and swore quietly. "Here's another reason now.

Kat

I'm not one to open up to a stranger, but I nearly kissed the woman's feet for shooing Whip and her husband away.

She gave my waist a squeeze before she let go. "They're in the bar now. If I know Mike – and it's a sure bet I do after thirty-five years – they won't be out again soon." She chuckled. "It's safe to warm up your backside if you want."

I turned around to face the lobby and watched her sink back onto the sofa. "I'm sorry for..." I raised still cold hands to my burning cheeks.

"No worries, honey. We girls have to stick together when our men turn into Neanderthals. My name's Yvonne."

I tried to muster a smile. "I'm Kat."

She smiled. "Doesn't that suit you? And your young man?"

"He's not my…anything."

Yvonne's smile deepened. "Ah. But he wants to be."

"No…maybe…I don't know." I perched on the edge of a chair and closed my eyes.

"What about you? What do you want?"

I shook my head. "Not…" I pressed my hand to my lips, remembered the feel of Whip's mouth on mine. "I don't know."

Yvonne laughed. "It's always the toughest question, huh? It was that way with Mike and me. Why would I want to tie myself to so much bluster, I wondered. Till he made me laugh more than anybody else." A wicked gleam came into her eyes. "But even after I figured out he was the one for me, didn't mean I had to let him know. I strung him along a couple months more – for the fun of watching him suffer." She sighed. "What a time!" The gleam came back. "Almost as good as when I finally gave in."

"But…"

"That's me. Not you. So I'll ask again. What do you want?"

"I…" Dammit. What did I want? "I want my land. My home. Just the way it is. No houses. No golf course."

"Hmm? You're from around here?"

"Yes. The other side of the river."

"Interesting. We're thinking of moving to the area, Mike and me. For our retirement home. Seems like a nice area."

"I think so."

"What do you like about it?"

I shrugged. "I've always lived here, except for college when..." I shook my head. "Anyway. I couldn't wait to get back. It's a nice town. Safe. Friendly. Small, but we're not far from anywhere. I love the trees. And the water. The river. Our...my creek."

"You have a creek?"

"It runs through our farm." I paused. "It used to be a farm. But...that's all going to change now."

"Really?" She had a way about her, like she truly wanted to know. So I told her.

"My father died. Now it's just my brother and me."

"And you two don't want to farm."

I laughed. "You never met my brother!"

"Let me guess. Doesn't like getting his hands dirty?"

"No. Or his five-hundred-dollar shoes either." I clapped my hand over my mouth. "I shouldn't talk about Paul that way. Not when..."

"When what?"

My eyes filled. "Not when we're going to bury our father tomorrow."

She took a quick breath in. "My goodness. Tomorrow?" She shook her head. "That's never an easy thing."

I sat there fighting tears, feeling more comfort than since Dad died. The way Yvonne listened was like a hug. "I...almost forgot...for a while."

"That's how we get through it," she said in a soft tone. "We get on with living, and we forget – for a while." She raised a shoulder. "But it doesn't go away. Trouble sticks around, waiting for us to remember."

"You're very kind. I've talked your ear off, and all you wanted was to have a quiet drink by the fire with your husband."

She laughed, a lovely cascading sound that made me think of Gram's wind chimes. "Actually, we were two minutes from brewing up an argument. An old one. You and your young man saved us."

"He's not…"

"Your young man. I know." She smiled her disbelief. "Too bad. You'd make a handsome pair."

"He's…my brother hired him. To…develop our land."

"Oh." Her eyebrows went high. "That does complicate things for you, doesn't it?"

"He's just paying attention to me so I'll agree to…do what Paul wants."

She tilted her head, started to say something, then stopped, shaking her head.

"What?"

"I won't be the worst kind of busybody, the kind that doles out advice when it wasn't asked for, when I don't even know the whole story."

"Go ahead. You've been so kind. And…men… I'm so…confused. By…everything. Please. Tell me what I should do."

She smiled and shook her head. "Oh no. You'll have to figure that out yourself. Nobody can but you." She turned her palms to the ceiling. "All I can do is tell you what I saw."

"Please."

"That young man wants you more than whatever your brother is offering. A man doesn't look at a woman the way he looked at you when all he wants is her land." Her smile shifted. "And here he comes now. Looking at you like it's Christmas morning and you're the best gift under the tree."

I looked up and found Whip's eyes on me. My heart did something odd in my chest. But there was something else besides Christmas in his eyes. A warning? I shifted my gaze to see Paul and Chrissy behind him.

What had Yvonne said? That we needn't worry about forgetting? For a few minutes I let myself forget how different Paul's goals were from mine. She was right. Trouble was still there. Waiting for me to remember.

WHIP

Until Paul walked into the bar, all my focus was on not screwing up with Kat. Did I forget the tricky tightrope I had to navigate so Paul would get enough and still protect Kat? Maybe I had. For a few minutes when my only thought was her.

Step careful, I thought. Don't rile the rattler. With their father dead, Paul would be more apt to strike, more venomous.

I gave a thought to my mother's words. She was right. Getting mixed up with either Patterson put me in rough seas. Was I ready for the storm their different hopes for the land might raise? How it might make Kat see me as the bad guy no matter what I did? Walk a tightrope while swimming upstream, I thought. And hope not to sink in icy waters.

Paul wasted no time. We were barely seated before he began. "So let's hear about that project, Whip. You convince my silly sister we can do great things at our place?"

I glanced at Kat. "I doubt it. But I won't presume to speak for her."

"So? What'd you think, KP?"

"Paulie!" Chrissy swatted his arm and simpered. I began to see the reason for Kat and Darcy's disdain. "Be civilized! Wine first." She batted eyelashes too long and thick to be real. "A toast to your daddy. Funerals take liquor, my mama always says."

"I'm set, thanks." Kat lifted her sherry, sipped.

"Paulie. Wine. Please?" More eyelash action. I started to wonder if that energy could be harnessed. Chrissy could put oil companies out of business.

"Jesus, who do you have to blow to get service here?" Then to the waitress who stepped to our table, Paul said, "Bring me your best Chardonnay. A bottle. And a dirty martini."

Kat cringed at his tone but kept her own friendly. "Fancy. Dad would be impressed." She smiled. "Remember when he made us try Southern Comfort, Paul?"

"Christ. I was never so sick in my life."

"Paulie! I never heard this story!" Chrissy pouted. "I wish I knew you as a boy." She pinched fingers near his cheek – with no actual contact. "You must have been so adorable."

Kat snorted. "Not that day! One sip and I couldn't breathe. But you told him to keep pouring – till…"

"Don't remind me. Old man thought it was funny, me sicker than a dog. Never touched bourbon again." He smirked. "I showed him. Switched to gin."

I watched the interplay between them and sent Kat a mental attagirl. It was a savvy reminder that the two of them shared more than land, things only siblings could know. Like my brother Trav and me. Like the friend who'd been like a brother.

A sound like a braying donkey raised the hairs on the back of my neck. Chrissy. How good would sex have to be to put up with such a laugh? "Paulie! You're so funny!" Another Chrissy titter. More like a hyena this time – a shrill machine-gun staccato.

I had to hide behind my menu. Poker face, I reminded myself. From the corner of my eye, I noticed Kat hiding too. Same wavelength, I thought, as my mind pictured synchronized swimming.

A loud burst from Paul yanked me back to the table. "Jesus! Where is that drink? Waitress!"

"Paul, please..." Kat said in a murmur. "Keep it down, will you? Some of us have to live here, you know."

"No, you don't! That. Is. The. Point." Heads turned, but he went on oblivious. "Just because you choose to hole up here in podunk... Jesus, KP! In case you haven't noticed, crummy little Oakton is not the center of the universe. There's a whole wide world out there." He threw wide arms into the air. Only the defensive swerve of our waitress saved him from being drenched in icy martini. Too bad.

"I like it here." Kat's voice was small, maybe to subdue Mr. Loudmouth and avoid a public scene. But like any bully, he pounced on what he saw as fear.

"How would you know?" he exploded. "Except for that *minute* you lasted in college, when have you ever seen anything of the world?"

I wanted to pound the guy. Till he was bloody. Which would make Kat even more embarrassed. I opened my mouth to say something in Oakton's defense. To defend Kat.

No need. She leveled steady eyes at her brother, and in a low voice that made me think of our scary grade school principal, she said, "Enough. We will *not* talk about this here. Go ahead. Roll your eyes all you want. But if you ever hope to gain my cooperation, you will *be quiet* and behave like a civilized human being acts in a public place. Do. You. Understand?"

I stuck my nose in my menu so I wouldn't break out in a cheer and earn a warning to use my indoor voice.

"Okay, okay. Jesus. I'm only speaking truth, and…"

"I mean it, Paul. You behave. Or…"

Major eye rolling. But he picked up a menu and shut up long enough for our frightened waitress to take our orders. Chrissy gave Paul ample time for blood to cool while she hemmed, hawed, and grilled the poor girl about the menu items. Was the chicken free range, were the vegetables organic, did they not have gluten-free, what was on the keto diet, yada, yada.

"Thank you, Madeline." When Chrissy finally made up her mind, Kat smiled at the waitress. "You're doing a great job. Do you like school?" The girl nodded and smiled as Kat asked, "Still planning on vet school? Good for you!" She turned to us. "I've known Madeline since she was little. Great family."

Score another for Kat, I thought. She didn't punch her brother's nose with the upside of small towns, but she put it on the table where he could see it. If Chrissy hadn't swept it away.

"I just *love* my Missy's vet. He takes such good care of my little precious, doesn't he, Paulie? I had to change Missy's groomer though. She gave my little girl a *terrible* trim! I could have cried! And poor Missy was so *sad* till we found a new groomer to fix it. Here, I'll show you." She shoved her phone at us. "There's my precious." Chrissy's baby talk was more nauseating than her laugh. "Precious is mad at Mommy for leaving her with Gramma, idn't she, Paulie?"

Next to me, Kat shivered. "Do you feel a draft?"

Eyelash wind tunnel, I thought. Out loud, I said, "You're probably still cold from earlier." I reached to drape her coat around her shoulders.

Her hand touched mine for a millisecond in the process and I watched that lovely bloom rise in her cheeks. "We spent too long out at the site," I said to draw Paul's attention away from her reaction.

"Yeah, tell me about that."

"What do you want to know?"

Paul's eyes gleamed. "Everything. What's the price range? The market? How big? How do we make ours bigger, better, sell for more?"

I glanced at Kat, who rearranged her silverware and started with location. "It's on the bluff. High ground like here. Down river. Near the park."

Paul nodded as if he could picture it and only needed details. Not likely. He was never one to hike the park. Not like Scott and I did. More than once we followed deer trails past park boundaries and out to the bluff. Sometimes it seemed like he was still there – one reason I appreciated the Twin Creeks site.

"Farmland?" Paul asked.

"Woods, mostly." I watched his eyes. I didn't see guile. But I knew it was there. "Maybe you remember the Jensen twins? It was theirs."

Paul shook his head. And then I saw the light go on. "Not the hot blondes. The cheerleaders?"

I nodded. "Gwen and Gabi."

"The Super-Gs. God, the wet dreams I had over those two!"

"Paulie!" Chrissy swatted.

"Years ago, sugar." Paul grinned. "I was what? Fourteen? And they were smokin' hot." His eyebrows waggled. "Older women. God!"

It was how I saw them once – as objects of my teenage lust. But I'd learned. "Two of the smartest women I know. Really good people."

"Oh sure." A lascivious grin brought another smack from Chrissy. "But Jesus. I mean *twins*! Closest I ever got to heaven, the two of had their arms around me. At the same time! All that firm young flesh. I'm hard just thinking about it."

Kat

A long line of people winds past me. The smell of flowers overwhelms, makes it hard to breathe. Feet pinch in Sunday shoes. Strangers pat my shoulder, touch my hair. Hushed voices say sorry, so young, looks natural, peaceful, better place. I don't understand. Why?

A high-pitched laugh makes me turn. Paul. Two blonde heads bend toward him, straighten, step to kneel by the box that holds my big brother. Too still. Not natural.

I blinked, heard Paul ask something about money, blinked again. The Lodge. Not the funeral home. Someone set a plate down. I heard the chink of silverware, Chrissy's cackle, water splashing over ice in a glass.

I tried to focus, make out words. But the sounds blurred, as if I were under water. I touched the tablecloth in front of me, squinted to make out the others – close enough to touch, but seeming far away, like I watched through the wrong end of binoculars.

I remember picking up a fork. Maybe I ate. I don't know. I felt a touch on my arm once, heard a low rumble. Whip Tyler?

My confused gaze follows my father's long strides. The snaking line parts, closes behind him. I stand on tiptoe to see the toppest part of his head stop at the door. I feel his rage all the way across the room. I strain to hear as Gram slips an arm to pull me close, says never mind. I watch Dad return to his place by Mother, fists bunched. Eyebrows lift on faces in the line. Voices murmur a name. Whip Tyler.

"Should I wrap that for you, Ms. Kat?"

I looked up to see young Madeline hover at my elbow, shook my head.

"Coffee? Dessert?"

I shook my head, but a steaming mug appeared anyway. I cupped shaky hands around it and tried again to follow the conversation. Something about zoning, rights of way…

Sometime later, we stood. I got in Paul's back seat, the new-car smell tanging my nostrils, my body aching from my brain's ping-pong swing between the Lodge and the funeral home, between present and past. An argument rumbled from the front. Chrissy wanting to get back to Missy, Saturday night's dance. Paul's voice, low and urgent, "Not if I can push this thing forward, get her to agree. We made progress tonight. Got to strike now before she…"

I wondered who he meant. Then I saw. Me. The land. Gram's will. Trouble coming. I shook my head, as if to clear my tumbling thoughts. It didn't help. I kept wondering how one brother ended up dead in a box, hearing the other say "closest I ever got to heaven…"

WHIP

"Luke sent these." I handed Kat a box early the next morning. "He'll be here later with the rest of the food. Said we should eat these now."

She looked at me like I was a stranger – or maybe I had two heads? "Kat? You okay?" I'd wondered since the night before. Lay awake going over all the bone-headed things I said, wondering which was the fatal mistake, what made her clam up so tight, what I could do… "How's your hand?"

"Fine." She looked away and set the box next to her coffee maker.

"Mind sharing?"

I don't know how to describe the look on her face. Blank. Like I spoke a foreign language. Like she forgot I was there. "Coffee? Can I have some?"

She nodded, pulled a mug off the shelf and handed it to me before turning to the other room. I put out a hand to touch her arm. But I pulled back. She'd bury her father that day, I remembered. Let her be.

That's what I told myself all morning. It wasn't easy. She barely said a word the whole time we worked on the pane of glass I brought from town, the fireplace.

Side by side, like we'd been doing it all our lives. In silence. Not quite a comfortable silence, but closer than you might expect.

She didn't need me. But I read out the installation instructions, added an extra hand, passed a tool, till the fireplace was hooked up and ready to test.

"Here's hoping it won't explode," I said as she moved to the switch. She sent me a startled look. "Just kidding. You went over that gas connection four times. You got it right, or the pilot light wouldn't be on."

She nodded and flipped the switch. We both stared to see flames came up around the fake logs in the grate. "Yeah!" We said it in one voice, smiled at each other like we were the first to invent fire. Just as quick, her face was shuttered, her head up, listening.

A minute later, Darcy blew in like the cavalry. "I had to beg, but I got Lulu to handle the last of the breakfast shift so I could run and change." Darcy slid her eyes from Kat to me. I shrugged and raised palms to the ceiling at the question in her eyes.

Darcy gave one sharp nod. Maybe she got my unspoken message that I didn't know any more than she did. Or maybe – Darcy being Darcy – she decided to take it – whatever it was – into her own hands. I was glad she was there.

"Honey, you've got to get moving. Whip and I will finish up here. You get showered and changed." Darcy jerked her head toward the other side of the house. "I don't suppose you've heard anything from the city slickers yet this morning? All right. While you're in the shower, I'll venture over and be sure they're up and around. Then they're on their own. But you," she pointed at Kat, "will be at the church on time."

Like the robot she'd been all morning Kat moved toward the hallway. She was barely out of sight when Darcy turned and hissed, "What's going on? What did you say to her?"

"I don't know! She's been like that since I got here. Since midway through dinner last night." Darcy narrowed her eyes and I felt an urge to confess – except I didn't know what crime I'd committed. "We got everything done the way she wanted. But she's been...quiet. Remote. You saw her."

"Paul? Did that bastard upset her?"

I shook my head. "Not that I saw. He was obnoxious at the Lodge, but Kat stood her ground, got him to dial it back, be less...pushy. But then a while later, she went...quiet." I lifted my palms. "Didn't eat. I tried to bring her back to the conversation, but... It was like... like she went someplace else. In her head." Again I tried to pinpoint when, what I said. "I don't know why. She came home with them, so maybe he...got to her." I shook my head. "But she was already..."

"Remote. At dinner. What about before?"

I felt my cheeks go warm. "She rode over with me. We stopped so I could show her the Jensen place. So she'd see how I work."

"And?"

I rolled my eyes. "I made a move. All right? Not a big one." Why'd I have to sound so defensive? "I backed off soon as I saw how..." Darcy's eyes narrowed. "It scared her. So I backed off." My hands went to my head. "But that's not why... I don't think..." Had I done this to her, made her shut down? I shook my head, remembering our laughter when we dashed to the Lodge fireplace. "It was okay. She was good. Read

Paul the riot act. And then..." Who was I trying to convince?

Darcy kept staring and I wanted to confess every impure thought I ever had. No waterboarding necessary. Just send Darcy. A small grin flickered on her face and I released a breath. Did I pass the inquisition?

"So you made a pass. Maybe you'll learn some finesse next time," she said. "You done here?"

"Pretty much."

"Good. Unload my car. Set up the bar in that corner. Luke will be here in two hours. He'll need your help while we're at the church." She gave me a critical eye. "Those the only clothes you've got?"

"I'll be gone before anyone else sees me."

"Oh no you won't, buster. It's all hands on deck. Give me your keys. I'll text Luke, get him to stop by your place and bring you some decent pants and a clean shirt."

"I can't be part of Vern Patterson's funeral, Darcy. He'd roll over in his grave. Before he's even in it."

"He's being cremated." She held out her hand. "Keys."

I sighed. "Luke knows where I keep the spare. I don't know how the man stands it."

She winked. "There are benefits." And with a swish of her hips she aimed toward the hall that would take her past the bathroom where I heard the shower running.

I told myself not to let myself think about wet hair streaming over naked shoulders and... I stood from putting the last wrench in the toolbox and took a hard grip – on the handle and my imagination – while I hauled it out to the porch where we stashed stuff the day before.

I took gulps of cold air thinking it was almost as effective as a cold shower. But not. My mind cruised back where it had no business going. Not when a simple kiss could scare her so much. Go slow, chump, I thought. Be a friend. Earn her trust. Keep your head clear. Don't think about…

As a pep talk, it wasn't bad. Till Kat and I stepped in the same room and my mouth went dry.

Kat

"Darcy? Will you..." I stopped abruptly – and for the first time since the Lodge – I felt awake. Wide awake. And like I wanted to drop through the floor. Whip Tyler with an intense look in his eyes. I tried to swallow.

"Your hair. It's wet," he said. "You'll get cold...your arms...your hair..."

I shook my head. To clear out the fog. "Where's Darcy?" Was that my voice? Why did I sound like I swallowed a frog?

"She went over...there." He pointed. "To rouse Paul." His voice didn't sound right either. I shook my head again, wondered if something was wrong with my ears.

"Oh. I'd better..." I turned on one heel before the reason I needed Darcy slammed back in my brain. I swallowed and angled my body back where it had been. "I'll just...um..." I took a step back.

He stepped toward me. "What's wrong? What can I do?"

I froze again. Or my body did. My damn head kept shaking like one of those stupid bobble dolls people put on their dashboards. "No. I just…Oh dammit all to hell." I turned around. "I can't reach the zipper."

I tried to act cool. Like a block of ice. But with all the heat my embarrassed body pumped out, I felt like a drip. I closed my eyes, tried to pretend I wasn't there, that the dress stood on its own power. Decades passed before I heard his footsteps behind me.

His fingers grazed skin at my waist before they grasped the tab to start the slow slide up. I reached to yank my hair away and as soon as I felt the tug stop, I shifted to escape. "Wait. There's something…a hook. Sorry, I'm not used to…"

His hands at my neck sent goosebumps in all directions.

"You are cold. Wait. Hold still."

"No. I have to…"

"Got it." I was ready to bolt, but his hands slid to my arms, held me there. "Still cold." He turned my body, nudged me so I had to step where he aimed. "Let's get that fireplace going."

"I've got to…"

"Get warm first. Just a minute or two. It's why you got the fireplace, right? Big old place like this, I'm surprised there wasn't one already."

Where was Darcy? "Not modern enough. Old Amasa wanted central heat." That odd voice. Mine?

"Amasa? There's a name. Your…?"

"Great-great. Biblical name. King David's general, or…something." I pulled against the hand that somehow had a firm grip on mine. "I really have to…"

"But you aren't warm yet." He ran his free hand down my arm, and there went the goosebumps again. "See." He grinned. "It's a great dress by the way. And you look great in it. But maybe a little…" The grin morphed into something intense that made my breath catch at the back of my throat. "Bare? For November?"

"There's a jacket." Darcy's voice made me jump like a trout after a fly. "Want me to get it for you, Kat?" She stood at the hallway door, one hip cocked, a smirk on her face.

"No. I'll… I need to… No." I fled past her to my room, where I took faltering steps to sink onto the stool at Gram's dressing table. Slow, even breaths. I reached for my brush as if it had life-preserver qualities. I couldn't do much about my flaming cheeks, but maybe I could tame my hair.

"Kat?" Darcy. A soft rap at the door.

I fanned my cheeks with one hand, took a swipe with my brush. "Come in."

"How many times have I told you, Kat girl? You can't brush curls like yours. Let me." Darcy picked up the hair pick she bought for my fifteenth birthday. "Pick and separate. Use your fingers to smooth the curls." She stepped back and smiled at the mirror. "See?"

I nodded. Couldn't do it myself, but I did see. Soft curls framed my face, drifted over my shoulders. No frizz. Face still too pink. Breathing not quite regular. "Funeral ready?" At least my voice sounded almost normal.

Darcy smiled. "Yup. And for that guy out there. He's hot for you Kat, honey. The man has good taste."

I turned, slipped on the jacket that matched the damn dress. As if I could hide my red face from Darcy's eagle eyes. "He just wants my land."

She snorted. "The way he looks at you? That's not about land!" She waved her hand in front of her face. "The sexual tension comes off the two of you in waves! Contagious waves! If we didn't have a funeral in," she glanced at her wrist, "forty-five minutes, I'd be jumping Luke in ten." She thought. "The walk-in cooler. Best spot for a quickie when we're open." She grinned. "For a longie, the butcher block in the kitchen's better."

"Eww! How do you expect me to ever eat there again? The kitchen?"

"Oh, honey. The kitchen, the pantry, every booth in the place." She laughed. "Look at your face! How do you think I got pregnant?"

I rolled my eyes. I made my voice as prim as mortified Miss Jorgenson whose job it was to teach the facts of life in sixth-grade health. "I am delighted to know you and Luke have a good sex life. I'd just rather not think about it while I'm eating a chicken salad sandwich, thank you very much."

She winked. "We make the best chicken salad in town! Extra zip!" She snuck another glance at her watch. "Alas. Hold that thought. We'll go out your dad's side, keep the pitter-patter of Chrissy's tiny little stilettos off your floors here as long as we can."

"Darcy... thanks." So much I wanted to say, how she took charge when I couldn't, how she steadied me, gave me something to think about besides... I couldn't find words.

She gave me a quick squeeze to say there was no need. "Step on it, girl. We got a funeral to get to."

WHIP

No matter that I had laundry to do and bills on my desk. Darcy's instructions had been crystal clear. And firm. "You hold down the fort here, so thieves don't clear the place like they did to the McClanahans in Valley Spring last month. Luke will be here by one. Help him get the food set up. Change your clothes. Finish setting up the bar. Be ready to pour." She'd looked to the ceiling as if her master list were written there, smiled, and said, "Any questions?"

A dozen cutting replies played in my head, but what would be the point? "Got it." My eyes went to the hallway. Darcy patted my arm. "Give her time," she said. "After today."

I nodded. Kat had to bury her father today. Not the time for...what I'd been thinking. I wandered between her kitchen and fireplace till I heard car doors. For a second, maybe two, Kat's eyes drifted to the window where I stood, and I tried my hand at telepathy – I'm with you, want you. Her eyes dropped. So did my hopes.

Nothing to do but wait. I slumped onto the couch and stared at our morning's work, my thoughts jumbling. This place, Kat, her brother, skin, the color green...

I came to sometime later and was on my feet before I knew where I was or who. I blinked, dazed and stupid as the room came into focus. It took longer than I'd like to admit. Kat's place. If Luke caught me napping, there'd be no end of grief.

I rubbed at my eyes as I stepped to the door and looked out. Nothing. No van. No Luke. Maybe the other door? Or the one...no two in the kitchen?

That's when Darcy's instructions came back. Thieves? Surely not. But I'd seen. The house was a sieve. So many doors, all the downstairs windows low to the ground. Better take a look, I thought.

As soon as I opened the back door, I heard Kat's dog. I was halfway down the driveway when I saw a blur of black and white disappear down the lane between the corncrib and what must be the far side of the vegetable garden. The blur came back with a ferocious bark, as if the dog yelled, "Wake up, asshole! We got trouble here."

I took off on a dead run. Was that a truck? What would they be after in the barnyard? Not livestock. Farm equipment? Seemed unlikely. But the dog didn't let up. So I ran toward him even if I didn't know why. At the barnyard gate, nothing. Except another open gate and a furious dog.

I sprinted across the barnyard. The farm kid in me noticed and was grateful that the ground was mostly dry. Only one mucky puddle by the open gate. I slid on takeoff as I hurdled over it and saw the intruder's parked truck.

He wouldn't get far, not with a snarling and lunging dog at his door. Nor did I need to hurry. I put hands on my thighs and concentrated on air. In...out...slow. Get...breath...back...first...

I eyed the truck, thought it looked familiar. Then as I got closer, I knew. The smell of his ever-present cigar gave him away. Rodney Richfield. Snapping pictures through his windshield.

I put a hand out to Dutch. "It's okay, boy. I got this."

The dog gave me a disgusted glance, as if to say, "Yeah right. Now I've got him cornered, you've got this."

"You did good." Three more lunging attacks on the door. I laughed. "That's it, fella. Give him hell. Scratch up his truck while you're at it. Nobody deserves it more." Dutch cocked his head, not convinced he should throw his cards in with me. But he let me close enough to put a hand on his head, a low growl still in his throat. "Good old Dutch. Let's deal with this asshole."

I rapped on the window – higher than Dutch could reach – and Richfield turned his head with his customary smirk. The same smirk I once almost wiped off his face. I worked for the jerk when I first came back. Once. That's all it took.

He hit the power button on the window and said, "Not paying your respects to old man Patterson, Tyler?"

Classic put-the-other-guy-in-the-wrong Richfield. "The family asked me to stay onsite. Keep the thieves from stealing the silver."

"Guess the family didn't tell you I'd be stopping by, huh?"

"Forgot to mention it. So many other things on their minds." Stay cool, I reminded myself. Don't let the asshole see you sweat. In my most civil tone, I said, "What brings you here, Rodney?" As if I had any doubt.

"Opportunity, boy. Young Patterson said he wanted an expert opinion about his land." He spit out the window. I questioned my wisdom, but I closed my hand around Dutch's collar. Let him talk, I thought. Examine the threat. "You got that dog under control?"

"For now. But I wouldn't get out. If I were you."

"Whatever. So the Patterson kid said you'd been on the job, what? Three, four weeks? With no plan what to do with this prime land? I got a dozen plans. Took me three minutes." He swept his hand – and the cigar – to indicate the hills sloping down to the sparkle of sun on water.

Kat's land. Not for sale. But why tell Richfield? Not that I had the chance anyway since the jerk kept running his mouth. "But then, you always was slow on the uptake. A project this big? Told the kid you can't think that big."

I pondered the fun it would be to drag the jerk from his truck. Let Dutch maul him. Toss him down the hill into the creek. Icy water closing over his head. Yeah, that would be fun. If he were more than an annoying gnat. I shrugged. "Could be. Time will tell."

Richfield's eyebrows lifted, surprised his bait didn't get me to bite. I waited, and sure enough, he took another tack. "What do you say we collaborate? You being a family friend and all. You swing the deal my way, I'll cut you in." He spit again before going on. "Kid mentioned his sister might be a roadblock. That's why he said to come today."

I figured. Paul tried to do the same with me. How many others, I wondered. Playing dirty with all of us. Kat most of all. On a level playing field, I believed Kat could hold her own. But Paul was doing everything he could to tilt that field his way. Maybe I could help tilt it back.

"Paul didn't tell you about the Conservation Department survey?"

"Shit. What's up their ass?"

Not a thing, I thought. But I also knew the guys in the department would find a way to stop any project Richfield touched. And for good reason. "Beats me. The sister called them." She hadn't as far as I knew, but I'd suggest it soon as I got the chance. Meanwhile, let this scum think she had. I shrugged. "Here's hoping they don't find some endangered creek larvae."

I tried to pay attention. The only father I'd ever have. His only funeral. Seemed like the least I could do. I pushed my spine against the hard back of the pew and tried to focus on Pastor Young at the pulpit.

"...everlasting life...Let us pray."

The sun through stained glass cast a stripe of rusty color across my lap. I watched one hand turn vivid red. The other caught violet as it reached toward my knee. And if I moved just a little...

"Hymn 306 in the blue hymnal. Please rise if you're able."

The organ was stronger than the voices wavering from the congregation. Still, I was surprised to see so many here. Friends from the museum, second cousins or third, distant relations with the trademarked Patterson high foreheads and bushy eyebrows. Gram used to quiz me. What branch of the family tree did the Howard Kinzers spring from? How were the Bowers related? I knew the tree better than the people.

"Please be seated."

The light dimmed and my colors were gone. The better to pay attention. I breathed in the aroma of freshly baked bread. Darcy's signature scent. My imagination filled in an undertone of lavender. Gram's signature. It made sense I'd feel her here. She'd send me a stern look and tell me to stop fidgeting. Then she'd open her big handbag and slip me her tiny magnetic Scotties to keep my fingers busy. So many Sunday mornings, I strained to line the white dog's head with the black's before the magnets slid them head-to-tail. I could use those little Scotties now. And Gram sitting beside me.

"To everything, there is a season…"

Maybe Gram was here. She loved that verse, asked me to read it at her funeral. Hardest thing I ever did. She knew it would be. "I've had my season, Kat. A long, good life. You read. Take in those words. No mourning now. It's your season to dance," she said.

I sat straighter as if she nudged me. I looked to the lectern and my heart jumped. Did I miss something? Reverend Young's eyes peered into mine.

"No matter our age, losing a parent is a difficult passage," he said. I wondered where that passage led. "Kat and Paul, I wish I could tell you otherwise. What I can say is you're not alone." He raised his eyes to include the rest of the pews. "Most of us here have lost a parent, and in addition to the loss we feel for Vern Patterson, we're reminded of others who went before us." I heard the rustle of stiff clothing against the pews. "Our earthly human condition is to feel loss not once but many times. Not separately, but in the cumulative. As love that makes the losses worthwhile is cumulative. It's love that helps us sustain and grow through the losses. The love we feel for the departed – both recent and past. The love of family and friends who gather to comfort us at times of loss. And the love of our Lord Jesus Christ…"

Cumulative. The word echoed in my mind, drowning out the rest of the pastor's homily. It was – would be – weird to live in a world without Dad. But it was the cumulative weight of loss I felt more. Gram. Mother. Scott most of all.

A sigh escaped and Darcy reached to squeeze my hand. I lifted my head to meet her eyes, nodded to show I was okay. It wasn't a lie, even as my emotions spiked like a seismometer during an earthquake. But clarity spiked higher than present grief.

I never knew how to mourn Scott, to accept he was gone – not like I had when Gram died. Losing her hurt like the devil, but was eventually pushed aside by happy memories, the knowledge she was satisfied with her season.

With Scott, I was too young. Memories came in hazy, faded snapshots. The way he'd tickle till I couldn't breathe or flip me over his shoulder in a fireman's carry. How big those shoulders looked in his football uniform…the sun glinting off his hair when we'd tramp through the timber to the old swimming hole.

I wished I could remember when Scott was alive better than the night he died. I woke to Mother's screams and tore down the stairs to the kitchen. There was a policeman. And Paul. But soon as I peeked around the door, Dad hollered for me to go back to bed. Later, all he said was there was an accident. Scott was dead. And, "Don't ever let me catch you near that water tower!"

That was the last time I heard my brother's name. On our side of the house anyway. And I quickly learned not to ask, to walk on tiptoe. Around Mother especially, but Dad too. I'd sneak into Scott's room sometimes – when I forgot or when swamped with the ache of missing him. I'd read his old Hardy Boys or pick up his model cars – till Mother found me there one day and gave me the worst beating of my life.

So it's not like I could ask what happened. No one helped me understand. Not even Gram. She might have if she knew. But I was too scared to ask. It was easier to go numb – like Mother and Dad. Like I had at the Lodge when Paul talked about "the closest I ever got to heaven," and I remembered those blonde heads bending over Scott's casket.

The only thing I knew was that Whip was there when my brother died. I heard his name often, in low bitter tones. "If not for that damn Whip Tyler," Mother would say before she pounded up the stairs and locked herself in Scott's room. "Never should have let him run around with that boy," Dad would mutter between clenched teeth. They blamed Whip. So I did too.

But the Whip Tyler who carted lumber and handed me tools – who asked for stories about our land – that Whip didn't seem like the devil my parents made him out to be. He seemed…nice. Trustworthy even. Not like… Maybe.

He wanted me to trust him, I knew. Okay, I'd give him a chance to earn my trust. He'd tell me – what happened, how it happened, why Scott died. Then I could understand, have my season to properly mourn, put my brother to rest at long last.

"Hymn 487 in the blue hymnal. Please stand."

I stood so abruptly, Darcy shot another questioning glance at me. My smile was real this time. So real I almost laughed. And I sang out with gusto, like stepping out from a dark cave into a bright spring morning. I was trapped in the dark for a long time. But Whip would fix that. Reason enough to sing.

"The family invites you to continue your remembrances of Vern at their home. And now…" He lifted his arm as he did at the end of every service. "The Lord bless you and make his face to shine upon you. Amen."

Reverend Young stepped down from the altar and stopped at our pew. He shook Paul's hand and squeezed mine with a smile. "Don't be a stranger, Kat, dear."

I smiled back, I'm pretty sure. I might have even promised to come to church. I wasn't paying attention. All I could think about was getting Whip alone, finally learning what I needed to know. And… I had to drop my head, let my hair hide the heat rising in my cheeks. Once I knew Whip deserved my trust, then…

"Let's get right back," I whispered to Darcy as the usher approached our pew to escort us out.

Her eyebrows rose before she nodded. "It's now or never."

I reached a hand to touch Paul's arm. "You want to go home and get food set up?" I saw the look I expected. "Or you and Chrissy could stay here and glad-hand with folks? Follow along in a few?" I gathered my bag and coat, sure of his response.

"Fine."

"Stall a little. Give us a head start to get things ready," I suggested as I nudged Darcy out the other side of the pew and headed for the side entrance.

WHIP

A moment after I let loose the specter of the Conservation Department, Dutch's ears went on alert. Then I heard it too. Tires on gravel. But since the dog didn't bristle or pull from my side, I figured it was no threat. Probably Luke.

But Richfield wouldn't know that. "Uh-oh. Sounds like they're coming back from the funeral," I said. "Better hightail it before the sister finds you here and gets in a huff. If the DEC doesn't squirrel the deal, that would for sure."

It was enough to set him moving. Wouldn't you know old Richfuck would find that one puddle and splash muck all over me? On purpose, no doubt. Same way he ran down that fawn on a site. Bastard.

I pulled both barnyard gates closed on my way back toward the house, where I saw Luke's van backed up to the kitchen door. Dutch ran ahead to escort Richfield off the property. When he came back with wagging tail, I crouched and whistled him to me. "Good dog! Good old Dutch!"

Luke stuck his head out the rear door of the van. "About time you showed up. Give me a hand unloading." He held out a tray, stopped, sniffed. "Hold it! Don't touch anything. What the hell happened to you?"

I sighed. "Long story."

"You can't tend bar like that."

"Didn't you bring clothes?"

"On the front seat." I stepped in that direction, but again he held up a hand. "Don't touch. Shower. I'll bring the clothes."

"Shower? Where?"

"Where do you think?" He shook his head and muttered, "Morons. I've got morons on my team."

I took a guess why laid-back-Luke had an edge to his voice. "Lulu was back today?"

He closed his eyes. "Yeah. Remind me to thank Darcy. Get the door, will you?" Then, "Don't even think about wearing those boots inside."

I looked down and acknowledged he had a point.

"Shower. Now. Make it quick."

"Luke. I can't use Kat's shower." I tried to make it sound reasonable. It didn't fly.

His eyes closed again while he mumbled, "Morons..." Then in a totally fake and syrupy tone, "No problem. Go on home. Shower there. Take your time. Maybe you could stop by the church on your way? Tell everyone to wait there till you're ready?"

"I'll go shower."

Kat

"You know Luke will have it under control," she said as we climbed into her car.

"Yeah. But I want a minute with…to…um…powder my nose." Okay, that was lame. Darcy knows I only bother with makeup when she forces me. "You know. Collect myself."

She gave me a sidelong glance that said, "Yeah right," clearer than words. But she let it go with a sigh. "Whatever you want, Kat. Whatever you want."

At home, I was out of the car almost before she got it stopped. "Can you check with Luke? I just want to…" I headed past the kitchen door and in through the dining room. Wine bottles and glasses were lined up on Gram's gateleg table. A beer cooler sat on the floor behind. No sign of Whip.

I rushed toward the kitchen, where I heard Luke say, "Idiot came walking up from the barn, splattered with mud and who knows what else. This after spending the morning with Lulu. You owe me serious sex favors for this day, babe." When he saw me in the doorway, his face went sheepishly comical. "Aw, Kat. I didn't mean... You know we're glad to do it."

I laughed. Reached out to pat his arm. "I do know, Luke. And I'm grateful. Don't know what I'd do without you both." I looked around. "Whip too. He's been a big help. Where..."

"He ought to be out of the shower by now." He looked at Darcy. "Whoops. His clothes. I forgot to get his clothes out of the truck."

"I'll get them." I dashed out the kitchen door, and then – to avoid their faces and the looks they might exchange – came in through the dining room. I made a beeline for the bathroom. I rapped on the door and went in.

"I brought your..."

I don't know who yelped. Him? Me? Maybe both? What I do know is that every word I ever learned evaporated from my brain. Except stupid, stupid, stupid!

In my rush to find Whip, to find out what I needed to know, it never occurred to me that I'd find him *naked*! What was I thinking? Luke said he was in the shower. Of course he was naked. Stupid, stupid, stupid!

I dropped his clothes and sprinted out the door. But not before I saw...what I saw.

WHIP

I grabbed for a towel. Of course I did. But not quick enough.

For one thing, it took a moment to be sure she was real. I mean it was her shower, the smell of her, the soap still damp. I had...thoughts. Okay?

And then, like I conjured her, she was there. Only thing wrong was the horrified expression on her face. Not the picture in my mind. Not even close.

So I grabbed for a towel. And something to say. Something to make her want me the way I wanted her. Or if that was too much to ask, something to convince her to keep a door open for the idea. Something.

If such words existed, I didn't find them. Not before the door slammed.

I wanted to go after her – started to actually. Until I heard other voices and decided showing up naked at her father's funeral reception was maybe not a great plan.

Thank God my bedroom was across the hall. Refuge. I leaned against the door and wished I'd never have to open it again. God! What was I thinking? Worse, what he was thinking?

Footsteps in the hall. A knock on the door. And nowhere else to hide.

"Kat? Are you in there?" Darcy.

I let out a breath, opened the door and pulled her in.

She squeaked. "Easy, girl." Then she saw my face. "What? Kat honey?" Her eyes narrowed. "Did that rat of a brother of yours say something?"

I shook my head.

"What then? You're scaring me. What's going on?"

"I just…walked in on…Whip…" I closed my eyes, but his image was indelibly burned on my brain. "He was…"

Darcy put a hand to her lips.

"It's not funny! He was…"

Her shoulders shook. "Jerking off?"

"Darce! No. He was in the shower." Then, "Well…" I clapped my hand over my mouth. "No. I mean… I don't know… Maybe?"

"Maybe? You couldn't tell?"

"He wasn't…you know. But he was…" I looked at the ceiling, the floor, out the window. Didn't matter where I looked, I saw…what I saw. "Um…big."

Darcy hooted.

"It's not funny!" But it was. Some minutes later, I wiped my eyes and said, "Jesus. You'd think we were thirteen."

"Except back then, a good giggle is all we could hope to get," said Darcy. She waggled her eyebrows.

"Stop it!"

"Honey, that is a hot guy you walked in on. And he is so hot for you. As you saw for yourself."

"I didn't…he wasn't…that wasn't about me." The heat rose higher in my cheeks.

She raised her hands. "Oh sure. Maybe it was J-Lo or Beyoncé that got him all excited." She shook her head. "Girl, have you gone blind? Do you not see how he looks at you?"

I covered my face. God, the room was hot. Okay. I'd seen. And even when I knew better, I liked it. What I saw. Too much. "But Darce, Whip Tyler? What's he even doing here?" I forgot he might be trustworthy.

"He's helping. Like he helped you yesterday and this morning. Being anywhere you are. Any time he can."

"But in my shower?"

"Luke said he came in all muddy. He told Whip to take a shower, get cleaned up so he can play bartender to the assembled guests who even now are arriving on your doorstep to comfort the bereaved."

I closed my eyes. "I've got to get out there, don't I?"

"You do."

I heard what she was thinking. "I know. You tried to talk me out of it. My idea to have people back here. Shows how smart I'm not." I heaved a sigh and stepped toward the door. Stopped. "Darce. How do I face Whip now?"

She grinned. "Ask him for a drink. Any luck? He'll slip you a stiff one."

I choked back a laugh as I stepped into the hall. "You are terrible. What would I ever do without you?"

WHIP

No sign of Kat when I came out of the bathroom – fully dressed. The door to her room was shut. Was she in there? I thought about knocking, but I heard voices down the hall. Guests. Who'd want a drink.

I got behind the makeshift bar just in time. Good thing I set it up before I fell asleep on the couch. Who knew a funeral made folks so thirsty? Hungry too if the stacked plates I saw were anything to go by.

It looked good. Simple but plentiful. Sandwiches, potato salad, raw veggies, booze. What Luke probably thought of as all the essential food groups. No doubt his catering business would see a boost after Vern Patterson's funeral.

I knew most folks there – and about half the time I could guess whether they'd want red, white, light, dark, sugared or diet. I made a mental note to thank Luke for sticking to basics here too. I'd never keep up with mixed drinks, but I could use a church-key, pour, and say nice-to-see-you about as well as the next guy.

While I poured, I kept one eye peeled for Kat. I figured she was making hostess rounds in the big room down the hall, the grand entrance where company would cross the wide lawn to the two-story porch and the front door. A door more for show than for regular use.

I was pouring red wine for Georgia Jeffries when Darcy appeared. She gave Georgia a hug and said, "White and a Sprite, please, Whip." To Georgia, she said, "Kat will be so glad to see you. She's tied up with some guy her brother wanted her to meet. The wine's for her." She put a hand to the front of her skirt. In a whisper she told Georgia, "I'm not drinking for the next six months or so. But don't tell Luke I said anything." She sent me squinty eyes. "You better not either, Whip Tyler." To Georgia she said, "Come help me rescue Kat."

Darcy slipped an arm through Georgia's and steered her toward the hall, but before they got there, Paul and his plastic woman appeared. How did she walk in those things? A tall man in an expensive suit inclined his head toward Kat as if afraid to miss a single syllable. She looked less enthralled, I was glad to see, especially when he lifted his head and I saw the open collar and gold chain at his throat. Robert Torvino.

I passed Paul a beer and said low, "You didn't waste any time."

He grinned. "No time to lose. Hot iron and all that."

"You picked a couple winners." I shook my head. "An ass and a snake."

"Afraid of a little competition, old pal?"

"Not when they show up at your father's funeral. You think that will fly with your sister?"

"You're here, aren't you?"

"That's different." It was. Wasn't it?

"Is it now? You saying you don't want the chance to turn this place into cold hard cash?"

"I could use the work. But that's not why I'm here today."

"Yeah, right. You think playing bartender will get you in little sis's pants?"

"Now look!" Across the room Darcy raised her head. And eyebrows. I lowered my voice. "Not that I owe you an explanation..." I took a breath. "I like Kat. She needed help with this shindig, so I'm helping. This is about friendship. Not a land grab."

"Focus more on land and less on friendship." He made it sound like a dirty word. "I gave you first dibs. But if you don't show me those ideas you say you've got and soon, I'll find somebody else. Count on it. Pal."

Kat

Why didn't I settle for punch and cookies in the church basement? Ten minutes into this reception I insisted on and I wanted to hide in my room.

But there I stood in Gram's sitting room, welcoming all those shirt-tail cousins. Another time, I might have enjoyed hearing their family reunion stories. Evelyn Bower remembered spinning around on Great-Gremma's piano stool. George Clement, eighty if he's a day, got giggling as he told about sneaking peeks at the African stories in Great-Grandpa Eli's *National Geographic*s.

The historian in me would love those stories – another time. The day of Dad's funeral? Not so much. I had too many other things on my mind. Scott. Whip Tyler and what only he could tell me. What Paul had up his sleeve. Whip Tyler naked in my shower.

But these were my guests, so I pasted on a smile and made nice till my eyes glazed and my cheeks ached.

"I suppose you'll have to sell the farm," said Evelyn. "It's sad to see these old places go. But you'll be better off with a nice little house in town."

"I'm not going anywhere."

"Oh, honey. Surely you're not going to rattle around in this big old house all by your lonesome?"

I was tempted to say I'd have orgies every night. I forced a smile. "I won't be lonesome. This is my home."

"Oh dear. I don't like that idea at all. Won't you be scared to death? Regina, did you hear? Little Kat here plans to live here. All alone in this big old place!"

"Why, Kat! This place must have ten bedrooms!" Regina shuddered. "You couldn't pay me to live in a place this big. Think of the cleaning!"

That's how the first half hour went. I kept assuring my cousins that I wasn't afraid to live alone, I had a good dog, I was staying. They nodded and didn't believe a word.

"Food's in Gram's – my – dining room." I tried to hustle them down the hall, sending telepathic requests that they bring back a glass of wine for me. Or three.

The Kinzer cousins continued the litany when they arrived. "I stayed with your great-grandmother – she was my Aunt Emma, you know. Two weeks every summer. Hot as blazes upstairs. I never slept a wink. And freeze in winter, I'll be bound. Give me central heating."

"We've got central heating."

"Hmph. You get yourself in town, girl. This place will make you old before your time."

By the second half hour, the Bowers came back through. "Wouldn't your grandmother be proud of what you've done… But the money you're putting into this place!"

"And there's so *much* to do!"

As the Clements wound back to the sitting room, the Bowers emerged from the rooms on Dad's side, and I noticed a shift in the thick cloud of doubt.

"Be sure you get a good price, Kat girl. You know Delbert McDougal over our way? That developer he sold to made a killing. But poor Delbert got a pittance. A pittance. Poor old fella couldn't afford a good nursing home. Had to go to the county home." Shudders all around.

"No worries. I'm not selling."

"But Paul just told us… Oh dear, did I get the wrong end of the stick?"

Where was Paul? Or Chrissy? I made my excuses and took my own turn to Dad's side. And there they were holed up around Mother's maple table with a man who looked vaguely familiar.

"What's going on over here?" I asked.

"KP, here's somebody you need to meet. I think you're going to like what he's got to say. Robert, my sister, Kat. Kat, this is Robert Torvino. He's interested in our land."

"Paul." I tried to keep my eyes from rolling.

"Just listen for once. Robert says we can make a fortune. He can help us do it."

"We have guests, Paul. We really should…"

"I'll walk with you, Ms. Patterson." As the man stood, I recognized him from photos in the newspaper. The unfinished hotel on the river in Valley Spring. The companies that didn't get paid. The wife of a contractor was an old classmate. Three kids under seven. Last time I saw her, they were moving to an apartment because they couldn't make their mortgage payments.

"How…kind. Mr.…Torvino, was it?" Shyster or not, the man was a guest in my home. And Paul knew I'd have to be polite. Dammit.

"Robert, please." The oil slick on the corncrib floor came to mind. "You're sitting on a gold mine here. Let me tell you how you can deposit that gold straight into your bank account."

"Perhaps my brother gave you the wrong impression. I have nothing to sell. Has Paul offered you refreshment?" I pointed across the sitting room to the hall, but the shyster was unshakable.

"He did mention you intended to retain some of your acreage. But when you hear what I can do for you… I'll make you a very rich young woman, that I guarantee."

"Really." I allowed my lips to turn upward in the smallest of smiles. "It's nice you have such…concern for me."

More cousins arrived. Paul and Chrissy walked past them down the hall. So much for the glad-handing I'd asked from those two. "Laura. Kenneth. It's been forever. How have you been? And the kids?"

Laura is about as shirt-tail a relation as they come. Not someone I liked. Or that liked me. So my enthusiastic – and prolonged – greeting took her aback. But did Torvino take the hint and disappear? No. He stuck like the burrs I had to pick off my jeans after a hike in the timber.

"Let's get some food, wine. We can catch up." I put an arm around Laura and aimed her toward the dining room. Where I caught sight of Whip bending over the cooler by the bar. I turned away quick, blood rushing to my face. And might have toppled except for Torvino's hand on my elbow.

WHIP

"Chrissy and I are out of here," Paul said. "You let me know when you come up with something, pal. If you come up with something."

And with a flurry of "Thanks for coming" and "See you soon," none of which sounded sincere, they were gone. Maybe other folks would take the hint and leave. They didn't. More kept coming. Kept drinking.

The bar was busy. So busy, I didn't see Kat leave the room. But I wanted to send up a cheer when Torvino, the snake went out the door. Seeing him at Kat's side had burned. That I had no call to act the jealous suitor was beside the point.

When the crowd finally began to thin, Darcy came through the hall with a load of dirty plates and glasses in her hands. I took her weary face as an excuse to close the bar. "I'll take those. You go sit down. Get Luke to give you some…tea or something."

A ghost of a laugh. "Good idea. Check the other side, will you? Pick up trash and such?" She stepped into the kitchen door and came back with a tray and a trash bag.

"Got it."

No sign of Kat. Not in the big room or through the open doors to the other side. But there was plenty of trash. I loaded a bag and put dirty glasses on a tray. I'm not in Darcy's league, so I didn't try to haul it all at once. I headed back toward the kitchen with the bag.

Halfway down the hall, a door opened and out stepped Kat. She stopped dead when she saw me, that lovely color rising into her cheeks. Then with a look of resolve, she grabbed my arm and pulled me through the open door, trash and all.

"I have to ask…oh hell!" She pushed me back against the now closed door and fastened her mouth on mine.

It took five seconds of pure shock before the trash bag hit the floor and my hands were free. One hand dove into her hair while the other slid to the small of her back, pulled her closer.

It was a kiss for my make-out hall of fame. By the time we drew apart we both breathed hard.

"I…can't…believe…I did that!" Her hands came up to cover her face.

"Me neither. Do it again!" I swung her around so she was against the door now. She gasped. "Okay. If you won't, I will."

Minutes later, her hands pressed against my chest. "I…can't…breathe."

I laughed and loosened my arms – slightly – as we swayed into a hug. Swimming was great sport, I thought. A cannonball was even better.

And then I heard a strangled sob. I put a hand to her cheek, tried to lift her face, but she burrowed into my chest so all I could see were her bright curls. "Kat? Sweetheart, was I too…rough?"

Her head moved. A muffled no. A huge breath. She took a step away, and this time I let her. But I slid my hand down her arm till I found her hand. I wasn't letting go. Not now.

When I saw her face, I got it. Or thought I did. "Rough day?"

A nod. A ragged breath. "Yeah."

I gave her hand a tug, thinking to fold her into another hug, but she resisted.

"No. I...have to ask you something." She raised teary eyes.

"Anything."

"I...need...to know...to understand..." She shook her head as if trying to rearrange words floating just out of reach. "What...happened? The night...Scott died."

My hand, reaching to smooth her hair back from her face, halted, hovered in air before dropping to my side.

"Please, Whip. No one...my family...we never..." A deep breath. "I need to know."

"I can't tell you." I shook my head. "I'm sorry. I...can't."

She stared at me, "why" written all across that pretty face. Then as she saw I meant what I said, she spun away from me. "You need to leave. Now."

I said it again – to his face the second time. "Leave. Now."

His hand grabbed at his hair, ran it through. Hot eyes bored into mine, but I couldn't read the emotion. Anger? Lust? He opened his mouth, the word "but" forming on his lips. Hands lifted before dropping them to his sides, his shoulders drooped. One nod. A quiet, "I'm sorry, Kat." He closed the door behind him.

I took two steps back, rammed into the bed, sat hard. My bandaged hand pressed against my heaving chest; the other clutched my elbow as if my pitiful hands could hold my insides from spilling out.

I shook my head in a futile attempt to dislodge scene after humiliating scene from this forever-long day. No luck. The squeak of a door, footsteps on the porch outside my room brought my head up, ears straining. Further away, an engine started. I closed my eyes and breathed.

Then I was up and zipping across the hall to the bathroom, shutting that door. Four steps to the window. Taillights glowed red as he braked at the end of the driveway. I saw him turn right. Gone.

Fine. I told myself to breathe and caught sight of my reflection in the bathroom mirror, amazed that my face still looked familiar. Pale, lips swollen, a slightly bruised look about the eyes, but not remarkably different from a few hours earlier. Alone again.

"Right," I told my reflection. "So you didn't learn what you wanted to know. You didn't know yesterday. You don't know today. Move on."

My hand crept to my mouth. Some things I had learned. I pulled my hand back to my side. "No point thinking about…" I said to the mirror. "Go thank your friends for all they did. Send them home to their own lives."

One more deep breath. "Stand up straight. Shoulders back." I opened the door and listened. No peep from the left. Good. All the front-door friends and neighbors were gone. And the cousins, praise heaven. The next breath came easier. Who was left on Gram's side? I stepped softly down the hall, ears on alert. Georgia, Luke, Darcy. Friends, real and true. One more breath before I moved to join them.

Georgia passed beer bottles through the window to Luke. I collected three wine glasses and did the same. I looked around. "I think that's it. You guys are the best." I slipped an arm around Georgia as we moved to the kitchen door. "How can I…" Why can I never say my deepest feelings without blubbering? But if there was ever a time to try, this was it. "I…there are no words…"

Luke pulled a platter from the fridge. "Sit. Eat." Darcy used a foot to push out a chair from the table where she already had a sandwich on a plate.

206

Georgia grabbed clean glasses from the dishwasher. "Red or white?"

Luke dived into the fridge again. "Beer for me. Milk for my bride."

"You guys..."

Darcy shoved a plate stacked high with sandwiches and potato salad at me. "Shut up. Eat."

When had I last had food? I couldn't remember. Was I hungry now? I looked at the food before me, at my friends. I was. "You too. All of you. Sit. Eat with me."

"Don't have to tell me twice," said Georgia. "I've had my eye on that salad all afternoon."

"Sit," I ordered Luke. "I can't take a bite till you all do. Gram's rule. And I am starving."

With the first bite, it felt like every cell in my body came awake, greedy and insistent. "Mm..." I dug in like a truckdriver on a long haul.

"Have another sandwich." Luke passed the platter.

"More salad first," I said. "Tastes so good." Felt good too. Every cell purred, content to savor the simple act of chewing among friends.

As my stomach filled, I looked at Darcy. She wasn't eating – not like the rest of us. I put a hand on her arm. "You okay?"

"Just tired."

I looked at Luke, his brow wrinkled in concern, and shoved back my chair.

"This was perfect. Just what I needed. Thank you." I stood up and started stacking empty plates. "And now I need you to go home."

They argued – as I expected.

"I don't like you being here all alone." Darcy.

"I can stay." Georgia.

"I'm fine. Go."

"But…"

"Go."

"You weren't alone here before."

"Close to it. Dad couldn't have fought off a kitten these last months. And I've got Dutch. He's a good watchdog. Go."

"You sure?"

"Positive. I'll call you tomorrow, Darce. And I'll see you Monday, Georgia. I've got to get cracking on that early schools exhibit."

The two women sputtered a few minutes more until I leveled my eyes at Luke. "Help me here! Get them gone!"

"You heard her. Let's give the girl some peace."

It wasn't that simple. When is it ever? "Vestibuling," a friend from school called it – the time between the decision to leave and people getting out the door. A full twenty minutes later, all three finally stepped into their vehicles.

Luke's van was already in motion when I remembered something. "Wait!" I dashed from the porch to the passenger door and yanked it open. I turned my back on Darcy and pointed. "Zipper. Free me!"

WHIP

So much for swimming. Just when I thought... No point. She threw me out. Right. Should have seen it coming. Did. Kept swimming anyway.

I whacked the dash with my hand – and swore. It hurt. Bruised hand, bruised ego. Get over it. Right. It would have been easier if she hadn't kissed me. Hadn't... Stop. I shook my head. Son of a bitch.

I turned down the blacktop toward town. But going home to my crummy little apartment held no appeal. A drink, I thought. Drown my sorrows.

I pulled the truck into a broad U-turn while I considered retracing my steps. Barging back in on Kat, not taking no for an answer. Or telling her what she wanted to know. But I couldn't do either one. I turned east, away from the Patterson place.

I want my dog, I thought. That's where I'd go. Juno was at my brother's farm – had been since I left for Joliet. I was supposed to pick her up. Was it only yesterday? I'd called Trav on my way to Kat's. "She's fine. Get her when you can," he'd said, and I knew he meant it. Trav's easy that way and so's Tess.

I glanced at the clock. They should be done with supper. I could slip in, get Juno, claim I was too tired to come in for coffee. No lie there. I was beat. Beaten. Yeah. That too. A beer and my dog. That's all I wanted.

I knew it for a lie. But I might as well keep saying it. I wasn't going to get what I wanted. So what if Kat smelled better than my dog. Juno was a lot less complicated. The dog loved me. No matter what happened so long ago.

I saw her tail in full wag as soon as I turned in the driveway. With my mother. So much for grab and go.

I pasted what I thought was a smile on my face as I braked. And readied my excuses as I hopped out. I bent over to rub my girl's ears. "Hey, Juno girl. Miss me?"

"We were heading back to my place when her ears went up. She must have heard your truck from a mile away." Mom's voice held the sound of Juno's full body wag, and I knew I should be grateful that two females in this world were glad to see me. But really? All I wanted was my dog.

"She's a good old girl, aren't you, J?" Maybe if I just kept making a fuss over the dog, I could get out of here. "Ready to go home?"

As I straightened, Mom lost the wag in her voice. "Something's hurt you."

"I'm fine."

"It's that Patterson girl, isn't it?"

"I'm fine. I have to go."

"You never could hide your feelings."

"Ma. I can't."

She sighed. "Just like your father. Okay. Take your sweet dog and go." She stepped back. "But Whip, honey, if you want to...talk...or...something, I'm always here."

I shook my head. Motioned for Juno to get in the truck. "I...know. But..."

I looked in the rearview on my way back out to the road. She watched me drive away. She was complicated too. And the same wall blocked my way with Mom as with Kat. I hit the steering wheel. "You don't know what you did to me, Scott," I said. "You don't know."

Kat

Out of my funeral duds and back in jeans, I felt better. More like myself anyway. My body felt wrung out, but my head was too full for sleep. If it were still light, I'd take Dutch for a walk down to the creek. But in the dark? No thanks.

Get your house in order. That's what Gram would say. Especially if she tripped over a bag of trash on the way out of her bedroom and remembered too well how it got there. There wasn't much left to do in the kitchen. I stacked a few stray dishes and glasses in the dishwasher. Maybe I'd find more out and around.

After so many people in my house earlier, it felt odd to hear my footsteps echo as I crossed the dining room. You're the one who wanted to be alone, I told myself. Wasn't it normal to feel a let-down? After all those anxious nights watching Dad breathe. After pushing so hard to show off my house. After enduring all those guests.

My house. I took a breath. Where I lived. With my dog. "Dutch, old friend. Come." He gave me a look that said a nap was a better idea. But with a grumble, he stretched, yawned, and padded to my side. "Let's go look at our house."

Good idea. I could pick up after the guests, and... Nothing out of place in Gram's sitting room. I'd have to cover the furniture again till I decided what to do with the room. I pondered on it for the hundredth time. It was the best room in the house, airy and bright with views to both east and west. Too good for no-man's-land. But I'd never hold court there like old Amasa must have. I wondered if Lovina tried to talk him out of it. Or maybe she appreciated no-man's-land when Eli's new bride moved in.

I shrugged because what else can you do when your ancestors aren't around to dispute your speculations. Or maybe they were. Was that why the cousins thought I should be afraid to be here alone? Dutch raised his head at my giggle. "But how I'd love to meet the family ghosts," I told him. He seemed unimpressed.

I was not afraid. But I checked to see the front door was locked. I'd check all the doors before I slept just like I had ever since I moved back home. "That's just smart, Dutch, old boy. Not afraid."

Through the door to our old living room, I spotted a beer bottle on the bookcases in the corner. As I moved to pick it up, I remembered curling up there when I was supposed to be dusting, sure the arm of the couch would hide me.

I sank down there now, no longer able to ignore the weight of the day. "How will I ever face..." Dutch leaned against my side. I buried my face in his fur. Waves of humiliation – and other emotions held too close too long – let loose in tears.

WHIP

The next day I holed up. I turned on the tube, cracked a beer, stared at the walls, poured out dog food. Downstairs I stood at the door watching Juno squat on the narrow strip of grass across the alley behind Oakton's Main Street. In a cold rain that matched my mood. I sat at my desk. Tried to work. Stared at a blank computer screen till I gave up and shuffled back upstairs to the couch.

I kept telling myself it couldn't matter. I'd only known her for a blip. Why was I so bummed? It wasn't like me. Not Mr. Keep-Your-Guard-Up. But…there was something about her. Something that got to me. Like her brother, I thought, as if it wasn't already weird enough. I flipped the channel. Again. Looking for something to stop these crazy vultures circling through my mind.

Forty-eight hours later, I opened the last bottle in the fridge. I caught my reflection in the hallway mirror. Not pretty. I ran my hand over the sandpaper of my face, pulled my shirt aside and took a whiff. Shower, shave, get more beer.

Juno whined. "Again?" We went downstairs. Sun stabbed my eyes as the dog danced around my legs.

214

"Okay, okay." I grabbed a tennis ball from the pile by the door and gave it a toss. Satisfy the dog, I thought. Then shower, shave, get more beer.

Luke pulled into the alley on the third toss. He got out and ambled to lean against my truck. When Juno brought the ball back, I started to toss it to him. He crossed index fingers. "No dog slime for me."

I shrugged and flipped the ball across the alley. He watched Juno dash and fetch it back twice more before he spoke. "You left in a hurry the other day."

I shrugged. Tossed the ball again.

"I saw her asshole brother leave a while before, so I figure you had words with Kat?"

"You could say that."

He nodded, watched another toss. "Haven't seen you at the Firehouse."

"No. Been hanging with my girl here." I took a pull from the bottle in my hand.

"Got another one of those?"

"Fresh out. I was going to get cleaned up. Get more."

"Good idea." He grinned. "I'll wait with slime-girl while you shower." He grimaced as I tossed him the ball. "Then I'll boil my hands before we go."

I started inside, then turned back. "Seems like you're always telling me to shower."

"Seems like you always need telling."

Kat

By Sunday night, I couldn't fool myself anymore. The cousins were right. The house was too big for me. Too many rooms that needed too much work. Too much money. Too much space for one lone female and her dog. Too much quiet.

I tried to tell myself it was exhaustion talking. And it could have been with all I'd done. Since before Dad's funeral and after. Without much progress, unless you'd count all the tired furniture and worn carpet from his living room parked on the front porch. Two days' work and all I had to show for it was an empty space. With layers of wallpaper waiting to be stripped so the room could be turned into...what? A second parlor that would be used even less than Gram's sitting room? What was the point?

"The point is you love that house." I didn't mean to dump my doubts on Darcy, but her call caught me at a low moment. And she was right. I did love the place, loved its history, the family feel the walls gave me. But what good was history when you didn't have someone to share it with. I was a family of one, the end of the line – at odds with the only family I had left.

I wanted kids once, love, marriage, the whole deal. Not anymore. Not with my track record. For a few fleeting minutes I thought about taking another chance. But not with someone I couldn't trust. Never again. I'd live and die alone. In a fifteen-room house.

If Scott were alive… I'd be the maiden aunt to his passel of children. There'd be laughter, birthday parties, Thanksgiving feasts. Happy times the house was built for. But Scott was only one more ghost. And it was probably only wishful thinking to believe he'd have loved the place as much as I did.

Paul and Chrissy's kids, if they ever had any, would never live here. Probably wouldn't even visit. I'd be the aunt that stood in their father's way, kept him and them from untold riches. But who else would I leave the house to? And how fast would they rip it down after I died?

And if I gave in? Moved to town like Paul and every sane person thought I should? Or I could build myself a tidy little cottage overlooking the creek. Either way, I'd still be alone. And die a little as I watched a wrecking ball smash our ancestral home.

I pushed myself off the floor where I'd collapsed. "Enough." Dutch raised his head from where he lay. "Enough wallowing, old friend. No wrecking ball in your lifetime or mine. This is home. And we might as well make it sparkle." He yawned and put his head back down. I smiled. "All right. I don't guess we have to do it all tonight."

I shut off the light. "Come on fella. Time for bed. Everything will look better after a good sleep." Dutch didn't look convinced, as if he wondered if I remembered how to have a good sleep. Me too. It's not that I was afraid. Certainly not of the dark. It just didn't seem as friendly as it used to. That's all.

I started at the creak of wind on glass. A noise I'd known my whole life. Once I thought I wouldn't know how to sleep without all the sounds of this old house shifting and settling for the night. Once those familiar creaks and groans brought comfort. But they had a less neighborly tone in the middle of an all-alone-in-my-too-big-house-night.

WHIP

"Whip, old buddy, how's it hanging?"

"Paul."

"How you coming on plans?"

"I thought you made another choice. Torvino? Richfield?"

"You're not afraid of a little competition, are you, Whip old pal?"

"You asked me that before. After your father's funeral."

"And?"

"Honest competition doesn't bother me. Getting blindsided does. Bad timing does."

"So you want to take your toys and go home?"

"Depends."

"On what?"

"Whether you play straight with me. Whether you want to respect the land or rape it."

"Yada-yada."

"I mean it, Paul. If I take you on as a client, you take my standards."

"If *you* take *me* on?"

"That's right."

"I'm doing the hiring here."

"My toys. My game. Or you get Richfield and Torvino who will rape your land. Ruin it. Guaranteed."

"How can you know that?"

"I know them. Know their shoddy work, know people they shit on – landowners who were promised big bucks."

"They didn't deliver?"

"You want names?"

"Yeah. And while you're at it, get me names who think you're so wonderful."

"Check your email tomorrow."

Kat

"Sorry I'm late!" I tore past Georgia's desk to drop my bag. "Flat tire." I checked the activities board and groaned. "Mrs. Wink's first-graders! I forgot they were coming today. Are they here already?"

"Renee's got them. No worries." Georgia cocked her head and winced as she heard a crash from downstairs.

"I'll go." Renee is a genius fund-raiser. And the world's worst tour guide for kids. They terrify her, which the kids figure out in the first ten seconds. I surveyed the situation as I hurried down the stairs. Chaos. Noise. Mrs. Wink held two boys by the hand, three chaperones collared some – their own probably since they wouldn't manhandle other people's kids. Renee raised a feeble, "If I could just have your attention…"

I reached for the old ship's horn and tugged its rope, held on through one prolonged blast. Every kid swung eyes at me and froze. "Hi, everybody! I'll let the first kid who sits on the floor in front of me – mouth closed and hands in your lap – blow this horn at the end of the tour!"

In a mad rush, kids plopped down. "Remember the rules," I said. "Everybody listens and everybody keeps hands in their laps – or you won't get to hear the horn blown by our lucky winner…" I bent down to the adorable boy with curly dark hair and angelic freckles sprinkled over his nose and cheeks. "…whose name is…" I shoved my fist-cum-microphone to his mouth and saw the unmistakable devils in the boy's eyes.

"Timmy! I'm in first grade, and I like horns! Can I blow it now? Can I, can I?"

"Glad to meet you, Timmy – and no. The deal was you get to blow the horn at the *end* of the tour. Got it?" At his disappointed nod, I gave his shoulder a tiny squeeze – and a nudge to remind him to sit back down. "It will be worth waiting though," I said to Timmy before casting my eyes to the rest of the class, "because one thing we'll learn today is what different horn blasts mean. The blast you just heard is what riverboat captains sound when they leave a dock or come around a bend in a river. One long blast warns other boaters. Who's heard that kind of blast on our river?"

Every hand went up. "I thought so. The barge captains blow one long blast when they come around the bend from Buffalo Rock toward Oakton. And now you'll know why – to warn other boaters to look out. Who has heard shorter blasts on the river?"

All hands again. "You've got smart kids this year, Mrs. Wink." In a conspiratorial whisper, I added, "Not like her class last year!" The kids giggled, already eager, I knew, to repeat my words to their older siblings who lorded over the lowly first-graders in the age-old pecking order of Oakton Elementary.

Grabbing kids' attention is easy. Keeping it's harder. "And smart kids always thank their tour guide. Let's all say thank you to Ms. Renee, who was filling in for me while I changed my flat tire. One, two, three, thank you, Ms. Renee!" I sent her apologetic eyes before introducing myself as Ms. K. Not Ms. P, for obvious reasons. Not Kat or I'd hear meows for the rest of the tour and for weeks around town.

"The first peoples and the later European settlers didn't have roads, so they used boats – to get here and to trade what they made for what they needed. That's why they needed ways to signal each other on the river. At the end of the tour, we'll get Timmy and four of his friends to show us what those signals were and what they meant. Now I want you all to turn on your bottoms while I move over there to show you what those first boats looked like."

Ten minutes later, horns blew and I ushered the first-graders to the courtyard, where we keep modern versions of old toys and games. The group took off in all directions with shrieks and hollers. That's why we keep the toys outside. They might forget the horn signals, but they'd remember playing here – and that was good enough for me.

I turned, ready to leave the kids in Mrs. Wink's capable hands, when one of the chaperones approached with a firm hand on young Timmy's shoulder.

"What do you say, Tim?"

The eye-devils rolled, and I had to smother a chuckle. "I know, Grandma." He beamed his angel smile at me. "Thank you for letting me blow the horn, Ms. K. It was really fun."

"You're welcome, Timmy. I hope you come again."

"I will." He raised beseeching eyes at his grandmother. "Now can I go play?"

"Be off with you!" We shared a laugh as he tore across the courtyard to where his buddies were setting up a game of nine-pins. She turned to me. "You're very good at your job. I think my grandson has a crush on you."

"Aw. He's sweet. And a handful?"

Her smile grew. "Comes by it naturally. His dad and uncle were terrors." Sharp brown eyes studied me. "His uncle has a crush on you too." At my confusion she added, "I should introduce myself. I'm Mattie. Mattie Tyler. Now I've met you, seen your work, I admire Whip's choice."

WHIP

I'd yet to sit easy after talking to Paul Patterson. But in a way he did me a favor. A project beats solitaire for hoisting a guy out of a funk. Or if not all the way out, at least enough so I could see what I had, not only what I'd lost.

I had my youth, good health, strength. Solid friends in Luke and Darcy. I reached down to give Juno a pat where she lay by my desk chair and smiled at the slap of her tail on the floor. A good dog. Beer in the fridge. My work.

I clicked on my computer and pulled up a plat map of the Patterson place and a topographical map of the area. I zeroed in to match one map to the other, checking and rechecking the scales of each map until I was reasonably sure I had it right. The creek that divided the property helped.

I blocked out what I figured would be Kat's hundred fifty acres, a triangular swath of woods bordering the creek, a hilly area south and west of the house, the field she'd said was once an orchard to the east.

Paul's land surrounded hers – about ninety acres to the east, sixty to the west. The east parcel was relatively flat, I remembered from my trip to those fields with Kat. Route 6 ran along the edge of the west plot, so it was easy to picture from the thousands of times I drove that road. It was more rolling than flat.

So the choice was either build on the east close to Oakton or on the west a few miles closer to the bigger town of Valley Spring. Or both, and on Kat's land too, if Paul had his way.

West made the most sense, I thought, to get the higher Valley Spring land prices, but take advantage of the lower Oakton Township taxes. Good selling points for buyers and for Paul. And a thick border of timberland along the southeast edge that would be Kat's property. A substantial buffer between Paul's development and her. From her house, she'd never know other houses were there.

I told myself I couldn't let it matter, what was good for Kat. But it did. So I'd focus on the west.

I did the math and started dropping in streets and houses with my site software. I added trees along the highway and streets I drew to create the house-in-the-woods feel I figured Paul's buyers would go for. Mixed-sized lots were the way to go, though I knew I'd have to sell him on that idea. I drew out a few five-acre lots along the back border near the mature trees, a few quarter-acres nearer the road, half-acre parcels in between. A neighborhood of about seventy homes.

I sat back and pondered how to pitch the plan to Paul. It didn't have the flash of a golf course or high-end McMansions. But affordable housing plots would bring in money faster and more homes would add up to higher profits in the long run.

I doubted he'd have a clue about how infrastructure costs factor into a developer's pricing. I clicked to the water and sewer feature in the software and kept working. Once I had preliminary numbers, I could run them by Stan Stevens for a reality check. And draft an email to give Paul more to chew on than names of satisfied clients.

I could copy Kat on the email, I thought. I should tell her about Richfield too. The conservation angle. Or not. Focus on the numbers first, I told myself. Then decide.

I rubbed one arm, then the other. As if I needed my coat. I didn't despite the November breeze. The heat from my cheeks provided enough heat to last through February.

"Mrs. Tyler. How nice to meet you."

She smiled. "Somehow, I doubt you really mean that, dear. And I don't blame you. I'm sorry I ambushed you."

I started to say something inane like, "Oh, that's okay," but I clamped my lips shut. Why lie? An ambush, it was.

"I'm not usually this pushy," she said. "Whip said you had an interest in early schools. Maybe we could have lunch and talk about that? After I help Mrs. Wink get the monsters back to school?"

I didn't respond. Not because I wanted to shut her down. More because I wanted to drop in a hole.

"Never mind," she faltered. "Not a good time. I'm sorry for your loss, by the way." She looked off in the distance, almost like she wished for a hole to drop in too. Odd thought to have about such a put-together woman. Smooth salt and pepper hair in a thick pageboy, manicured hands pulling a gorgeous wool wrap closer about her slim body, perfect posture. She was the kind of woman I hoped to be when I grew up. If I grew up.

Her eyes studied me. "I only met your father once. When your brother died."

My turn to study her. "You know what happened? How it happened?"

She cocked her head. "No. I was hoping you might tell me."

"I don't know."

"You must have been very young."

"I was. I'm not now. And I need to know."

"I wish I could help. But Whip wouldn't talk about it. And believe me, I tried to make him." Her eyes closed as if in pain, opened at the sound of Mrs. Wink's voice.

"Boys and girls, it's time for us to go back to school. Line up now and be ready to say thank you to Ms. K as you walk by. Like we practiced. Timmy, you had your turn to be first earlier. You and your grandma will be our caboose now."

One by one, the kids walked to me, held out their hands to shake, to say, "Thank you, Ms. K," before skipping ahead to catch up with the rest of the line. A few added, "It was fun," and one little girl said, "I like your hair."

I'd have enjoyed their sweet goodbyes except for the uncomfortable anticipation of another encounter with Whip's mother. As she approached again with Timmy, he said, "Thanks, Ms. K. I *really* liked blowing that horn." Then she took my hand and asked, "How about that lunch?"

I hesitated. "Can't today."

"Dinner then. Friday? Come see my schoolhouse?"

WHIP

"What are you doing in town, Mom?"

I didn't mean to make it sound rude, though I could see she took it that way. But I was up to my neck in the sewer plan for Patterson West when she walked in. And I don't like surprise drop-ins, especially when I've got maps and papers spread all over my desk and two weeks' worth of garbage piled by the door.

Juno was glad to see her. But while Mom appeared to enjoy Juno's love-fest, she clearly had other eggs to fry.

"I spelled Tess today at Timothy's field trip. Chaperone duty. To the museum."

Uh-oh. I braced and was right to.

"Tim and I met your girl. I think the little guy's in love."

I shouldn't feel jealous of a six-year-old. Except the kid probably had a better chance with Kat than I did. "She's not my girl."

She waved her hand, batting away my protest. "I like her. We had a lovely chat."

I frowned. "Mom..."

"Oh, don't worry. We didn't talk about you. Much." She paused while the barb stuck deeper. "Anyway, she's coming to dinner on Friday. To see my schoolhouse. You come too."

"I don't know, Mom." I bent down to scratch Juno's ears, stalling and hiding, which I should have known wouldn't fly with Mom. "Kat doesn't want to see me."

"That's not the impression I got. In fact, I'd say, she's as miserable as you. About whatever happened between you."

"I'm not miserable."

She gave me the look, the one where her head cocks and eyebrows lift – the don't-lie-to-your-mother look.

I let my eyes roll. "Mom. Stop. Kat doesn't want to see me. Period."

The look shifted to the what-are-you-not-telling-me stare. But two can play that game. I stared right back.

After a long moment, she sighed. "I guess I'll have to cancel then. I can't entertain someone who isn't willing to eat with my son."

"Mom…"

"No. I thought this was a nice girl. She's certainly good with children. But if she won't eat with my son, well, she must be…horrible. I won't have her in my house."

"She's not horrible."

She smiled, the gotcha smile. "Didn't think she was. So you'll come to dinner on Friday."

"You should trust me on this. It's not a good idea."

"Friday," she said with her I-won-and-you-might-as-well-admit-it smile.

I raised my hands in defeat. There's no fighting that smile. I could always back out later, I thought.

"And don't even think of backing out. You bring the wine. Flowers would be nice too," she added as she sailed out the door

Kat

I don't know what I was thinking. Why did I agree to dinner at Mrs. Tyler's? I considered backing out a dozen times a day all week, searched for an excuse that didn't scream "scaredy-cat!" Couldn't find one.

"All I want to do tonight is strip wallpaper," I told Dutch. "But no. I've got to get myself cleaned up and presentable. For an ordeal." A skirt, I decided, but a simple one. And the soft green sweater Gram made. For confidence.

I grabbed a bottle of wine from the fridge. Plenty left from the funeral supplies. Never go empty-handed was Gram's rule.

What I didn't count on was another flat tire, left front this time. Does a tire ever go flat when you aren't dressed up? Since Murphy's checked out the right front on Monday and found nothing wrong – and since I'd be late if I took the time to change it, I plugged in the air compressor to inflate the tire. Maybe it wouldn't leak before I got back home again. I could hope.

I knew roughly where the Tyler place was. Dad and I delivered seed corn to the O'Briens up the road and I remembered seeing the schoolhouse. And the rigid set of Dad's jaw as we passed it.

It was a charmer, that schoolhouse, with a fresh coat of red paint and bright white trim. I saw that much from the car. A narrow porch – maybe an addition – ran along the front, sheltering a vivid blue door. A truck I knew to be Whip's was parked behind a Prius of the same blue.

"Ms. K, Ms. K!" Timmy ran down the drive from the left, followed by a smaller girl and three very big dogs. I was halfway out of my pick-up when I heard his voice and seeing the size of the dogs, wondered if I should climb back in. "Don't worry, Ms. K." Timmy slid to a stop in front of me, breathing hard. "They won't bite you." He grinned. "Unless I tell them to."

I couldn't hold back my own grin. The kid was infectious. "Hello, Timmy. Who's this you've got with you?"

"My sister. She's only four. Her name is Tallulah, but we call her Tally. She's not old enough to blow the horn at the museum. Not like me. I'm six. And a half."

I crouched down and offered my hand. Timmy grabbed hold and shook vigorously while Tally slid behind her brother. "I'm glad to meet you, Tally," I said and was rewarded with a shy smile.

A loud whistle blew from up the driveway that led to the farmhouse and other outbuildings. "Gol-darn it! We just got here."

From the schoolhouse porch, a voice said, "You know what that means, Tim. You too, Tally-girl."

"We got to go. It's the rule." Timmy made it sound like the end of the world. "And once you go in Grandma's, we can't see you or talk to you or nothing."

I smothered a laugh. "My mother had that rule too."

"She did? Back when you were a kid?"

Now I did laugh. "Yes, and you don't need to make it sound like the dark ages. Scoot now so you don't get in trouble."

"All right. Next time come see *us*." He raced off, Tally close at his heels, even if she was only four.

As I straightened, Whip came down the porch steps. "Juno, stay." The chocolate Lab looked as crestfallen as Timmy. Until I clucked and she came scampering. "Juno! Off!" Her hindquarters, ready to jump, slumped and her eyes held an expression that communicated clear as words, "You never let me have any fun."

Whip walked toward us. "Say hello," he told the dog. She plopped her butt on the ground and held up a paw. "Kat, meet Juno. Juno, this is Kat. Be nice."

I took Juno's paw in my hand. "Does he mean you, girl? Or me?" The dog's tail thumped, but it wasn't an adequate outlet to her excited quivers.

"Juno." She cast a mournful look at his stern tone but adapted the leap she wanted to make to a sideways flop that invited me to rub her belly.

"Oh, you're a shameless hussy, you are." I crouched to comply. "You know how to get what you want, don't you, girl?" And so did I. Every minute I talked to his dog was a minute I didn't have to talk to her human. Oh well. Might as well get it over with. "I called the conservation office. They're sending someone out next week. So...thanks."

A call from the porch gave me an excuse to leave it at that, and I was grateful. "Whip, don't let your dog monopolize our guest. And wipe her paws before she comes in my house."

I straightened and stepped toward the front door. I held out the wine. "Mrs. Tyler. Thank you for inviting me."

WHIP

She didn't look at me. She played with my dog, oohed and aahed as she followed Mom around the schoolhouse, studied her wine like it held the secrets of the universe. And would not meet my eyes.

You'd have thought Mom and Kat were childhood friends the way they got on. I was invisible. Not that it mattered. Before, I thought if I just kept swimming, I'd get to her. I knew different now. Unless I told her what I could not tell her, it made no difference how hard I swam.

But it did matter. She mattered. And I couldn't hide it, even if I tried. I did try – avoiding Mom's knowing glances, keeping my few words quick and to the point. Trying to be invisible like Kat obviously wanted. Didn't work.

Maybe if I'd been able to keep my eyes off her, I'd have pulled it off. I kept my voice in check, but my eyes would not behave.

Ears neither. My attention kept wandering. And still I learned more about Mom's schoolhouse than I ever hoped to know – when it was built, when it closed. How Great-Grandma Tyler came to teach there during the depression and made $35 a month, how she boarded with the family and ended up marrying the oldest son.

"That's what happened in my family too," Kat said. "Almost exactly. Except it was the youngest son for my Great-Gremma – Emma before she had grandkids."

Mom laughed. "I wonder how many farm families could tell the same story. Ma Tyler – no Grethel for her, ever! She still lived in the big house when I married Whip's father. She'd tell stories – how isolated young people felt out here in the country. Few chances to meet other young folk. So when she got hired to teach here, all the boys jostled for her attention. But Whip's Great-Granddad had the inside track, sitting down to supper with her every night."

The two of them had a fine time, sharing tales back and forth, looking at relics from when the schoolhouse was filled with kids, digging into old ledgers. Why I had to be there was a mystery to me. But, if Kat was there, I wanted to be too, pathetic as that was. So I hung on every damn word she said like some lovesick pup and tried not to get caught doing it.

Faint smudges under her eyes showed dark against her pale skin. And the set of her shoulders was stiff, like she carried a heavy load she couldn't set down. I noted the scratch on her hand. No more bandage.

Her conversation with Mom seemed normal enough. Animated even. If you didn't know her. If you hadn't seen her easy and warm the way she was with Darcy and Luke. Once or twice she'd been that real, that easy with me too. That first morning in her kitchen. Before she knew who I was. Out in the field, talking about the ditch full of snow. The way we laughed after I almost hit those deer. Before I kissed her.

They were all glimpses – enough to keep me swimming, dammit – of how it could be with us. Not just the way she'd felt in my arms, though I wouldn't soon forget that. But those few times we really talked, the way she listened when I showed her Twin Creeks, the way we made up the travelogue for the dark. The way she felt about her land.

One minute I told myself it couldn't be hopeless. The next, I'd think give up. Yeah. Fun night. It went on for hours. And was over way too soon.

Shortly after Mom put dessert on the table, Kat made noises about getting home. Which threw Mom straight to action mode.

"Whip, honey, you walk Kat out. Check that tire before she leaves. Make sure it's still got enough air."

I would have anyway. I'd planned on it soon as Kat mentioned the flat that made her later than she'd planned. She protested, but I expected that too. What I didn't expect was what Mom said next.

"You're not having good luck with tires, are you dear? Monday at the museum. Wasn't it a flat tire that made you late? No time to get it fixed yet?"

Kat rolled her eyes. "Different tires. You know how sometimes things break down in spurts? That's me and tires this week. I just hope the washer doesn't go on the blink tomorrow. I'm behind on laundry."

Mom said something. I don't know what. My mind was too busy picturing that big empty house and all its doors and windows. No way she was going home alone.

Kat

"Don't be ridiculous!"

Whip's jaw tightened. "I won't. If you won't."

"I'm not."

"Two flat tires in one week? No puncture in either one? You don't find something suspicious in that?"

"Well…"

"Get in. I'll follow you home. Make sure you're okay."

"And then?"

"And then I'll go. I am well aware you don't want me around."

What could I say to that? I looked at the ground.

"Kat. Get in."

I did. And fumed the whole way home. I did *not* need looking after! By any man. Certainly not Whip Tyler! I tried speeding, hoping to get in the house before he got there. He stuck too close. Halfway home I gave up trying.

I didn't go so far as to admit I was a little nervous going home by myself. Not then.

At home I put the pick-up in the garage and stepped out to tell him to go. To hell is where I had in mind. Sitting across from him at dinner – the way he stared at me the whole time – took every ounce of patience I could muster. I was done with Tylers – never wanted to see another one as long as I lived. Timmy crossed my mind, and his adorable little sister. Not even them. Temper sizzled.

As I pulled the garage door down, an odd shiver crept up my spine. I put it down to anger. When he stopped his truck, I moved fast, ready to let him have it. But when he opened the door and Juno leapt out, another shiver hit. Fear.

"Dutch!" Where was my dog? I was on the porch, calling his name by the time Whip came up behind me.

"What's wrong?" He grabbed for my hand, pulled me to a stop.

"Dutch. Where's Dutch? Didn't bark. He always barks. Twice if he knows you. Forever if he doesn't. Dutch!" I pulled away from Whip, got to the door.

"Wait!" He grabbed me again.

"He's mine!" I tried to breathe around the unreasoning panic.

"I know." Somehow Whip's arms were around me. "We'll find him. Can he get inside?"

I nodded. "Dog door. Gram's porch."

"North side?"

I nodded again, fumbling for my keys. "He must be inside. But…"

"But he'd be out here. If he could."

Full-blown panic. "I have to find him!" I wrenched at the storm door to get at the lock.

"Wait." Whip's hands were on my shoulders. "I'll go first."

I bristled. "It's my house! My dog!" The lock gave way and I swung the door open, but before I could step across the threshold, he pushed me aside.

"I'll go first. You come behind. Turn on the first light you get to. Got your phone?"

No time to answer or protest. I was on his heels, nearly tripping as Juno shoved past. Why hadn't I connected the overhead light to the switch by the door? I scurried across the alcove and ran my hand along the wall between kitchen and dining room. Light flooded the room.

"He's here." I blinked to see Whip kneeling near the door to Gram's porch.

I was beside him before I could blink again. Dutch lay motionless a foot from his dog door. "Oh God. Is he…"

"He's breathing. No blood."

"Thank God. But…"

"Drugged, I think. Smell it?"

I sniffed. Faint, but sweet. Slightly medicinal. "But who…?"

"First things first. You stay here. I'll be right back."

"You think whoever drugged him is still here?"

He shook his head. "Not likely. But let's be sure."

I hardly noticed him leave as I pulled Dutch's head on my lap. "Wake up, Dutch. Please. Wake up." Juno dropped to the floor, laid her muzzle on my leg.

Whip was back. "Nobody. How do I get upstairs?"

I pointed to the corner. "There. And off Dad's kitchen. But we're wasting time. We have to get Dutch to the vet."

"We will. Juno, stay." With a squeeze to my shoulder, he was gone. I heard something tumble. Cleaning supplies stashed on Gram's narrow winding stairs. Juno whined.

"It's okay, girl. He'll be back. Dutch. Dutch! Please. Wake up!"

A grunt, then footsteps overhead, doors opening, closing, footsteps receding as he made his way south. He must have found light switches. I winced at a crash. Maybe not. Or maybe he found…somebody? My heart pounded. But then I heard his footsteps coming closer. Downstairs again. Approaching fast, breathing hard.

"Anything?"

He shook his head. "Attic? Cellar?"

Tears leaked from my eyes as I nodded. "Attic's always locked."

"The door down a hall south of the other stairs?"

"Yes."

"Okay." His breath was coming under control. "Locks from the outside? Not in?"

"Yes. Please, we have to hurry."

"Cellar?"

"Outside."

"No access inside?"

"No."

"All right. Nobody in the house but us. Let's get this fella some help." He scooped Dutch up and stood with a grunt. "Juno, stay. Guard."

WHIP

I called Doc Becker from the truck. "I'll meet you at the office." One door down from his house. Gotta love small towns.

Kat cradled her dog in the passenger seat, crying and crooning over his poor still body. As soon as I got off the phone, I reached a hand to squeeze her shoulder. I didn't lie and say he'd be okay. Poor guy looked in a bad way. He was breathing. True enough. But his breath felt too shallow, too slow.

I didn't tell her what I saw in the other kitchen either. Maybe she'd left the drawers and cabinet doors open, stuff spilling out of them. But every other room I searched – and I'd hit all of them in that big barn of a house – were tidy. Even the room with the ladder and the half-stripped walls had no scraps littering the floor.

So it didn't seem likely she'd left the mess. Somebody was looking for something. Wanted it badly enough to drug her dog to get inside. Somebody who might hurt Kat as well as her dog. I thanked God I was there.

"Stay put," I said as I pulled up to Doc's office. "I'll come around and get him."

"Hurry!"

A minute later I slid the poor mutt onto the steel table in Doc's examining room. Relieved to get him there. Hoping it wasn't too late.

"Is he...will he be okay?" Kat had a hard time getting out the words. She bent over the table, stroking Dutch's fur.

Doc sent me a look that said he needed room. I put my hands on her shoulders, pulled her back into me. Held her there. He put his stethoscope to the dog's chest and held up a hand for quiet. A long minute until he spoke.

"Remind me. How old is Dutch?"

"Six." Kat had her hands to her mouth, so it sounded muffled. "Is he..." I tightened my hold, pulled her closer.

"I'm guessing drug or poison," Doc said. "I can't tell which."

"I don't keep poison. Not even in the outbuildings."

Doc nodded, sent her a small smile. "Good to know. It could be a bad plant, but..." He straightened. "I'll take a blood sample to see what we're dealing with."

I felt Kat sway, like her knees gave out. "You okay? You want to go in the other room?"

She shook her head, took a breath. "No." Her hand crept up to grasp mine. It felt good to hold her, to know she wanted me to. But I didn't fool myself. She'd have held on to anybody then.

Doc shaved a patch on Dutch's leg, inserted a needle, frowned as the vial filled. Kat and I both held our breaths. "He's dehydrated. I'll start a saline IV before I take this into the lab." He hooked up the bag of fluid in sure and efficient steps and gave Kat's arm a pat as he moved toward the door. "The IV will help. He's a

246

strong, healthy dog in the prime of life. All in his favor. I'll be back in a few minutes."

"Can I touch him?"

Doc smiled. "Absolutely. Love beats medicine nine times out of ten."

I loosened my grip, but stayed at her side, the two of us stroking her dog, hands touching like we'd been together for years. She looked up at me, tears welling but no longer sliding down her cheeks. "Who would do this? Who would drug my dog?"

I shook my head. I saw no sign of break-in. And I checked all the doors. Only one had its deadbolt pulled. I wondered if the intruder had a key. "We'll find out. When Dutch is better." If. Let it go now, I thought. Time enough later to wonder who – and why.

"Dutch is a good watchdog. He wouldn't let..."

"First things first, sweetheart." Time enough later to say she'd never be alone in that house again. "Let's get this guy back on his feet. Then we'll figure out the rest."

"I wish he'd hurry." Kat echoed my thoughts.

I put my hand over hers and squeezed. "Dutch is strong. Hang on."

Doc came back. "Blood is spinning. I want to check his heart again." We gave him room to wield his stethoscope and watched his reactions. When he smiled, we both let loose a breath. "Heartbeat is stronger. A good sign. I'll check his blood."

Kat's tears flowed as she stroked Dutch's head. I felt like crying myself – even more when I thought I saw his tail twitch. "Kat. Look."

She raised her head and followed my gaze at Dutch's tail. Nothing. Did I raise her hopes for nothing? And then there was a small thump. Not a full-out wag. But his tail definitely moved.

"Doc!" I called. "He's moving."

Doc hurried back and smiled wide. "He's coming out of it."

Kat put her head down on his fur and cried. A minute later her hand reached out to find mine. The three of us stood there spellbound by the increasingly steady rhythm of the dog's tail.

"He'll be groggy awhile yet. Leave him here overnight. I want to check him again in the morning, see there's no lasting problem."

I could see Kat didn't want to leave him. Couldn't blame her. I hadn't liked leaving my dog at Kat's – not when there was a dog-drugger lurking about. But I said, "Can we stick around awhile, Doc? Till he wakes all the way up?"

"Sure thing. And then you can carry him back to the kennel. Better your young back than mine."

An hour later, Dutch was settled and comfortable. He'd opened his eyes and sighed, thumped that tail. He squirmed once when I picked him up. He was asleep again when I bent to set him on the blankets Doc positioned in a corner of the kennel.

Kat went down on her knees by him for a long moment, until Doc said, "He'll be all right now, Kat. I'll check on him in a couple hours, give him an exam in the morning. You come in about nine. He should be ready to go home then."

Kat stood and reached her arms to give the vet a tight hug. "Thank you, Doc. Thanks so very much. I don't know what I'd do without Dutch."

Doc patted her shoulder. "You're welcome," he said as he guided us toward the door. I said my own thanks, and Doc said in a low voice, "It's a good thing you were there to help tonight, Whip boy." I couldn't have agreed more.

Kat

All I remember about the ride home was clutching a damp green bandana in my hand. Not a color I ever had. When the truck stopped, Whip said, "Give me your keys."

The next thing I remember was watching flames dance in the fireplace, Juno's big head draped over my leg. Did I leave the fireplace on? I must have said it out loud because Whip answered, "You're cold. Stay here by the fire. I'll check the house again. Juno, stay."

Stupid tears started again, and Whip's dog put a paw up. I hugged her close, which she took as invitation. With a small jump, she was in my lap. "I bet he doesn't let you on the furniture. Me neither. Get down." She knew I didn't mean it, probably from the way I tightened my arms around her. I laid my head back against the couch, let my eyes drift closed, absorbing the heat from the dog and the fire.

I stirred. Cold. I rolled seeking warmth and nestled in. Arms came around me, held me. I reached to stroke

Juno's head – and sat up with a start clasping the blanket to my chest. Dark. Bed! I was in bed with…

"Kat. It's okay."

"What are you doing here?"

Whip sat up too. "You wouldn't let go. When I carried you in…"

"That's ridiculous!" It had to be. "I don't remember…"

"You were asleep. On the couch."

"Dutch… Juno…" At her name, I heard a tail thump. The night came rushing back – except for the part where he said I wouldn't let go.

"Right. Dutch will be fine. I checked the house when we got back from Doc's. You were asleep. I thought you'd be better off here, so…"

"And you stayed?" Outraged virgin mode again. I clutched the blankets tighter, did a quick scan under… Sweater. Skirt.

"You held on…when I put you down."

No problem finding heat now. It was all in my stupid face. Whip slid his legs over the edge of the bed, stood. Fully dressed. "Look. Nothing happened… You…we fell asleep." In the dim light I saw him raise a hand to his head. "I'll spend the rest of the night on the couch."

"Couch?" I took a deep breath, tried to pluck reason from the air. "No. Listen. I…appreciate…your help…with Dutch…and…all. But I don't need a keeper. Go home. Take your dog." Juno whined.

He stopped at the door. "No."

"What do you mean no?" My voice rose. "Go! I don't want you here!"

"Too bad. I'm staying."

"Didn't you hear me? I said I don't want you here!"

"I heard you. And I'm staying. I won't leave you alone in this house. Get used to it. Juno, stay." He closed the door behind him while I watched, my mouth hanging open.

WHIP

"What the hell?" My whole body levitated – two feet straight up. Then I was on my feet, heart pounding, eyes wide open. Not focused, but open. I took a step toward Kat's room. Another intruder?

No. At the doorway down the hall, I saw her silhouette – and understood the scream that brought me so rudely awake. Her table saw. A faint gray lightened the blackness of night through the east windows. Not yet daylight.

I staggered to a wall and leaned. She did it on purpose. I saw the smirk on her face from fifteen feet away. Her way to say "get out" again, as she had in the middle of the night.

Nice try, Kat, I thought. But it won't work. I sniffed the air. Nothing. Okay. I'd make the coffee. I pushed myself off the wall and turned toward her kitchen. I hesitated. Coffee first. Get my brain working before showing her the mess in the other kitchen. To shore up my argument why I was still here. Why she shouldn't be here alone.

Kat

I listened hard for a door to slam, a truck starting. Nothing. What was wrong with the man? Why didn't he go when I made it so damn clear I wanted him gone?

I sniffed in righteous indignation. Tried not to remember how he hugged the couch pillows while he slept this morning. Or how his arms came around me in the night. I turned off the saw and gave it a pat. It wasn't the saw's fault the man didn't find its whine enough reason to leave.

I sniffed again. And smelled something rich and delicious. Coffee. What the hell? The guy had the gall to make coffee in *my* kitchen? I'd put a stop to that! Five steps and I detected another aroma. Savory. Sweet. What?

"Here you go." He pushed a steaming mug down the counter as I rounded the door into the kitchen. "Omelet will be ready in a jiff. Sit." He turned back to the sizzling pan on the stove and ignored me. While I stood there with my mouth hanging open and my damned traitor stomach growling.

"Where do you keep your cinnamon?" He opened a cupboard door, rummaged, opened another. "Found it." He turned with a grin as he sprinkled it into a bowl of eggs. "Secret ingredient."

I aimed virtual poison darts at him. No reaction. The man was like a wad of gum you'd step in on a hot day. Impossible to get rid of. I stood there watching him pour eggs from *my* bowl, into *my* skillet, at *my* stove and searched for words that would penetrate his thick skull.

No words came. Dammit. I didn't mean to drink the coffee. But there was the empty mug in my hand. I slammed it down. Still no reaction from Mr. Dense.

"Now listen…" I started. "What are you doing?" Which wasn't what I meant to say at all. Damn the man. He sidetracked me.

"Apples. Ever had an apple and cheddar omelet? You won't believe how good it is." He turned the skillet one way, then the other, skimming edges with a spatula. *My* spatula! "I make a killer sausage and pepper jack omelet too. But I found the apples first."

He sprinkled more cinnamon over the apples and frowned. "Ought to have nutmeg too. Oh, good. Your fridge is limited but your spice rack's solid."

More sprinkling. And my damn stomach growled again. It smelled good. Too damn good. He carried two plates to the table and leveled his eyes on mine. "A few hours yet till you can call Doc's office and check on Dutch. Might as well eat."

Dutch! My heart bumped as it had last night when I saw my poor limp dog. He'd be okay. Doc said so. But what did it say about me that I let my irritation with Whip put Dutch out of my mind?

255

I sat, picked up a fork. "It...was good of you to help...last night. With Dutch." I bent over the plate. Please God, I thought. Don't say anything about the middle of the night.

Maybe he read my mind. Maybe he didn't want to talk about it either. Or breakfast mattered more. Was he staring? Like at his mother's? I raised eyes to peek. No. He was at the door, whistling for Juno, who came bounding in.

I bent to her. No better buffer than a dog. "Hi, good girl. Couldn't you find Dutch's dog door?"

"I closed it off last night," Whip said. "After...you were asleep. I didn't want her to run loose. She doesn't know the boundaries here. Didn't want to chance it longer than a quick pee."

"Oh. Right. We lost dogs on the road. When I was a kid."

"More traffic than she's used to," he said. "Juno. Down. Let the girl eat while it's hot." He sat and went at his own plateful.

One look at Juno's sorrowful eyes, and I sent her a mental promise to save her a bite, no matter what Simon Legree said. I was three bites into the omelet before the flavors slowed me down and got my attention. I looked up and said, "This is good."

"You sound surprised."

"No. I...well, yes. I don't know men who cook. Except Luke."

"I can make six – no seven – dishes. My Aunt Sue taught me. Said every human should be able to cook something even if Jake – my uncle, her husband – would starve without her." He chuckled. "She got that right. If you want a blood-rare steak off the grill, Jake's your man. But that's the full extent of his culinary talent." He took another bite. "Sue's a saint." He shook his head. "Had to be to deal with Jake – and the jerk I was at seventeen. Macho and mad at the world." He shrugged. "But I liked to eat. So I learned."

I stared and then looked down at my nearly empty plate. Mad at the world? I wondered but didn't know how to ask.

He kept talking. "This omelet was one Aunt Sue concocted after a trip to see family back east. Vermont? Maine? Don't remember." He waved his fork as if to suggest that geography past the Illinois state line couldn't matter much. "She talked about apple pie with a thick slab of cheddar." He pushed his now empty plate away and picked up his coffee mug. "Said it was great, but she was no hand with pie. So she tried the combo with eggs. First dish she taught me."

Silence. Till I felt compelled to say something. "It was good." More silence. While I searched for words that didn't make me sound like a simpleton. Nothing.

When he spoke at last, I jumped. "When was the last time you were in the kitchen?" He angled his head. "Over there."

I blinked. "I...don't know. Yesterday? No. Day before probably...Why?" I sat up, on high alert. "What?"

WHIP

She was up and out of her chair before I could say more, out of the room before I could get to my feet.

"Kat, wait." She didn't and it was too late to warn her. Ready or not, I thought, there she goes. I refilled my mug and followed.

I found her kneeling on the kitchen floor, gathering scattered papers in one hand. Blazing anger in her eyes. Aimed at me. "Why didn't you tell me?"

I shoved a hand through my hair. "No time." True enough. And lame.

"*My* house!"

"*Your* dog!" I fired it back, surprised at how my anger flared in response to hers. Her shoulders sagged and I felt like a class-A heel. "Look. Job one was to be sure nobody was in the house. Doors and windows intact. Then, get Dutch to the vet. Fast as we could." Less lame. I saw her accept it. "After…I was going to tell you. But…you were…out. Fast asleep."

Her head came up, fires banked, but still smoldering in her eyes. "What else did you find?"

"Nothing. Nothing out of place. Far as I could see. Except. You keep the doors deadlocked? All but the one we came in last night?"

"Always."

I nodded. "Smart girl. Any chance you left that one open?" I pointed toward one leading to the front porch.

She scrambled to her feet and pushed past me. I followed to the room with the ladder. "Here?"

"Yeah. The bolt was open. I closed it on my first look-see."

She shook her head. "It was locked."

"Not last night, it wasn't. Wait. Where are you going?"

"To check my house. Like I would have if Dutch…"

"I checked it. Twice. There's nobody here."

"*My* house," she said, heading for the stairs. I made a sound, some protest I didn't swallow in time. She swung back to face me, and I raised my hands in surrender.

"Your house. Go ahead. But…" I swallowed. "Maybe take Juno with you?"

She rolled her eyes. "Come on, girl." My dog went to her without a backward look.

Et tu, Juno? I thought. Right. My idea. There was nobody up there. I was sure of it. But still. I listened and tracked Kat's path through the rooms above – mostly from Juno's loping gait.

I pictured where they were as I followed the sounds. Two big rooms to the south, another that stretched across the house east to west. I heard her open, then close the door to the upstairs porch and breathed a little easier. I couldn't imagine anybody getting up there, but still. The pace of footsteps slowed.

Navigating that smallish hallway, I thought. The storeroom above her bedroom, approaching the other set of stairs...

I plopped down on the couch where I'd slept and sipped casually at my lukewarm coffee as the two of them came through the door to the curved stairway. As if I was there the whole time. It seemed like a good idea – to show...respect.

"Anything out of place?" I asked.

"No." The edge in her voice was still there.

I kept quiet, let her reach her own conclusions.

It didn't take long. "You have a theory."

I raised both hands. No way I'd front my ideas before she did. But I did chance saying, "You're sure you pulled the deadlock on that front door?"

The slit-eyed stare turned on me.

"Okay. You're sure. Then whoever came in used a key. Right?"

The stare didn't subside, but she nodded, said – in a not-too-friendly tone, "Go on."

"So...who has keys? To your house?"

"Who knows?" She was up again, pacing. Stairs to kitchen, back again. "This house is a hundred fifty years old. Who knows how long ago this set of locks was put in? There could be keys all over the county!"

At least she was taking it seriously. I kept quiet. Nodded.

"Stop being so, so...damned...stone-faced!"

The who-me look didn't fly. "I guess you leave it to the sheriff?"

"I'm not calling the sheriff! There's nothing missing, no *crime* to report."

"Breaking and entering is a crime."

"Not if he used a key."

"He?"

"He, she, whoever." She paced some more, stopped. "You think it was Paul."

Sure I did. But it was the last thing I'd say out loud. "What do you think?"

"I don't see why he...I wouldn't stop him...there's nothing here he wants."

Again I said nothing, did nothing, though I itched to hold her, comfort her like in Doc's office. Fat chance of that. I nudged the dog at my feet, angled my head toward Kat. She's young, Juno. Not fully trained yet. But what a good heart. One quizzical look at me, another jerk of my head in Kat's direction, and my dog made me proud. Seconds later, Kat sank to the floor, cradled sixty pounds of insistent Lab.

Minutes later, she raised her eyes. "If it was Paul...I don't want the sheriff involved."

I tried to make my face stay still. Not a great success. "That's up to you..."

She stood. "Yes. It is."

"But..." I knew it wouldn't sit well. It still needed saying. "Sheriff or no sheriff, it's not safe. You here alone."

"This is my home. Mine," she said through clenched teeth.

I nodded. "Should be enough. But it's not." Time for hard ball. "Not when your truck's vandalized. Twice. Not when someone breaks in. Not when your dog is drugged."

"My car…" I watched her put it together while she paced. I sipped at my coffee, cold now and not appealing. But it gave me something to do while she stewed and chewed.

She jerked to a stop and swung to face me. "I will not be pushed out of my home."

"Don't blame you. Get somebody to come stay awhile?"

"Who?"

I shrugged. "I don't know. Family?"

She glared. "Not bloody likely. You saw my cousins at Dad's funeral. No chance."

"A friend then."

"I don't have friends." She spat it. "You don't make friends when you can't have kids over…" Her voice broke. She whirled and took three strides to stand by the window. Her hand gripped the back of a chair, knuckles white and straining.

I gave her time to collect herself before observing, "I've never seen tighter friends than you and Darcy."

A sigh. A nod. "She's the best friend in the world." Another sigh and a swipe at her eyes. "And she's pregnant." She turned and added in a quieter voice, "They've got their hands full – the business, the baby…"

"They work hard. Both of them." It was true.

"I won't have them babysitting me."

I took a breath and wondered if I should say what I wanted to say. What the hell. "Right. So I guess that leaves me."

"You?" The way she said it, you'd think I suggested she scoop up manure from the barn floor and take a bite.

"Look. Doc will open up soon. You go. Pick up Dutch. Think it over." I pulled my keys from my pocket. "I'll stay here." I put up a hand to stay her refusal. "Till you get back. You think of someone else who can stay with you in the meantime, fine. If not…" I held out my keys. "There's clean laundry in a basket by my bed. Jeans and shirts on the back of the bedroom door. Laptop on the coffee table. That's enough to keep me in business here till you figure something else out."

An hour later I pulled out my phone in the Firehouse parking lot. "Darce. Can you come out?"

"Out? Where are you?"

"Parking lot. Here." I saw her face at the window.

"You can't come in?"

I looked at Dutch on the seat next to me. "No. If it's not a good time…"

She was halfway out the door, half into her coat before I could finish.

"Kat. What's up? Why couldn't you come in?" Dutch roused to lick her hand, thump his tail twice, and was back asleep before I could answer.

"I didn't want to leave him alone. I just got him from Doc Becker's. Somebody drugged him last night."

"What? When? Is he okay? Are you okay?"

"I'm good. He's…going to be fine. Still tired, but Doc says he's going to be fine." I swallowed hard. "He was…unconscious last night. When I got home. From Whip's mother's house."

"Oh, Kat. No." She put a hand to her mouth, eyes wide as she stared at me. "And you took him to Doc's? Last night? You should have called."

I shook my head. "It's okay. Whip helped me."

She raised an eyebrow a la Scarlett O'Hara, the way we practiced in ninth grade. "You gave Whip the green light. Hooray! You two will be great together."

"Darce." I shook my head. "No. It's not like…that. He…followed me home…is all." I squeezed my eyes shut. "And spent the night." The minute I said it, I wished I hadn't. "Nothing happened – exactly… I'm telling this all wrong."

Darcy leveled her eyes at me. "Then slow down. Start at the beginning. Tell me everything. And I mean everything."

I took a breath and began. Except for reminders to slow down, she didn't say a thing until I said, "And now he's decided to move in. My house, and he's practically forcing me to let him stay…" I looked at my friend and didn't love what I saw. "What?"

"You don't want me to say it, Kat, but Whip's right. You shouldn't be alone out there."

"Not you too. I've lived in that house most of my life. It's perfectly safe."

"Kat. It's not." She shook her head. "In town, maybe. Even then, I wouldn't like it. Not with all those doors, all the places somebody could hide." She crossed her arms. "No. Not with somebody flattening your tires, going so far as to drug poor old Dutch…"

"But…"

"What if it had been you? What then, Kat? You expect your friends to sit back and say okay fine?" Darcy's temper is famous for a reason. "Not this friend. I'll drug you myself, lock you in a closet."

"But…"

"Honey. I'd move in with you. I would. But what use would I be? Pregnant lard-ass cow."

"You'll never be a lard-ass. And I'd never ask you…" I knew she'd say I didn't have to, so I made my voice firm. "Not an option."

"Kat…"

"No. And that's final."

There went the eyebrow. "So… I guess that means Whip."

I rolled my eyes. "Really? I have to?"

"Yes. You have to."

I chewed on my lip, gave voice to what bothered me most. "I don't like it. Feels too much like…"

"Justin."

"I was such a dope, Darce. Such a doormat."

"You're not now. And Whip's nothing like Justin."

"How can you be so sure?" I hung my head. "I let him take over my whole life, Darce. Like some dumb rag doll."

"Justin was a creep who preyed on you when you felt…weak." She covered my hand on Dutch's head. "Do you feel weak now?"

"No…but…"

"No. You're a strong, capable woman. And Whip is a good guy."

"Justin seemed like a good guy at first too." I winced at my feeble tone, hated the wobble in my voice.

Her hand squeezed. "That's what predators do, honey. He saw you were lonely, away from your true friends. Away from my vibe-meter."

A tiny laugh bubbled to the surface. "I forgot the vibe-meter."

"No! The most reliable tool in all of humankind? The vibe-meter set off alarm bells the first time I met Justin."

"You pegged him first thing."

"I did. Saw how he undermined my friend Kat." She huffed. "Bastard!" Her hand squeezed again. "But you're the strong woman who sent him packing."

"Took me long enough. Longer to get him really gone. I shouldn't be glad he found some other poor girl to browbeat."

"You tried to warn her. You can't help it she didn't trust the vibe-meter."

I shook my head, wishing... I shrugged. "Can't help someone who doesn't want help. I learned that." I turned my hand over, squeezed back. "If you hadn't been there..."

"You'd have come to it yourself. You wouldn't stay with a guy your friends hated."

I rolled my eyes. "You don't hate Whip."

She grinned. "Not one bit. I like him, Kat. And I was ready not to, for your sake. History and all." She raised her hands. "But he and Luke have history too. Even so, what clinched the deal? Made the vibe-meter hum? The way he helped before your dad's funeral. Didn't have to be asked. Just showed up. Pitched in. Helped."

I couldn't deny it. I closed my eyes and saw Whip hauling lumber, pouring drinks for my horrible cousins, carrying Dutch into Doc's office.

Darcy wasn't done. She'd never quit till the deal's closed. "So he offered to stay at your place. Looks like more helping." She smiled. "Guy's crazy for you. I have to admire his smarts. And you're overdue for that kind of crazy. If you ask me." She sighed. "Which you didn't. So you'll step into that good crazy. Or you won't. The vibe-meter can't tell the future. Except this. He'll be your friend until – unless – you make the first move. He won't push himself on you. The vibe-meter knows."

"So you think it's all right that he stays at my place? That he's...safe?"

"Depends what you mean by safe. Do you mean you might learn to like him? Want him?" She patted her heart before her tone went serious. "Or do you mean will he sneak into your bed and ravage you in the middle of the night..." I jumped. "What? Did he *do* that?"

I waved my hands in the air, shook my head so hard my brains rattled. "No! Well. Not exactly."

"What *did* he do? Exactly?"

I leaned one hot cheek against the truck window, wished I could swivel my head clear around to give the other the same relief. "He...was there. In my bed."

"Oh my God!"

"But he left...when I...kicked him out."

"Oh. No good?"

"No! Nothing happened!"

"Well why the hell not?"

"Just. Stop. Okay?" I gulped at air. "It wasn't like that."

"You're blushing like it was like that." She grinned.

"Listen. I woke up. He...was there." I couldn't tell her what he'd said, that I wouldn't let him go. "I...fell asleep. He carried me...to bed...he said. We both had all our clothes on, for Pete's sake!"

She raised that damned Scarlett O'Hara eyebrow again. "And?"

"I woke up. And...he...left. Went to sleep on the couch."

She gave me another long look. "So, you ask me if he's safe? A guy who's certifiable, he's so crazy for you? In your bed? And he leaves? Because you told him to?" She stopped trying to hold back her laughter. "Oh yeah. He's safe. The bigger question? Are you?"

"Stop! And...and...go back to work!"

WHIP

After Kat left, I wandered through the downstairs again. Checked doors, windows again. Still locked. But far from secure. Too many low windows and doors everywhere. Too much glass an intruder could break.

If it were my place, I'd put in an alarm system, change all the locks. I heard Kat's voice in my head. "My house." I'd have to keep my lips zipped. Or she wouldn't let me stay.

As it was, she didn't like it. But I'd stay put...until... Till I know she's safe, I thought. No use thinking about anything else. Even if it might kill me to be so close and not allowed to touch her.

It won't change, I thought. She made her feelings perfectly clear. Unless... No. I couldn't tell her. So we were at a stand-off. And I was opening myself up to a world of hurt.

Juno followed as I wandered back to the kitchen – the new one – and cleaned up the breakfast dishes for something to do. Then she whined.

"Okay, girl. Nothing to do in here. Come on." I grabbed my coat and opened the back door. "Good for both of us to get our boundaries clear."

Outside, Juno did a happy dance and a quick squat before her nose went down to explore a host of new scents. Until she heard a bleat. Fluffy. In a fenced enclosure to our right with a concrete structure that looked like an old smokehouse and a longish dilapidated building. The old ewe was rounder than I remembered. Overfed? Or pregnant? Hungry. That was certain from her insistent bleats.

"Hold your horses, mama. Can't get you grain till I find it." Didn't take long. Not with the ewe trotting along the fence toward the back corner of the garage. A bin and grain scoop just inside the unlocked door. Juno followed me inside and nosed around. "You're out of luck, girl. Just because it smells like a milk house doesn't mean you'll find milk." It was an old-fashioned set-up, a far cry from today's high-tech operations. But the buckets and strainer, the utility sink, that lingering milky smell – milk house.

I bent to scoop oats to feed the still bleating Fluffy when Juno gave out a happy yelp. She raised her head with the you-can't-catch-me look that let me know she shouldn't have whatever she'd found. She lunged for the door, but I was closer and slammed it before she could get out.

"Oh no you don't. What've you got?" She crouched and gave a low growl. "Leave it!" She whined a protest. "Juno!" She pouted like the toddler she was and dropped her treasure.

I picked it up and forestalled her jump with a stern, "Sit!" A yellow Styrofoam tray. I sniffed. Beef, with a tinge of something... So this was how he got the drug in Dutch. The worm.

"Not for you, pup," I told Juno. I bent to rub her ears. "Don't want to make another vet run." I held the tray out of reach and opened the door.

A faint whirring sound had Juno's ears perked. I looked around but wouldn't have seen anything amiss until I followed Juno's nose. Above the door, a small round device. Camera. Aimed toward the house.

I froze and the hair stood up on the back of my neck. As if it pointed at me instead. As it had minutes before. When I thought I was alone… I cringed. When I might have done any number of things a guy does when he's alone. Did I pick my nose? Take a leak? Scratch my balls? What did the worm behind the camera see me do? It was a damn invasion of privacy!

My privacy. That's all I thought about. For the first minute. And then I really got pissed off. The worm wasn't spying on me. He was watching Kat. My hand went up to swat the damn thing down. Until her voice rang out in my head. "My house."

My hand dropped. Did she put it there? A security system? No. All that talk about how the intruder got in. She'd have said. Wouldn't she? Still… Either way, she should be the one to take it down. Not me.

Another whir, quiet enough to escape notice – unless you were right on top of it. I took a closer look, careful to stay behind the camera's eye. Where did it aim? The house, I thought. Back porches, the kitchen door, Kat's bedroom window. My hand went up again, and it was tougher to resist the urge to bust the damn thing. Catching me scratch was one thing. Leering at Kat made me want blood.

I paced the small room. Fuming. Slapping my fist into my palm. Itching to knock the worm five ways to Sunday. Like I wanted to do when Paul shouted at her… It had to be him, I thought. Worse than a worm. A brother should protect his sister, not spy on her. I wanted to crush him.

Right. As if she'd thank me for that. No. Kat was an independent sort who valued being able to take care of herself. She wouldn't thank me for stepping in like some macho protector. Or for tattling on her brother. Her reaction to the intruder's mess made that clear. So I'd be the bearer of bad news again. She'd be mad, and I'd get the brunt, deserve it or not. I'd see suspicion, accusation in her eyes again.

Too bad, I thought. This wasn't about me. She had to know. And yeah. She had to be the one to decide what happened next. To take care of it herself. But...like it or not, I was here to stay. To protect her, like it or not. From the worm behind the camera, the worm who'd drugged her dog, the worm who was her brother.

The worm who was my client. I shrugged. Too bad about that too. Paul Patterson wouldn't be the first client I sent packing, nor likely the last. I couldn't let myself wonder if Kat would be the last woman I'd lose or just the only one who mattered.

I shook it off. Let the worm behind the camera think he won. For the time being. I stepped outside with Fluffy's oats. Let him see me here, that she's not alone, I thought. Let her decide what comes next.

I fed the ewe and took the scoop back inside without a single glance at the damn camera. I'd take Juno out front where we could meet Kat, intercept her before... We headed toward a gate to the front lawn till I thought twice. "No unlocked doors, girl. None we can't see." We went in through the kitchen, locked the door behind us, and went out the front.

A loop ran through my brain. "Stay afloat long enough to keep her safe. Later...so what if you drown. Stay afloat long enough..."

Kat

Dutch was still asleep when I stopped at the hardware store. But his tail gave a thump and one eye opened as I came out. "Coming back to yourself, boy? Hope so. Wouldn't mind your company next stop."

I sat for a moment after pulling into the space marked number five. No big deal, I thought. I'm just going into a guy's apartment. His empty apartment. I scanned the alley wondering who lived in the other upstairs apartments on the block, wondering how many watched me, how they'd start tongues wagging all over our small town.

Dutch stretched and sat up. As if to ask what we were doing here. "Right. Let's go get Whip's stuff. Wanna come? Of course you do. What a good dog."

I opened the door and waited while Dutch assessed the distance to the ground. "I'm asking too much. Poor old Dutch." But he jumped down and stayed by my side as I hurried to Whip's door.

Once inside, Dutch led the way as if he'd been here before. Familiar territory. Down a short hall, up a steep stairway. I looked at these apartments before I fell in love with my Victorian garret, so I knew the layout. Kitchen in back facing the alley, barely big enough to turn around. Another hall toward a fair-sized room at the front, bedroom off that.

Laundry basket at the foot of the bed, shirts and jeans hanging on the door, laptop on the coffee table – all exactly where Whip had said I'd find them. If I thought the kitchen was small, the bathroom was smaller. I bumped my elbow on the wall as I unplugged his razor from the outlet above the sink. He'd have to hold his breath in here, I thought, while my brain traveled to the last time I'd seen Whip in a bathroom. Mine. Standing naked in my shower. I turned away quick and bumped my other elbow.

I tossed razor and toothbrush in among the laundry, laid shirts across the top of the basket, and motioned toward the stairs. "Ready, boy?" Dutch thumped his tail and rose from a dog bed near a window. "Good idea." As his nails clicked down the stairs, I scooped up the dog bed, slung it atop the shirts, and hoisted the whole load onto my hip. "So he gets dog hair on his shirts. Fine with me."

WHIP

Juno and I were on our third tour of the lawn's perimeter when I spotted Kat's truck on the road. I got set to send her a signal, get her to stop out front, but I didn't have to. She hopped out and closed her door while Dutch scrabbled on the other side. He wanted out, wanted to check out this new dog on his turf. After what he'd been through, Kat hurried to do his bidding. Couldn't blame her.

I tightened Juno's lead. You can't know how they'll take it when two dogs meet for the first time. Dutch approached in a quick lope and I felt Juno quiver at my side. I hung on. He pulled up about a yard away, barked, and waited. No tail wag so he wasn't sure yet. But Juno was. She crouched in full wag, barked once, which Dutch took to mean, "Let's play!" He wagged back and I loosened my grip.

"They'll be okay," Kat said. "Dutch, this is Juno. She's a good girl. You'll like her."

Dutch angled his head at her and back at Juno, now straining on her lead. He seemed to take Kat's word. He came close and the sniff-fest began. I released Juno and off they went racing and chasing.

"He looks good as new," I said, watching them.

"Yeah." Her voice cracked. "He was still pretty dopey when I picked him up. But Doc said he checked out okay. No restrictions. I wasn't sure..." She sniffed. "He's okay."

I wanted to touch her, squeeze her shoulder, something. I jammed my hands in my pockets instead. "As long as they stay close. Juno doesn't know..."

"Dutch won't let her go by the road. It's in his breed to herd, to protect." She whistled and the dogs came dashing over. She bent over them both. "Dutch. No road. Keep Juno safe." You could almost see him nod. "And slow down a minute." He flopped on the ground at Kat's feet.

Juno tilted her head and crouched in another invitation to play, but when Dutch didn't budge, she dropped too. "You've got him well-trained."

"He came that way. Mostly." She crouched to pet her dog. "Dad got him from this trainer over in Morris. Specializes in Border Collies. He doesn't let his dogs go till they know something like two hundred commands." She stood, brushed grass off one knee. "Dad never learned more than a handful. Thought Dutch would manage the sheep all by himself. When that didn't work, he stopped trying. After I moved home, Dutch and I took to each other." She bent again. "Didn't we, boy? I spent a day up in Morris, tried to learn what I could." More pats. "But Dutch still knows about twenty times more than I do." She ruffled his fur, smoothed it again. "He's a good boy, he is."

"I hope he rubs off on Juno. She's got a lot of stubborn pup in her."

"And why not? She is a pup still." Kat reached a hand out to pet Juno, which was enough invitation for my dog to belly forward and thrust her big head in Kat's lap, pushing her off balance and down. She'd have to brush grass off more than her knee now. I could help her with that, I thought before I made myself step on the brakes.

How should I tell her about the camera? And where? Not while she faced the house. I hadn't seen one, but there could be another one out here. Tell her where he wouldn't see, wouldn't know we were onto him. So she'd get to choose what happened next. Not the worm, not me. Her.

"So...I got your stuff in the truck." She looked up and just as quickly turned her gaze back to the dogs – both crowding her lap. Lucky dogs. "I picked up new locksets at the hardware. Super deadbolts, Mac Harris said. I'll get them on the kitchen doors today. So...there's really no reason for you to stay..."

"Sure there is. You're still alone out here." I took a breath and tried to smooth the edge in my voice. She wouldn't get rid of me that easy. "Besides, now Dutch and Juno are such good buds, it'd be a shame to part them so soon. Don't you think?"

Her eyes lifted to mine and held with a look that said it was a lame excuse. She untangled herself from the dogs and pushed to a stand. Brushed the grass off the seat of her jeans. While I watched and contemplated drowning.

"Suit yourself. Just stay out of my way." She turned toward the truck. "It's a big house. You can stay on Dad's side."

I caught up with her, guessing the tree at the edge of the driveway offered as good a cover as any. "Kat, I..." I chickened out. "What's this?" I pointed at something round set into the lawn, stones, set in some sort of circle. "I can't figure it out," I said, trying not to sound like an idiot. "It's too small for a garden. Too rocky. But those rocks didn't just…I don't know…surface there. Not in such a perfect circle."

She rolled her eyes. But she stopped walking and faced me. "It's a millstone. My triple-great-grandfather ran a mill. On the creek. Carding wool mostly. We think. But this is a grinding millstone so he must have done that too. The next generation must have hauled this up here. Where it's a nuisance for mowing." Not to her, I thought. Not with the reverence that colored her voice as she spoke about her ancestors. But I could imagine her dad grousing as they steered a mower around it. Or her brother.

"I expect they used a push mower when they planted it? Not such a nuisance then." I looked at the sweep of lawn. "Had to take a long time though."

"Still does. Altogether there's more than an acre to mow. Mostly out here, but the north and south sides add up too." She looked at me, at the lawn, shrugged. "Well…" She started toward the truck again, but this time I was beside her. I aimed her steps so the tree would be between her and the house, stepped ahead so she'd have to stop or run into me. And you know what she chose.

"What are you doing? I said to keep out of my way."

"Wait a minute." I glanced back toward the house. If there was another camera there, it would see me, but not her. I took a breath. "I need to tell you something."

She narrowed her eyes. "What? Did something else happen?" She started to turn back toward the house, so I took hold of her shoulders to keep her facing away.

"No. I found something."

"What?"

"You didn't install a security system. Did you?"

Her face told me the answer.

"I didn't think so. Okay. So. You know that room at the back end of your garage?"

"The milk house. Used to be. Not since we got rid of... What about it?"

"I...Fluffy kept staring at the door, bleating her head off, so I figured that's where her feed was. When I was in there getting her grain, I...well, Juno...found a meat tray. Smelled bad."

"That's how... Dutch?"

"I think so." I loosed one hand to push it through my hair. "But there's more. It's why I wanted to talk to you here so you can decide without being watched."

"Watched? Who? Wh..."

"Don't look." I took her shoulders again. "Nobody's in in the house."

"I don't understand."

I nodded. "Yeah. The thing is..." I swallowed once like a coward before I came out with it. "There's a camera. Like you'd see in a store. Above the door of the milk house."

"A camera?" The confusion on her face deepened before her eyes went wide, unfocused and afraid. "Justin." It was barely more than a whisper.

My hand tightened on her. "What'd you say? Who's Justin?"

Kat

A hundred emotions rushed at me – none of them good. I tried to shake them off – shake the jumble in my head to find coherent thought. But the shake went to my belly, to my knees, so I had to grab Whip's arm to hang on.

"Who's Justin?" Louder now. Sharp. Rough.

I brought my eyes to his, squeaked out, "No…nobody." I pulled back, started to turn, but Whip was in my face again. How did he expect me to gather my thoughts when he kept staring at me like that? I pulled away again, pushed my palm toward his chest. "Back off. Give me a minute."

He took one step back but kept staring. Unspoken questions shot from his eyes. Darts and I was the dartboard. "Wait."

I needed to lean – on the truck – not him. I put my hands on the chill of the truck fender, grateful for its support. I closed my eyes against the swirl in my head. Not Justin. Too long ago. Couldn't be. Could, said the milk-toast part of my brain. Not likely, said the sliver of rationality left. I breathed deep, told myself to focus. Here and now. Not then.

"Camera? Milk house?"

"Yeah. Above the door." He was beside me now, close enough to feel the gravitational pull of his shoulder.

I straightened in a flimsy show of strength. "You left it there?"

From the corner of my eye I saw him nod. "Your place." He looked out toward the fields like me. "I…thought you should be the one to decide what to do."

I took a ragged breath. For a fleeting moment, I let myself wonder what it would be like to dump all the damn decisions I insisted on making in someone else's lap. Like what to say. What to do. No clue.

"Besides," said Whip, when I didn't reply. "I thought you might be able to use it somehow."

"Use it? The camera?"

"To send a message. To the…worm who put it there."

"A message."

"Yeah. He got me on tape this morning. Before I knew the damn thing was there. So now he knows you're not all alone here."

I turned my head, met his eyes. "And when the sheriff gets here…"

"Right." Whip's hand went through his hair. "You called them? The sheriff?"

I shook my head, moving to the driver's door. "Not yet. But I'm going to now. Meet me out back. Let him see you unload your stuff."

The idea started to hatch before I turned the key, but it wasn't till I rounded the last bend in the driveway that the idea morphed into a plan. In the few remaining yards up the incline to the back doors, I wondered if I could pull it off. Whip stepped out the kitchen door – a straight line of sight from the milk house. Damn the torpedoes, I thought as I jumped out of the truck and rushed him.

I took him by surprise, almost toppling us both as I leapt into his arms. He recovered, thankfully, in time to stop us crashing on concrete. Nor did he recoil when I crushed my lips to his. I felt his intake of breath before he crushed back, and I wondered when – and how – I'd breathe again.

As plans go, it was undoubtedly effective. I struggled to surface but the undertow was fierce, stealing breath and brain. In the end, it was clapboard edges digging into my spine that wrenched my attention from the flood of sensations. I loosened my grip on Whip's hair and pushed his chest away from mine. Tried to think.

Great gulps of air and still not enough oxygen. *Think!* Something I was supposed to do. What? It came rushing back. Camera. I darted a glance at the milk house door, back at Whip. "Inside," I croaked. His eyes, already lit with a thousand campfires, flared.

"No. Wait." More gulps of non-oxygenated air. "Your stuff. Back of the truck."

He held my eyes. Did the campfires dim? I couldn't tell and couldn't – if I were to save myself – make the effort to see. He nodded. Stepped back and oxygen poured in to fan my burning cheeks.

I jerked myself through the door and stumbled to the counter where I could lean again.

WHIP

I'd have been happy to let my stuff rot. Or blow to Indiana after that kiss. But Kat had that stunned, scared look in her eyes, the same as when I first kissed her at the Lodge. Maybe in the minute or two it took to haul my stuff in, she'd settle and be ready...to talk, to clear away the roadblocks she'd put between us.

As if my thoughts were orderly. Or what I wanted was talk. Jesus. One taste and I wanted to devour her. Wanted to start that kiss all over again – and finish it too. In the light of day, the dark of night, and everything in between.

I should have known it wouldn't go that way. But my brain was fogged in a sex-starved haze. So while I wrestled the laundry basket through the door, I called, suave as an overheated sophomore, "So, where were we?"

Which was when I should have asked "Where are you?" Not in the kitchen. Nor in the next room or the alcove off that. Odd that my brain, only now emerging from my pants, should pick this moment to wonder what she called these rooms. Dining room? Family room? Office? Didn't matter. She wasn't in any of them.

I don't mind saying this was not the scenario I played in my head during that stupid two minutes I went to the truck instead of holding on to her. I started down the hall toward the collection of other rooms I didn't know what to call but came to a quick stop between closed doors on either side. At least I knew what those doors led to – bedroom on one side, bathroom on the other. Both doors closed tight. To keep me out.

I got it then, a big boatload of logical thought. Ice-cold water dousing the fires she lit. On purpose. For the camera. Not because she wanted me. Hadn't she made it abundantly clear she wanted nothing to do with me? She put on a show. For the worm behind the camera. I was just a handy prop.

My poor bedraggled brain drained from my pants into legs that paced down that hall and into the next son-of-a-bitchin' room, the one where she ran the fucking saw that screamed me awake mere hours earlier. I pitched the laundry basket down in a spill of underwear and shirts, black dots of rage dancing in front of my eyes. In a few more seconds, I'd have upended that saw and who knows what else. But I tripped over a hunk of two-by-four, so I almost went to my knees.

I righted myself and gave a vicious kick that sent that hunk of lumber hammering into the woodwork six inches from Kat's foot. How long had she been there? She jumped and looked at me like I wore a black hat and had a six-shooter cocked in each hand.

I pointed an accusing finger. "You used me. Didn't you?"

She hung her head. Embarrassed. Guilty. "I... You said to use the camera..."

My eyes rolled as if propelled. I took a step toward her. "So you...you made this big show...kissing my brains out...to...what? When you *know* how I feel about you? How I..." I stopped. Closed my eyes and tried to get my breathing under control.

"I'm...sorry?"

Around went my eyes again, despite efforts to rein them in. "It was a lousy thing to do, Kat! Don't..." What? I forced myself to take a deep breath. "I'm not some toy. Don't use me." I turned, took long strides toward the front door. "I'm going for a walk. Don't...come on to me...not unless you mean it. Because next time? I won't be walking." One glare and I went, letting the door slam behind me.

Kat

I felt awful. Like a worm. Wasn't that what he called…whoever put up that camera? I'm not one bit better, I thought. Worm.

Whip was right. It was a lousy thing to do. And if I'd thought it all the way through, I'd never… I wouldn't have twelve kinds of egg dripping off my face. Or a heart that pounded in my throat.

I lifted my hand to my lips and felt heat rising. Again? Still? I thought I'd known passion before, but this? This was Kilauea erupting, hot lava scorching everything in sight. Not safe. And I wanted more.

I pulled the door open to follow him, to…apologize, beg maybe… I don't know. He hadn't gone far – and he'd come back with a stomp, dogs bouncing at his heels.

"In!" He pointed to the door. "And stay there."

I stepped back. Until I saw he meant the dogs, not me. He didn't meet my eyes – not even when his next words were meant for me.

"Lock the doors. Kitchen too. Stay inside."

He was halfway across the lawn before I managed to find my voice. "Wait. Please."

He stopped, sighed without turning. "Don't worry. I'll head to the fields." He ran a hand through his hair. "I won't go out back, won't wreck your little charade."

"What if..." He kept walking. Maybe he didn't hear. It wouldn't be surprising, the trouble I had getting sound past the lump in my throat. I started to run. I had to make him stop, make him listen, make him...see. "Whip! Wait!" No response. I shouted, "What if I don't *want* it to be a charade?"

He pulled up short, so quick I almost mowed him down. His hand was in his hair as he turned – quicker still so I cowered back a step. "Look." The fury was tamped down. Still there, but under control. I thought. "I get it. You wanted to show...the camera...something. And I was handy." His eyes bored into mine. "Fine. But I'm telling you now. Don't do it again. I am not some...toy."

"I know. I'm...Whip, I'm sorry. I...didn't mean... I was scared..."

He held up a hand. "Crying isn't going to work. Not this time."

"No...I..." Why couldn't I talk? Make him see.

"If you're so scared, you need to call the sheriff – not involve me in some...farce."

I took a ragged breath. "I will. I was going to. And then... I forgot." Could my face get any hotter? But I had to go on. "It wasn't a farce, Whip. Not...all."

He rolled his eyes and started to turn away again.

"Wait. Please. Hear me out."

"Fine." A hand came up in a gesture that said I-won't-believe-a-word-you-say-but-go-ahead-give-it-your-best-shot as clearly as if printed on the *Chicago Tribune*'s front page.

"I...I'm scared. Not just about the camera." I closed my eyes, tried to summon courage. "You...scare me too."

"Me?" Hand though hair. "What have I ever done to scare you, Kat? Jesus! I have been upfront with you all the way. Tried to protect you from that...rotten brother of yours. Stayed here last night so you wouldn't be alone in this mausoleum of a house." Eyes to heaven. "Everything I've done has been to keep you safe, for God's sake."

"I know. That's..." I raised my eyes to his. "That's not what I meant." I swallowed hard. "You...make me...feel...things. *That's* what scares me."

He narrowed his eyes. "You trying to tell me that...kiss...was because you feel something for me? Give me a break!"

I grabbed at his hand to keep him from turning away again. "N...no. Not...not...at the start. But...I... Things changed."

He didn't say anything for so long, I hugged my arms tight to my body. Bolstering myself to keep explaining. Make him see.

"It was a lousy thing to do. To...jump you that way. Why I did it." I swallowed. "I shouldn't have put you in that...position. You're...right to be mad." I snuck a glance at his face. A marble sculpture would give more away. "But...I don't think...I...would have done it if...I hadn't...didn't...want... To kiss you. Deep down, I mean."

"And that scares you." A different tone to his voice?

I nodded. "Yes."

"Why?" He looked off to the south hills as if my answer didn't matter at all.

"Because...you're...different...from other men I've known."

His gaze swung back to me. "Different."

I nodded. "And...I...I haven't been very smart...with men...before."

"So, I'm different. And that scares you." Something – maybe a laugh – flashed across his face.

I hesitated a beat while I studied the ground between us. Then, "Yes."

He let out a breath. "So what do we do now, Kat?"

I shook my head, shrugged. "Maybe you come back inside while I call the sheriff? There are...things you should know. But...I'd rather not go through it twice... If that's okay?"

I felt his eyes on me. "And us? You and me?"

"Can we take that slow?" What a wimp I was.

He barked out a laugh. "Slow, she says! Honey, did you ever pour molasses in January?" He shoved his hand through hair and looked at me. Then he sighed and slung an arm around me. A light hug as we turned back toward the house. Nothing to make my pulse race or blood hammer in my ears. "Okay. You're the traffic cop. But fair warning? I like kissing you. And I'll want to do that again – sooner than later."

Me too, I thought. My hand went to my mouth. Did I say that out loud?

WHIP

"By the way," I said as we went in the front door. "I don't think there's a camera out front."

Her hand went to her mouth. "I…didn't think about that."

"I guessed as much." Too bad. She might have jumped me again. My mouth twitched. Or not, considering how I bit her head off the first time. "I got a good look. Didn't see anything out there.

"Why…why would someone…spy on me?"

"On us." That lovely flush crept up her neck. "At a guess, to see when you're – we're – not around?"

"So he saw me leave last night? So he could drug poor Dutch? Break in?"

"He used a key."

"Right. I got new locksets."

"For all, what? Nine doors?"

"Seven. No. The hardware didn't have that many in stock. And the budget only stretched to three. For now."

I lifted my hands. "It's a start. I'll help you install them."

I watched her lift her chin and expected her to say she didn't need help. She didn't, I knew. But part of me wished she did. "Sheriff first," she said.

"Even better. Did you get lunch in town?"

"No."

"I'll put something together while you call. Depending on what I can find in your kitchen."

"Soup? In the freezer."

"Perfect."

I figured she'd want privacy to make the call. And I needed a moment myself. To recover? Celebrate? Figure out my next moves? Or lack of moves? She wanted – needed, I guessed – patience. I could give her that. Unless it killed me. But since the unattainable seemed possible for the first time, I could do anything.

For the first time, I glimpsed the shore I'd been swimming to. A future. Right here. I looked around, trying to see myself in this big impractical house. Lots of room for a home office, I thought. And all those upstairs bedrooms to fill with kids. My heart flopped around inside my chest. Hungry mouths. Braces. College tuition. A laughed sputtered. So much for going slow. The thought echoed when she stepped back in the kitchen.

"They're sending a deputy out. Sometime this afternoon," she said. She looked up. And away.

Keep your feet on the ground, I thought. "Soup's almost ready."

She nodded and stepped to the drawer opposite the stove where I stood – carefully, as if not wanting to get too close. I brushed a hand down her sleeve – casual, light. Just a friendly little touch and watched her whole body go still. Frozen.

I let my hand drop and she moved again, gathering silverware from the drawer, a jar of crackers from a shelf. As we ate, she seemed withdrawn, preoccupied. I was too, but I suspected different things consumed our thoughts. Mine were all on her, wanting to touch, taste, devour her. Hers? I had no idea, but it didn't feel like they were on me.

Not done swimming, I thought. Or the shore was just as tricky as the current.

#

Lunch was awkward – more my fault than his. It's not that I had second thoughts about what I'd said. Not exactly. It was that I couldn't seem to breathe with him so close. I felt like a seventh-grader at her first dance. Tongue-tied, shy, embarrassed to be alive. Could he hear me swallow? The way my heart raced?

Worse was imagining what he'd think when he heard about Justin. I said I hadn't been smart about men. What an understatement. I was a disaster. Why would any sane man want to tie himself to me after hearing that sorry tale?

But maybe Whip wasn't sane. What did I really know about him? Except that he...ignited something in me. Damn cheeks for one. All the damn time. Did he notice? I didn't dare sneak a peek – not when I felt his eyes boring into my skull. I wished for something more substantial than hair to hide behind.

Eat, I thought. So what if you can't taste it. Get it gone. One spoonful and the next. Finally I could push away from the table. As I carried my bowl to the sink, I managed a few words. "Got those lock-sets to install."

"Want help?"

I shook my head so fast I was surprised he didn't hear my brain rattle. "No. I..." What excuse could I give? "I can do it myself. Need to...show I can do it. The...camera."

From the corner of my eye I saw him hesitate, shrug. "Okay. I'll...clean up here."

I shook my head again. "You don't have to..."

"Might as well be useful. My mother trained me well."

I nodded once and bolted for the door. So not good with men. The air helped. If I didn't think about the milk house. Act natural. Don't look. I retrieved the locksets from the cab of the truck and glanced at the instructions before I remembered I'd need tools. I'd go through Dad's back door, I thought. No go. The deadbolt held firm. Good, I thought. Except I'd have to go back through Gram's – my – side. Where Whip was.

I thought. Until he opened Dad's door and handed out my toolbox. His other hand cupped the base of my neck, nudged me close. He nuzzled at my cheek, whispered in my ear, "Smile for the camera," before he drew back into the doorway.

Payback. Fair was fair. I pasted on a smile of sorts and got to work. I hadn't planned to replace locks. But it was high time. Made sense. It was right to start with the back doors too – even though those were more modern than the rest. But we used the back doors, rarely opened the others. Deadbolts had always been enough.

Until last night, I thought, and bent to the task. But if he – the worm – tried again, his key wouldn't fit. I didn't let myself wonder who that worm might be.

I had the first set installed, new key on my ring, when the crunch of gravel sent the dogs scampering to the side yard. A white car with the sheriff's emblem came around the curve by the poplar and pulled up in front of the garage. Not in the camera's range.

Whip stepped out. I knew we had the same thought. "It's okay. He's backing up the hill now." His hand came over mine. "They like to face out. In case they get a call. Now the worm will see him." He paused. "Do you want me to make myself scarce?"

"No. I... Stay. Please," I said as the deputy got out of the car.

"Ms. Patterson?"

"Yes. Kat." I stepped forward.

"Chad Miller. You called about a break-in?" The deputy paused, looked toward Whip.

"Milly?" Whip said, moving forward to shake the deputy's hand.

"Whip Tyler. I heard you were back in town. How you been?"

WHIP

Milly was a year behind me in school, played JV football with Scott and me. You know it's a small school when a fireplug like Milly can make the team. But he was tough, a scrapper. A good guy.

"Didn't know you were a cop, Milly," I said.

"Six years now. About the time I became Chad again," he said.

He cast an appraising eye at me, at Kat, and I watched him connect the dots – the rumors after Scott died, me here with Scott's sister who had wide eyes turned my way.

"You two know each other?"

"Way back, ma'am." Milly…Chad…reached to shake her hand. "Knew your brothers too, back in the day." He grinned. "Met you once, I think, when I was here haying. Dinner." He rubbed his stomach. "Your mom was a helluva cook."

Her lips turned up, but her eyes stayed uneasy. "My gram. Ham or roast beef?"

"Good is what I remember. And there was this pie…"

"Rhubarb pineapple. Gram's specialty. I'll give you the recipe. After... Come inside."

Milly followed her in, stooping to pet the dogs, chatting about food and the hard work of haying. Putting her at ease. Or trying. She gestured toward the mess of papers on the floor, on the counter. Told him about finding Dutch, how we got him to the vet.

I felt Milly study me. "Handy that you were here, Whip," Milly said, and I wondered how to respond.

Before I could, Kat jumped in to answer the implied question. "It was. Whip followed me home from his mother's last night. Even though I thought it was silly." She sent me a glance. "I'm used to being alone, always felt safe before. But it was good he was here. Dutch..." Her voice broke as she kneeled by her dog. "He might have died. Doc said we got him there just in time."

"I checked the house – before we took the dog to Doc's and after we got back. Found this mess. Everything locked up. Except the front door." I pointed.

"It was. Earlier. Deadbolt from the inside." Kat stood. "So..." She glanced at me, nodded. "Whoever...was here had a key."

"And the camera?" Milly asked.

"I found it. By accident. This morning." I told how I went to the milk house looking for feed, how Juno found the meat tray, the whir that made me look up. "Seemed like...somebody...wanted to keep tabs on Kat, when she was gone, that sort of thing."

"You left it there."

I nodded. "Kat was at the vet, bringing the dog home. I thought she should decide what to do."

"And you called us after Whip found the camera?"

Kat nodded. "Till then, I thought...well, I thought this," she gestured toward the papers scattered over the floor, "was my brother's doing...a family matter."

"Would your brother drug your dog? Break in when you weren't here?"

She fixed her gaze on the floor, shrugged. "Paul...can be...impetuous."

"Where's Paul living these days?"

"Downers Grove."

"Not so far. Hour and a half?"

"Less, I think. He...likes to drive fast."

"So you think he broke in. But you don't think he's behind the camera?"

"I...don't know. He's not...happy with me these days." She swallowed. "But it...feels like..." The color rose in her cheeks. "I had some trouble...in college. Boyfriend trouble."

Kat

I hated thinking about Justin, the mistakes I made. And I liked talking about him even less. But I had to get it out. I moved into Dad's dining room, suggested we sit at Mother's table.

I swallowed, took a deep breath, and began. "If you check the records," I told the deputy, "you'll find an order of protection issued against Justin Carpenter. He…" I couldn't pin all the blame on him. "I made mistakes with Justin, trusted him when I shouldn't have." I told myself to stick to the facts. "It ended…badly. And…he…bothered me…after."

"Did he hurt you?" I flinched at the tone in Whip's voice.

I shook my head. "N…no." I swallowed. "He…followed me…a few times." More than a few. "Enough…so… It scared me."

"How long ago was this?"

"Eight years. April." I was thankful for the deputy's matter-of-fact tone.

"And you've not heard from him since?"

I hesitated. "That May. A phone call. He left a message. He was engaged…wanted me to know." How wonderful she was, how she satisfied him like I never had. More hateful things. "I tried to reach out to her – to warn her." I took a deep breath. "And that started more calls. Him showing up. Again." I shook my head. "I reported it. Changed my cell number. Came home."

"Nothing since?"

"No."

Whip was on his feet. "You think he'd spy on you? Train a camera on your bedroom?"

The violence in Whip's tone scared me. "N…no?" I gripped the arms of the chair where I sat. "Why would he? After all this time? But…it's possible?"

"Where's this guy live?"

"I don't know. I…never wanted to know. Sycamore when we were…together. Now? I don't know."

"I'll google him." Whip reached for his phone, but the deputy held up a hand.

"We'll take care of that," he said. To me, he added, "Like you said, it would be odd for him to turn up again now. But you were right to bring it up so we can check it out. So…I'm guessing you want the camera gone?"

I breathed out. "Yes. Please."

"Wait," Whip interrupted. "We need to know who put it there. Can you figure that out, trace the device somehow?"

The detective grinned. "I can't. But our IT guys might. Let me get all the details down, make sure my report is complete."

He made notes, repeated them, looked at me to verify he got it all right. Then to Whip, "You want to add anything?"

Whip shook his head. "Just get the IT guys here quick."

The detective nodded. "I'll call it in from the car. Excuse me."

"I'll walk you out," said Whip.

I stayed where I was, glad to have a moment alone. Gladder not to have to face Whip. What kind of idiot must he think I was?

Dutch stirred at my feet and cocked his head as if to ask, "What are you doing here? You never sit here."

"I never used to sit here," I said. "You forget, Dutch. The whole house is mine now." I shrugged as I stood. "I know. I'm not used to it either." But as I peered out at the two men in my driveway, I said it again. "The whole house is mine. And I protect what's mine."

WHIP

"What do you think, Mil…er…Chad?"

"Don't fuss yourself, Whip. I never minded the nickname. Made me feel like I belonged on the team."

"You did."

"It was a good team. We missed you when you left."

The things he didn't say swarmed so I figured we might as well open the hive. "Didn't want to go. But…under the circumstances, it was probably better."

He nodded. "We missed the both of you."

I had to blink and turn my head, but he didn't seem to notice. Or if he did, he went on anyway. "Scott would like you being here now."

"You think?"

"Oh yeah. As tight as you two were?" He sighed. "There were rumors, some that blamed you. Not the guys on the team. We knew you. And we knew Paul Patterson."

"I…" What could I say?

"So. We'll get a geek out here to check out the camera. See if we can tell who's behind it. Could be the stalker.

But my money's on her brother." He leveled eyes at me. "And you need to be ready. Because once we find out, the rat – whoever he is – will surface. Just seeing me here could flush him out."

"We…I thought he should see Kat's not on her own."

Milly nodded. "Good plan for a start. We'll do what we can. Drive-bys, look-sees. But we don't have the manpower to sit here. Get her to take a trip. It's the best way to make sure she's safe."

"I thought the same thing," I said. "For about two seconds. She won't go."

"You brought it up already."

I shook my head. "No point. She's…invested. Dug in. Paul too, in a whole different way. It's an odd set-up." I dragged a hand through my hair. "Upshot is, he gets farmland. Not the woods which he sees as the best for development. For money."

"He wants what she gets?"

"Unless I can convince him he'll make just as much another way." We were outside now. One hand on his car door, Milly gave me a stare.

"You in the middle here, Whip?"

I shook my head. "I'm on her side. All the way. Paul's a client. Maybe. Says he wants to hire me. He's approached some other guys too. Not the reputable sort. So… I figured I can protect Kat's interests if I work with him. Maybe." I shook my head again. "But no matter what, if he comes after her – or what she cares about – he'll have to get through me first."

"So you are in the middle," he said, opening the car door. "Tell Kat I'll be back in soon as I make my report."

Kat

When Whip came back inside, I was boiling water for a cup of tea. It seemed a good time to test the British theory that tea is the antidote to any bad thing.

Justin was in my head, showing up outside my classes, shouting up at my dorm window, parked outside the library where I worked. The reason I cried on the phone to Gram and sneaked off campus, my tail between my legs. All because I wasn't smart enough to see it coming.

I shivered. And saw Whip watching from the door. I wished myself away, wished I'd never brought up Justin. And when those wishes didn't come true, I turned away, busied myself at the stove, reached for teabags in the cupboard.

"Geez, Kat." He prowled the room. Back and forth.

I went still, watched his shadow cross the floor, knew without seeing how he ran his hand through his hair. Who knows how long he might have paced if the whistle from the tea kettle didn't jar us both. I poured steaming water into a mug, reached for a second. "Tea?" I asked.

"No!" He stopped pacing, took three steps toward me. Too close. "How long did he stalk you?"

Stay calm. "A few months. That's all." It seemed a lot longer, but he didn't need to know that.

There went his hand. "Jesus. The guy sounds certifiable." He paced again, two steps away, three steps back. "But he didn't hurt you? Lay hands on you?"

I shook my head. He didn't need the details. "I don't know what you're so angry about. It happened to me, not you." The temper felt good. Strong. In a more measured tone, I added, "It was a long time ago. I'm...smarter now. It won't happen again."

"Damn straight it won't! He'll have to go through me first!"

Tea sloshed as I slammed the mug down on the counter. "Ouch! Dammit."

"Here. Run your hand under cold water." He had me by the arm, steering me toward the sink. I shook him off.

"Let go! It's nothing." Then, because he kept steering, I growled, "Back off!"

"What...I'm just trying to..."

"Run my life, dammit! Jeepers, you men are all alike! I can take care of myself! I do *not* need you or anybody else telling me what I can do, what I can't. Understand me? Never again!"

He took a step back, raised palms toward me. "I wasn't..."

I took a deep breath. "You were." Calm. I reached for calm. Another breath. "Listen. I made a big mistake once. Let myself get...lost. Let a man call all the shots. Let him be more important than my own self-respect."

Another breath. "I won't…can't…let that happen again. Not ever."

"I…"

"I mean it. You're what made me think about Justin. You deciding I'm not safe alone, insisting on staying here. You do *not* get to make those decisions. I do!"

"But…"

"No buts! Do you think I don't know this place is too big for one person? Do you think I'm willing to take a chance that Justin…or…whoever…might take some kind of potshot at me? Or my dog?" I pushed him out of my way so I could prowl like he had. "Okay. Two people and two dogs are safer here than one alone. I get it. But if you think I'm some hothouse flower who'll swoon over the first sign of trouble and lay down and let some *man* take over? Forget it!"

"I…"

"And furthermore, if this," I made air quotes with my fingers, "attraction you say you feel for me has anything to do with thinking I'm some incapable ninny, you can just pack up your…laundry basket and hit the road! I don't need it. Or you!" I squared up to him, narrowed my eyes, and stuck my finger at his chest. "Don't you laugh at me!"

WHIP

I tried not to, but the laugh was too big to swallow. I raised my hands as if she held a loaded gun. "I'm not," I said. "Not at you. I promise." I bent over the counter, trying to catch my breath between spasms. "Sorry. It's me," I gasped. "I'm the one who's funny. Here I am going all he-man, thinking I'm protecting my woman, when you...you are magnificent, Kat!"

She stared, eyes still slitted, still fuming.

"I mean it. Look at all you do, all you can do. This place, bringing it back like you have, the carpentry, the...*sheen* you put on it all. Hothouse flower is the last thing you are." I sobered. "I've never had much use for hothouse anything – nor ninnies. Not into saving somebody else. I swear it."

"You damn well better not try."

"Got it. But do I want you to be safe? From any creep who'd stoop so low? To spy on you, hurt your dog? Guilty."

She rolled her eyes, but I kept going.

"Or hurt you...scare you? I don't care how long ago it was. You're strong. I know it. But this guy? He scared you. I've got eyes, Kat. You're not the type to take out a protection order for no reason." I stepped close, cupped her chin, made my voice gentle. "He scares you still, or you wouldn't go pale talking about him all these years later."

Her eyes, fiery a minute before, dropped, closed tight like there were tears behind her lids. "That doesn't mean you get to act like some...Neanderthal." Her voice shook, but when her eyes came back to mine, the fire was back.

I smiled. "Right. I...reverted. Can't promise it won't happen again. I got as much Neanderthal drilled into me as the next guy." I shrugged. "Hard to crack."

Her eyes went to slits. "Try."

I laughed and was relieved to see a snap of humor soften her face. "Will do." I gave her a wink and added, "Might be I'll need reminding. Might be I can count on you for that?"

"Trust me."

I wondered, should I press my point? "And maybe you could count on me?" I held up my hands. "Not to take over. But to help...handle whatever comes next? If I promise not to handle it for you, will you let me handle it with you?"

"I...don't know." She turned away. "It's hard...for me to...trust...now."

I had to know. "Trust in general? Or trust me?"

She sighed. "Part of the same picture. I guess."

"Because of your – of Paul? The land?"

"Not that." She shrugged. "You said you'd do what you can. I believe you. Mostly." She lifted her hands. "But you're a Neanderthal. By nature. So...not easy to trust...that you won't think you're in charge all the damn time."

Relief brought another laugh. I caught at her hand, pulled her around so she had to look me in the eyes. "Try."

Kat

A rap at the door made both of us jump. How did we forget the deputy was still there? Our eyes locked a second. Longer?

Whip grinned. "There's somebody at your door." He stepped back.

I rolled my eyes at him before I went to let the deputy in.

He doffed his hat and stood holding it in two hands. His demeanor had changed. No less professional, but there was something different. I couldn't put my finger on it until I realized he had bad news.

"What is it?"

He nodded as if grateful to be asked. "Our IT guys are backed up. They'll try to get someone out here, but not till tomorrow morning at the earliest." He glanced at Whip. "I can disable the camera for you. But…"

"Whoever put it there knows we're onto him whether we disable the camera or not – and might not wait till tomorrow to…do something. Is that it?" He looked surprised, glanced at Whip, who shook his head. I saw. The Neanderthals thought the little woman was too dense to put it together all by herself. Score one.

The deputy nodded. "Could be he'll be scared off. Or…not."

"Right." I took a long breath, sucked in my cheeks. "Well. Forewarned."

"I looked up Justin Carpenter. Got a photo on my phone. This the guy you knew?"

I looked at his phone and raised quick eyes to the deputy. "A mug shot?"

He nodded. "Arraigned on domestic violence three times in the last two years. Charges didn't stick."

I felt the blood drain from my face, put a hand back to grip the table, pulled out a chair and sat hard. "Domestic…"

The deputy nodded again. "He's on the Sycamore PD radar, but they couldn't tell me if he's left town lately."

"So…he could be…the guy behind the camera."

"Or…not. They'll investigate. Will let us know." He fiddled with his hat again. "But for now…we can't say."

Juno plopped her head in my lap, and I bent over her to get a grip on myself. I let myself take one deep breath before I straightened. "Thank you for checking."

"So what now, Milly? We wait? Not knowing who might… Or when?" Whip was like a wolf straining at a leash. "That…sucks!"

Milly nodded. "It does, Whip. Big time." He lifted his palms, hat dangling from one hand. "I can check back. Give you my direct number. But you'll get a squad car just as fast – probably faster – dialing 911."

I stood and held out my hand. "I understand. Thank you, Deputy. I hope we won't need to call you again, but please know how much I appreciate your time and your...professionalism. I'll see you out."

WHIP

I trailed behind them, hoping for another private word with Milly, get his advice...or something. But Kat wasn't having it. I saw how she rankled when Milly looked to me. She had staked her territory and made her position clear. She was in charge here and I'd better not overstep – or she wouldn't let me help at all.

We stood together as we watched Milly leave, heard the gravel crunch from the other side of the house and the acceleration of his car as it hit the highway. Now what? The place was vulnerable. So many doors, windows. "We should..." I turned to lay out a plan – not that I had one.

But she was already on the move. In long strides, she sorted through tools on the back porch she still called her dad's. She picked up a hammer and without giving me a single glance, strode determinedly toward the milk house.

"Kat. Wait!"

"No. I'm tired of being watched."

"But..." I stopped. Couldn't disagree. The jig was up one way or another. And I couldn't help but enjoy the crack as she reached up with the hammer and dispatched the damn camera with a single blow. Or smile as she chased down fragments and whacked them into dust.

She grinned as she dusted hands against thighs. And then she picked up the hammer, marched back to the porch, and bent to the task of unscrewing the old lockset and fixing the new one in place.

Dutch sauntered onto the porch to collapse at Kat's side. Juno looked to me, tongue lolling. "Might as well join them." I took a seat on the porch step. "Down." My dog dropped at my feet, her pout worthy of a teenaged girl. Dog language for "Why can't someone – preferably her – touch me?" I relented and put a hand on her head. Why else would you have a dog? And I wanted to be the one to intrude on Kat's attention.

"You know we might get…company tonight."

"Might."

"Any chance you'd come stay at my place? Or Darcy and Luke's? It'd be…safer."

"No."

"Didn't think so. Had to ask." No response. I let a moment pass before I asked, "What can I do? To…help you…be ready. In case?"

Kat

I sat back on my heels. "You're asking?"

He grinned. "Trying."

Okay. I'd try too. "What do you want to do?"

"Short of scooping you up and getting you far away from here?"

"Yeah. Short of that."

"You've got a lot of doors, Kat. A lot of windows."

"So you think we'll have trouble. Tonight."

He shrugged. "I think you – we – ought to be…ready. In case."

I looked down. "I don't understand what he wants. Why he'd come here."

"Why he watched you?"

I shook my head. "If it's Justin…well…there was a lot about Justin I didn't understand."

"Maybe it would help us be ready...if I knew more? About him?"

I stiffened, not eager to trot out my ninny-time again. Neanderthal, I thought. Makes damn sure to keep his own secrets but thinks he's entitled to mine. I yanked at the plastic holding the deadlock and felt it slice. I sucked on the finger and muttered, "Damn packaging."

"Can I...?" At my glare he raised his hands in what was becoming a familiar gesture. "Sorry." A sheepish half-grin.

It was enough to settle my anger. He could be at risk too because he was here. So he had a right to know. And it came out easier than I expected.

"Freshman year. Northern." I pulled a face. "I thought I'd love it – on my own at last. I was wrong."

"Homesick?"

I nodded and saw from his face that he knew what it felt like. "Like being pulled up from the roots," I said. "And bombarded with all these people who didn't care – didn't notice I existed. I didn't fit in, couldn't relate or connect. Not in my classes, the dorm..." I closed my eyes, tried to block out the crushing loneliness, trying to feel as invisible as I seemed to be, this geeky country girl eating alone in the dorm cafeteria.

"You couldn't quit? Transfer someplace else?"

"No. Too many people...expected...more of me. I expected more of me."

Whip smiled. "I'm not surprised."

"Yeah well, I didn't live up to my expectations. Not in classes either. I did the work, but till midterms I had no idea if I was doing enough." I sighed, made myself keep going. "I met Justin right after my first exam. I was…scared…huddled over a coffee at the Student Union. He slid into the booth, said hello." I turned the last screw and sat back on my heels. "And that's all it took. He was older, a grad student, a commuter. He…had a way about him. Attentive, interested." I closed my eyes. "I fell hard. Like the sun came out after days of rain."

I bent to gather my tools. "Till the week before finals. Three papers due, two exams looming. Up against a wall – because I'd spent so much time with Justin instead of knuckling down. But when I said I couldn't see him – one night – he freaked."

Whip opened his mouth, but I held up a hand.

"Let me get through it."

Temper brewed behind Whip's eyes, but he pulled it back and nodded.

So I took a breath and went on. "A week later, Darcy drove up to take me home for Christmas break. I was so glad to see her, excited to introduce her to Justin, and just as eager to get home. I couldn't let him see how eager. He'd fished for an invitation, but I made some excuse. It didn't sit well, the idea of him here. The breathing space felt good. Being back, with Gram and Darcy, I saw…things I didn't see at school. For one thing, I saw how I'd pushed people away, people who might have been friends. And that Justin was part of that. He didn't want me to have anyone else. If I spent less time with him, maybe I could bring up my grades, keep my scholarship."

"And did you? When you went back?"

I lifted my hands. "I wish. I did insist on one night a week to myself, blamed it on folks at home laying down the law about my grades. He didn't like it, but I finally got him to agree. A few weeks later I had the chance to join a study group on a second night. He really didn't like that." No need to go into the scene he pitched. "But I did it anyway. And our relationship got...stormier. Jealousy can feel...flattering. Until it...smothers." I sighed.

"But breaking up is hard to do?"

I snorted, and the laugh brought back my resolve to finish the story once and for all. "Harder than I thought. It's easy to feel...trapped...like this is the bed I made so I have to lie down in it." I shook my head. "I volunteer a few times a month, do repair work at a home for battered women. They – the ones that make it out – are some of the bravest people I'll ever meet. They don't think so, but they are." It was a soapbox of mine, and I sent him a fierce look inviting him to argue. He didn't. His nod felt...good.

"I was lucky. And still it wasn't easy. He kept calling, kept showing up until Gram said I needed to get a protection order – to keep him away. It helped, but..." I waved a hand to chase away that nightmare time. "I came home. Finished my second semester from here. He couldn't get to me here. So he gave up. Or I...thought he did."

I narrowed my eyes at Whip. "I won't make that mistake again – trusting someone that doesn't deserve it."

WHIP

"Then I'd better deserve it, huh?" I tried to say it lightly, to swallow the jealousy, the fury her tale stirred. I reached out a hand, rested it briefly on hers. "I will try, Kat." Then, "Does Paul know? About Justin?"

"Gram sent him to get me from school." She sighed. "So… I don't like to think it, but he could be…using it. To scare me." She shivered.

"You're cold. Why didn't you say?" It was more than the cold, but I let it go, satisfied she acknowledged Paul's wormlike nature. "Let's go in, crank up that fireplace." I pulled her up, reached for the toolbox.

"I've got it." She grabbed the handle. "I'm perfectly capable of carrying my own tools."

I stepped back. "Right."

"Try harder." A small smile. "But you can get the door."

"Yes ma'am." I looked at the sky. "Wind's up. Almost dark."

She nodded. "Then let's batten down the hatches."

Inside, once she stowed her toolbox by the kitchen door, I reached for her hand. "Kat. One question.

About Justin." At her wince, I added, "One more. Then I'll leave it alone...unless..."

"Unless he shows up? Is that when the Neanderthal will show his true colors? Piss on some trees?"

"I get you don't want that. But..." I shrugged. "It doesn't sit well, Kat, knowing he was able to get by with what he did to you."

"It's over."

"As long as he stays away from you. But answer me this. Did he hurt you?" It's hard to keep your tone light when you're talking through clenched teeth, and I could tell she read me better than was entirely comfortable.

Her eyes held mine a long minute. "He never hit me. Shoved me. Once. That's when I got the protection order."

My hands squeezed again to involuntary fists as they had throughout her story. I made myself release them one finger at a time, while I said, again as lightly as I could, "You're a strong woman, Kat Patterson." I looked around. "A strong woman with a lot of first-floor windows."

"I've been thinking about that. WWMD."

"Excuse me?"

"It's something my brother used to say. 'What Would MacGyver Do?'"

"MacGyver? From television?"

"Duct tape, Swiss Army knife, paper clips – though I was thinking marbles for this situation."

"Hold up. You and Paul watched *MacGyver*?"

"Not Paul. Scott. He liked fixing things." Mischief lit her eyes. "And sometimes he blew stuff up – when Mother and Dad weren't looking."

A flood of images rattled through my mind. Scott pulling a red pocketknife from his jeans, a flattened roll of duct tape from his pack, rigging up a surprise in a teammate's locker, resetting a SIM card with a paper clip. MacGyvering. It took me back. "Okay then, Ms. MacGyver. What do you have in mind?"

An hour later, we'd spread an eight-inch swath of duct tape, sticky side up, a foot inside every window and spread marbles across the next foot of space. It wouldn't stop anybody, but by the time he got loose from the tape and slithered over the marbles, we – and the dogs – would certainly hear him coming.

Kat moved her dad's shotguns from the rack near the other kitchen to her bedroom. "He won't know they're not loaded," she said. "He's not the only one who can use scare tactics."

I didn't quibble. My rational mind agreed with her, but the Neanderthal in me hoped I'd have a chance to at least slug the guy. I'd do whatever it took to keep Kat safe. But I didn't have to rub her independent nose in it.

Kat

I never expected to have fun that evening. With Whip Tyler. But we did. Whip got into the MacGyver-ness of the task and kept suggesting more elaborate, devious, and ridiculous booby traps. I saw what he was doing. Keeping my spirits up. Taking my mind off what might happen. Not because he took the situation lightly, I knew. But worry wouldn't change whether the worm broke in or not.

Not that he could ward off all my worry. But he helped tamp it down. Poor Juno helped too when she stuck her nose into a mat of duct tape and couldn't shake it off. Couldn't outrun it either, though she tried, racing from one room to another and back. Or when she pawed at her nose and the tape stuck on her paw.

When Whip got her to stand still, she looked offended at our laughter, as if she wanted an explanation. "What's wrong with you?" she seemed to say. "That stuff's dangerous. Why would you leave it lying out in the open?" Dutch's reaction made us laugh too. With a cocked head, his expression replied, "What do you expect from a human?"

So between Whip and the dogs, my mind had the chance to brew up another kind of trouble. It was watching his gentle hands quieting poor Juno and tugging away that awful tape that did it. Much more distracting than his MacGyver-esque schemes.

Those hands. I saw – felt – them wrapping my injured hand, lifting hair from my collar, brushing my neck, skimming down my bare arms. His hands, the way his skin glistened in my shower...my breath caught in my throat.

And then we were done. Seven doors, nineteen windows – all MacGyverized. What now, I wondered as the worry raised its head? How would we fill the hours before – if – anything happened? The answer came when Whip asked, "What else can I do, Kat?"

Before I could think, before I could rein myself in, I closed the distance between us and said, "You could take my mind off...everything." At his look – the great stone face had nothing on him – I lost my nerve. "Or...not...if you don't want to."

His hands reached out to grab my arms, not rough, but not gentle either. "You know I want to," and the flash in his eyes made me bold again.

"Then let's..."

SALLY CROSIAR

WHIP

I pushed her away. I can't believe I pushed her away.

Kat

"But…I thought you…"

"I do." He saw me flinch at the anger in his tone. He let me loose and clutched at his hair with both hands. "I… Look. Give me a minute here." He dropped his forehead to mine and took a ragged breath.

I stood paralyzed and afraid in his grasp. If my feet hadn't nailed themselves to the floor, I'd have turned tail. But I couldn't move. Or I'd stumble and make a fool of myself. A bigger fool of myself. The biggest, fattest reddest-faced fool.

And…being so close to him…that's what nailed my feet down. It felt good. Like…more. Shock nailed me too because more didn't feel like I thought it would – like scratching an itch. More felt…life-changing. And terrifying.

"Kat. I… Are you sure?"

I couldn't speak. Couldn't breathe. It didn't seem to matter.

"Because you have to be sure. I can't... I don't want... There are still...things you don't know...things I can't tell you. I...wish I..." He raised his head, lifted my chin. "Look at me, Kat. Please."

The wanting – for me – blazed from his eyes, and bone-deep relief made me weak. He swallowed and I followed the contraction of his throat, saw his pulse throb. My knees turned to water.

"I want you...so much." His eyes closed and a second later, the grip on my arms tightened. "But you...have to...understand...I..." His eyes squeezed shut again. Another ragged breath, and they opened to show stern resolve. "I can't tell you...Kat. I can't."

I looked at him in confusion. "What?" Why weren't we kissing?

"The night..."Another swallow and I let my hand drift up to touch where the blood pulsed below the skin of his throat. His hand covered mine, held it still. "This is important. I can't tell you what happened the night Scott was killed."

I blinked. The night Scott... It came rushing back. After Dad's funeral. When I thought all I needed was to know. But that need was nothing compared to this. "Okay."

"Okay? But...it mattered so much...before."

Something spurted through me. Anger? Frustration? Impatience. "Yes! It mattered! *This* is what matters now."

"Are you sure?"

I nodded. "Yes! Yes! Oh for sweet Jesus' sake, stop talking!"

And finally, finally, he used his mouth for more important things. And took my mind off...absolutely everything but him and the fire we built. Together.

WHIP

"So…was this what you meant by slow?" I ran a hand up her back and smiled at the little shiver it caused. "Wasn't that what you said? What? Six hours ago? That we should take it slow?"

She raised up. "Mm?"

I smoothed curls back from her face. "You're a woman of surprises, Kat Patterson," I said as I eased her head back against my chest where it belonged. "And I do like surprises."

"Mm."

"Sleepy girl." I grinned as I nestled her closer.

"I'll get up in a minute."

"Where you going to find a better place to be than right here?"

She levered one elbow against the bed, braced a hand on my shoulder. "You've got a shit-eating grin on that face, Whip Tyler."

I laughed. "You put it there, sweetheart." I planted a light kiss. A smile played on her lips before her head sank back down. "That's better," I murmured as I toyed with all that wild sexy hair. My eyes drifted shut.

I don't know how long we dozed. Not long enough was my first thought when I felt cool air where her skin used to be. "Stay."

Her hair brushed my shoulder. "Hungry."

I forced one eye open. "What time is it?"

"Don't know. Time to eat."

I heard Juno's tail thump once before her big head squirmed between us. "Now you've done it."

"You hungry too, girl? You are, aren't you, good girl? You too, Dutch? Whip. The dogs are hungry. I'm hungry. Aren't you?"

"Starving."

"Thank God," she breathed as I pushed myself up. She, on the other hand, rolled to her back and stretched. Her long lean silhouette beneath the sheet made me forget all about food.

"Or we could stay right here..." I put a hand on either side of her body and leaned down.

"Food," she said, even as her hand cupped my neck, pulled me down...

"Damn it, Juno! Down!" At the best of times, the dog's obedience is spotty. Kat's giggle morphed to a snort which my dumb dog took as an invitation to play.

Kat sat up and swung legs over the side of the bed. "Food." She sent me a wink. "Later, maybe you'll sleep through the night, huh, girl? Meanwhile, I'll bet you need to go out." At Juno's eager bark, Kat stood and wiggled into something worn and plaid.

"You make flannel look good," I said. I reached over to tug on the hem, short enough for a tantalizing view of long legs.

"Oh no you don't." She danced away. "Come on, doggers, let's give you a pee and then we'll rustle up grub." She headed out the bedroom door, the nails of eight paws scampering beside her.

I almost sank back, almost let myself lie there and relish how we'd pleasured each other. Till I remembered the worm. I shoved my legs in my jeans and was out the door calling, "Kat, wait!" when I heard a door open.

It was less than a minute. Not that I could have changed anything. It was already too late.

The cold hit me as I opened the door for the dogs. At least twenty degrees colder since the sun went down. Was that snow? Only a light dusting, I saw as I stepped to Gram's porch, but yes. Snow. I pulled my robe closer and turned to wait inside when I heard a sharp bark. "Dutch? Juno?"

A barrage of barking and both dogs dashed – to me, out to the yard, back to me. "What's up, guys?" And then I saw it. Fire at the west end of the old chicken house.

I don't remember what happened next. Alarm jangled in my brain along with a jumble of gotta-do-fasts. Call 911. Dogs. Fluffy!

I was halfway across the porch when Whip's voice pulled me back. "Kat? What's wrong?"

"Fire. Chicken house. I have to get Fluffy. She's…there." I pointed, not trusting words. "In the chicken yard." I hurried toward the porch stairs, but Whip's arm reached out to stop me.

"Wait. Go inside. Call 911. Get dressed. Shoes. I'll get her."

Whether my next moves came from blind obedience or because he made sense, I don't know. Where was my phone? Jeans. I looked down at my robe. Bedroom. Whip pushed me back to the door. "Go, Kat. Call."

"Yes." And then I stopped. "But. You…" Jeans, no shirt. Barefoot like me.

"Go. Make the call!"

I heard him swear as his feet hit the concrete, but he didn't slow. I didn't either. Do what's next.

Three minutes later, the dispatcher assured me fire trucks were on their way and I was dressed and back out the door, Whip's boots and coat in hand.

WHIP

I wrenched the gate open, called to the dogs. "Get Fluffy!" Would they herd? No need. The ewe was already running back and forth by the fence. It was a simple matter to grab her. Less simple to hold on.

"Dutch, hold!" Kat was there. "She'll take to lead. Put these on!" She thrust a bundle at me, dashed for the milk house door, and was back before I'd sorted what she gave me. "Quick! Get those on while I deal with this."

The coat was easy. Stuffing wet feet in boots was not. Kat made use of the time to loop the lead around the ewe's neck.

"Come on, mutton head! You're as bad as Stupid."

Me? No time to ask. I grabbed the lead so the two of us could pull. Damn ewe dug in her heels until a burst of shattering glass scared her into a bolt, almost trampling us both. I heard Kat swear, saw her drop a hand off the lead.

"Are you hurt?"

"No. Can't let her loose. Barnyard." We ran – to keep up with the ewe – till Kat gasped, "This way." We pulled hard to turn the hell-bent creature and raced while Fluffy demonstrated her neurotic sheep-ness, bleating like a possessed creature and bunching back legs to leap the barnyard gate. Way too high for the dumb ewe to clear. We grabbed to hold her back.

"I've got her." Barely. "You get the gate." My best bet was to sandwich the beast between legs and fence, a move that did not earn Fluffy's approval.

"Can you get the lead off?"

"Working on it." The idiot animal didn't make it easy. A hundred fifty pounds of heaving squirm and a loop cinched tight and tangled in the matted wool around her neck. "Hold still, you imbecilic... Almost..." And then, "Got it!" Not a second too soon.

Kat swung the gate open and I took half a step back to dodge one flailing hoof — too late. The damn ewe didn't flatten me, but I did see stars.

We leaned against the gate as it clanged shut, gasping for air like...like we'd run a hundred-yard dash after a scared-stupid sheep. But we had to get back to... Sirens. I found Kat's hand, squeezed. "It will be all right. They'll shut down the fire before it spreads."

I wish I'd known what I was talking about.

"Gotta get the dogs inside."

"Juno, come! Dutch…"

"I've got them." I forced myself to walk, a collar gripped in each hand. If they ran, I'd never hold them, and we had to go around to the only open door on Gram's porch. Damn the MacGyvering and the worm who pushed us to do it all. At the door, I let go of Dutch's collar with a stern "Stay!" and pulled at the door. "Inside. Stay!" I shut the door on them and dashed back around the corner of the house.

Where it became abundantly clear there was nothing for me to do. Except watch from a distance. Stay out of the firefighters' way. I stood on the concrete stoop outside Gram's kitchen, eyes glued, wincing at every falling section of roof. Telling myself lies. "Doesn't matter. Won't have to tear down the old wreck now. Doesn't matter." Tears streaming anyway.

I'd trailed Scott there when he was sent to collect eggs or tend his rabbits. Darcy and I played there, hunting litters of newborn kittens in the old nesting boxes after the chickens were gone, clearing space for an old table and stools to cozy up our clubhouse.

Tongues of fire leaped toward the two-hundred-year-old oaks that shaded the north yard in summer, making me clutch at my heart. Sheets of water from the firefighters' hose beat the flames back. And I praised God for the swarm of yellow coats in the old chicken yard who saved the trees Double-Great-Grandpa Amasa planted for his bride.

Minutes later, the chicken house was gone and the fire fizzled into embers. As the night grew dark again, I scrubbed at my eyes. Two shadows pulled away from the other yellow coats and approached the stoop. Their grimy faces came into focus and relief surged. Until I saw how Whip limped. I jumped off the stoop and ran to his side. "Are you hurt?"

He shook his head and gave a rueful smile. "Bruised shin. Fluffy."

"We've got it under control, Kat. Just dousing it good before we head out."

"Luke. You're here." Whip's arm came around me as I stumbled.

"Yup." He shot me the lopsided grin Darcy blathered about when they first met. She had an eye for quality, that one. "Can't run a joint called the Firehouse and not play for the team." He sobered. "Sorry we couldn't save it for you, Kat."

"It doesn't matter. I was going to take it down anyway." It would have been more convincing if my voice hadn't cracked.

"Too bad you didn't get the chance to do it yourself."
Whip's arm tightened. He understood. My eyes went wet
again.

I swallowed hard. "You saved the trees, Luke. Tell the…
Tell them all how…" Another swallow. "How grateful…
Those trees…they're…family…to me. Thank you. Tell
them all how much I…" My voice fizzled.

Luke smiled. "I'll do that. The guys will like hearing it."
His smile dimmed. "That fire didn't start itself, Kat."

I straightened. "No." And in my heart, though I didn't
want to, I knew how it did. "It had to be Paul." I looked
at Whip. "Not Justin's style." Whip gave me a long look,
nodded. "Paul. Trying to scare me. To get what he
wants." I squeezed my eyes shut, but the voice in my
head insisted I face it. I opened my eyes and vowed I
wouldn't close them to Paul's dirty pool again. "He won't
stop."

Whip cupped my cheek. "I know you didn't want it to be
him."

I snorted. "I didn't want it to be anybody." I stepped
away from him. Away from warmth. "But we don't
always get what we want, do we? Paul's going to find that
out."

WHIP

"What are you thinking, Kat?" If I hadn't already fallen hard for the girl, the steel – in her spine, in her voice – would have pushed me over the edge. She was all fire. And ice. I felt sorry for Paul – and looked forward to watching his comeuppance.

But that was for later because as she turned to answer my question, her eyes went wide and a sobbing gasp made me reach for her. "What?"

"The corncrib." She clutched at my arm. "It's going too."

I turned, pulling her with me, to see fire licking against the sky where she pointed. Another fire. More intense than the first, and closer to the house. Kat's house.

Luke shouted to his buddies. "Cooper! Back the truck out! We got more to deal with!"

We moved as one toward the new threat. Like our being there could stop flames already out of control. It took ten paces before my brain engaged. "Kat, wait! Let the pros do it!"

"The house. It's so much closer…Oh, Whip!"

"You stay here! Not an inch closer!"

She gulped, eyes like saucers. But she nodded and I sprinted after Luke.

"The house, Luke. Let the crib go. Save the house!"

"On it. Stay back!"

Right. I'd helped – a little – with the chicken house. Because it mostly burned itself out. The crib fire was bigger, way beyond my paltry skills. Best thing I could do was stay with Kat. Keep her safe. I turned and she was beside me. Too close. Shouting.

"Luke! The gas tank!"

I jerked my head to follow her arm. Pointing at the tank every farm has to gas up tractors, the farm truck, the family car. Not more than twenty yards from the corncrib.

Kat

Too late! My head spun in horrible regret as I felt my body fly and land with a whoomph that knocked the air from my lungs. I struggled for breath. Nothing. Done for. I accepted I was dying even as I fought for air. I never expected death to feel so...heavy.

The weight rolled off me and a gasp brought in a smoky lungful of choking air.

"Kat! Oh God. Did I hurt you?"

I blinked, turned my head. Whip. Bending over me. Flames dancing behind his head. I pushed against the ground, one hand on grass, one against the rough jab of gravel.

"Thank God. Can you get up? Never mind, I'll carry you. Save you!"

Save me? I blinked again and the fire came back in focus. My eyes went to the gas tank. I thought it ended everything, the house, my life. Still there. I pushed Whip away, scrambled to my feet, gripped at his arm as I swayed. "The tank...what happened?"

"Don't know. The bang…I thought…your hand…did I do that…when I landed on you?"

"Hand?" I looked down. Blood. A trickle. "It's fine." I looked past him to the yellow coats, the burst of water from the hose they wielded. It looked like chaos, but Luke turned and walked back to us with a smile and an answer to the question on my face.

"Tractor tire blew. That machine is toast, Kat. Crib too. But we've got it contained, I think. Whoops. Called that too soon. Get her back, Whip."

His voice stayed calm, but he jogged back to add his weight to the hose aimed now at the poplar tree going up like a candle, wind sending sparks toward the corner of my house.

WHIP

I dragged at Kat's arm, circled her waist to pull her back. She didn't budge. "Kat, come on. We've got to get back."

"The house…"

"I know. But they'll save it. If…"

"If they can…"

I quit talking and scooped her up and over my shoulder fireman style. Seemed like the thing to do – until she began to pound and kick.

"Put me down!"

"When we're away. Someplace safe. Ouch!" The girl knew how to fight. I could admire that – later. "Knock it off, you little…" I grabbed to contain her flailing legs before a foot made contact where it shouldn't. I got as far as the garage where I dropped my uncooperative cargo and pinned her against the wall. She kept fighting. "Kat… Stop! I'm only trying to protect you, for God's sake."

"Who asked you to?" She landed a fist in my gut that left me gasping and let her wrench away. Back toward the fire. But I couldn't let that happen. "Let me go, you…big…ox! You shouldn't…even…be here!"

I saw red. "Tough shit! I am here. Can't you see? I can't lose you too. I couldn't save him, but I will by God save you! Even if it's from your own stubborn self!"

All fight went out of her. And I squeezed my eyes shut as I heard my words echo back.

"What?" I clutched at his coat, my body still pinned. "Whip! What do you mean…you couldn't save him? Who? Who couldn't you save?"

He stepped back – so fast my legs weren't ready to hold me. I flung myself forward – to avoid sliding to a heap, to not let him retreat from this…revelation. His arms came up almost in self-defense, catching me even as he took another step back, turned his head away.

"Whip! Answer me! Who couldn't you save?" I shouted. And didn't care who heard me.

"Leave it, Kat. Just…" Another step back.

"No! Tell me!" I launched at him again.

He winced – maybe from my full-frontal assault, maybe from the sudden glare of a headlight that caught his face. And I knew.

"Scott. Wasn't it? You couldn't save Scott. You'd have tried. But you couldn't…"

Pain marched across his face. His brow, eyes, jaw, skin dotted with soot and ash, all clenched tight. The hand he raised clutched at his hair. And a wave of feeling for this man nearly made my legs buckle again.

But I couldn't let up. I had to make him tell me, get the demon that chased him out in the open at last. Excise the wound. "Tell me. Please, Whip. Don't keep this bottled up. Not now!"

"I can't." Still wouldn't look at me.

"You can. It's all right." I swiped at tears. Mine? His? I grabbed at his coat, leaned into him, our faces close. Breath mingled. Why not tears? "Please. Scott would want you to."

WHIP

I pushed her away. "No! I can't!" I had to make it final, had to stop her. If I sounded harsh, so be it. If it ended any chance with her... I turned toward my truck. Had to get away.

A voice came out of the dark. "Um. Sorry to interrupt. But. Thought you'd want to know. Fire's out. Still smoldering, but...thought you'd want to know?"

Fire. Luke. The night's events slammed at me like a semi going seventy. How could I forget the fire? A glance at Kat said she had too. I looked away fast. The sight of her, those glistening eyes, curls tumbling every which way... It was enough to do me in. Almost enough to send me back, fasten my arms around her. Loosen my tongue. I took a step back. Can't, I told myself. Get out while you can.

Except of course I couldn't. Firetrucks blocked the driveway, hemming my truck where it sat. Walk, I thought. Get away.

Ten strides across the lawn told me I couldn't do that either. Three miles back to town. Dead of night. Dead tired. Desperate to get away. But... I shook my head. Stopped at Luke's side. "Keep her here," I said. Saw him nod, frown in confusion. "Can't tell..." I kept striding. It wouldn't be far enough, I knew, her on one side of the lawn and me on the other. The other side of the world wouldn't be far enough to lose the ache around my stupid heart.

Kat

How did I forget the fire? I hauled at my hair, held it off my face. And saw the night was dark again. Except for headlights that stabbed as I cast my eyes toward the corncrib. Smoke plumed to the sky, but from a mound of embers. Not wicked flames.

Like a campfire, I thought. Sitting tired and quiet, content to do nothing but gaze at embers. I was plenty tired. It sat on my shoulders like a slab of concrete. But there was no quiet. Yellow coats still buzzed with activity. Some aimed a hose, some coiled another, some stowed equipment.

A mound of rubble sat where the corncrib had been – glowing like that dying campfire. The skeleton of the poplar stood charred and stark. I swung my eyes to the house. Still standing.

I sank to my knees, the relief was so strong. I leaned into strong arms, ready to let the rest of the world float away – until I realized they weren't Whip's arms. "Luke." I blinked, tried to work my tongue through the desert of my mouth. 'It's over?" My eyes searched the dark past Luke's shoulder.

"We licked it, Kat. Couldn't save those old buildings for you, but we kept the fire contained." He laughed. "Good thing you warned us about the gas tank when you did. If that thing had blown, we'd all be smithereens."

I blinked again. Confused. The fire. I shook my head, trying to make sense – of the night, my muddled brain, Whip… Where was Whip? I pushed too hard. "It's…over." A sob pushed past the lump in my throat and morphed into a cough that rattled up from my heels.

"Here now. You took in too much smoke. More than you're used to. We've got water and oxygen at the truck. Come get a hit. Clear out those lungs."

"I'm okay," I said as he tugged at my arm. I went with him. Maybe Whip was there.

WHIP

I wasn't far across the yard before I ran into Milly. "Heard the sirens. Had a bad feeling when dispatch called me. But no real damage?"

Not if you don't count me, I thought. Plenty of damage to me, but...my problem. Nobody else's. "Two outbuildings gone. A tractor. Maybe more. But the fire didn't get the house." Kat's house.

"Odd the fires were so spread out, so much distance between them." Milly didn't say it like a question, but I answered him anyway.

"Luke said the first one was set." I pointed behind me. "Second must have been too."

Milly squinted in both directions. "Any theories?"

"Just the obvious."

"Paul? Or the old boyfriend?"

I shrugged. "Kat thinks Paul. Not the other guy's style. She said."

Milly trained his eyes on me. "You okay, Whip?"

I rubbed a hand over my face. No. "Yeah, sure. Tired is all."

"Worried he'll be back?"

"Paul will always be back." And he'd always stand between what was and what might have been. "Look. I know you said you couldn't assign somebody to stand guard or whatever you call it. But this changes things. Doesn't it?"

Milly nodded. "This changes things. I'll call in the arson squad from the valley."

"And a guard?"

He nodded.

"And you'll stay till the new guy gets here?"

His brows rose. But he stopped short of asking. I answered anyway.

"I'm wiped." I looked at his cruiser, saw a narrow opening I could nose my truck through. If I drove across the lawn. "You take care of her. I'm going home."

I didn't wait for a reaction. Didn't stop when I heard Luke call my name. I went straight to the truck and left the Patterson place behind me.

Kat

"Here, Kat. Drink this."

The first glug of water caught me too fast, making me sputter.

"Slow down. Swish a little before you swallow."

Heaven. Amidst all the horrors from that long night, I wouldn't soon forget the miracle of cool water slipping over my tongue, sliding down my parched and scratchy throat.

"Attagirl. That should do you."

"Thank you." I drank deep and closed my eyes. Briefly. Gram's voice played in my head telling me to face it, eyes wide open. Right, Gram. My open eyes lit first on Luke and the other yellow-coated fire crew tending to their equipment.

"Thank you," I said to Luke.

"You said that already." He grinned. "Still nice to hear."

I took the hint and stepped to another yellow coat. I didn't know him, but it wasn't hard to imagine his wife anxiously waiting for him to get home. Didn't have to imagine the "aw shucks" on his sooty face as I reached out to shake his hand. "Thank you."

I made the rounds, eyes searching for Whip, while I shook each firefighter's hand and thanked them for being there, for saving my house.

And if it didn't take the sting away from what remained lost – Whip, the trust of a brother, Whip – saying thank you did serve to steady me, to make me stronger in my skin.

"Ms. Patterson."

"Detective Miller." No uniform so I almost didn't recognize him. "I didn't know you were here."

"You were busy. That was a nice thing you did. Thanking all the firefighters."

"They deserve more than my thanks." I looked at the house. "Because of them, my home is still standing."

He smiled, then sobered. "Two fires, so far apart. Doesn't seem accidental."

"No." I glanced to the north where the chicken house no longer stood, back toward the still-smoldering corncrib, and squared my shoulders. "Someone sent me a message tonight. Wants to scare me into giving in." I narrowed my eyes. "It's not going to work that way. Not when he put so many lives in danger, threatened them and my home."

"So you'd like the arson investigator to look into the fires?"

"Will he be able to tell who set them?"

He smiled. "She's good at her job. If there are clues, she'll find them. And she tells me there are always clues."

"She. I shouldn't assume. I'll look forward to meeting her."

"I guessed you would. She's on her way."

WHIP

Shows what a state I was in. I left my dog behind. And didn't notice till I walked into my apartment. No flapping tail or rooting snout to nudge me through my broody funk.

I sank to the couch. Staring at nothing. Missing smiling green eyes, the span of soft skin I wouldn't touch again. And my dog.

I told myself to get a beer and get over it. But the fridge was so far away. Old promises, new questions weighed like an anvil. And held me where I was.

Various pains surfaced. My throat, my dry-as-dust mouth, the bruise on my leg. The reverb I couldn't tune out in my head.

"Scott would want you to tell." Kat's eyes fierce and pleading through the dark.

"Don't tell my family." Scott's last words, his eyes fading from that same clear green.

Their words echoed louder with every bounce. Those eyes gripped vise-tight. Loving them both constricted all my choices, like a corrupt sheriff's noose in an old B-movie. Not a thing I could do to smother either demand. Nowhere I could hide. No choice left.

I sat and let the despair of loss – my lover, my friend – soak through my skin. How long? No clue. Till sleep overtook me, and even then, scenes from the two worst nights of my life reeled through my dreams.

How many times had I relived Scott's fall? Awake or asleep. His hand slipping from my grasp, the fear, the thud when he landed. That thud was more than a sound. I felt it. In my bones. The jarring. The pain. His hand clutching at my shirt as he begged me to never reveal the part his worthless brother played to cause his death.

It was a familiar nightmare – until the water tower burst into flames and Scott's face morphed into Kat's. His "don't tell" into "tell me, tell me, tell me…" While sparks flamed and her hair flew.

No escape. Not even in sleep. I woke in a sweat, watched the dream play out again on the ceiling. Slept again, dreamed again until an insistent angry buzz entered the dream and brought my head up with a jerk. Heart pounding, sweat streaming from every pore.

The buzz still buzzed. Angrier, more insistent. Phone. I groped in my pocket – like the phone might be a line to sanity. If I could unglue the dry wad that was my tongue.

Not sanity. Darcy. "Whip? Where the hell are you? Luke said you left…You have to go back. Kat needs you."

I blinked. No water tower. No flames. Faint daylight showing at the window.

"Whip! Are you listening?"

"Give me a minute…" I put the phone down on my leg, felt the vibration of her voice while I tried to gulp air. No go. I coughed…smelled…smoke. I lifted the phone back to my ear, interrupted. "She's not alone. Milly.

Detective…set up…protection. He'll…keep her safe."
I stabbed at the end button.

He would. Right? I had to believe it. But Darcy's voice
joined the Scott and Kat litany as I stared again
through the dark.

Kat

The last thing Luke said before he left was, "Call Darcy. She'll need to hear your voice."

I remember nodding. And then the arson detective was there with questions. What time did I see the fire? What had the buildings been used for? I trailed after her quick stride, stood while she walked the perimeter of each fire, waited what felt like hours in a dazed stupor until Detective Miller put his hand on my arm.

"You're asleep on your feet. Nothing for you to do here. Not till daylight anyway. Go. Catch a nap. Elaine will be a few more hours. Go."

I nodded and made my way across the yard, the stink of scorched rubber and burnt corn making my eyes blear. I gave a thought to dropping my clothes at the door, to a shower, but all I could manage was to kick off my shoes before dropping on the couch.

Sleep was instant, deep, and dreamless. Until... I rolled, reached to nestle my head on the warmth of his chest...and woke. Alone.

Whip. I spread my hand where his body should be, found two dog heads. I buried my nose in their fur as if I could detect his scent there. But all I smelled was fire.

I sat up, eyes to the window. Daylight. What time? I groped for my phone. Not in my pocket. Coat? There. On the floor. I reached, shook. The phone dropped with a thud. Almost eight. So late…

The phone buzzed in my hand. Darcy. "I'm sorry, I'm sorry. I…"

"Never mind that. Are you okay? Why didn't you answer? I've been worried out of my mind."

She'd called. Had Whip? I squinted at my phone, couldn't make out… My eyes were so bleary. "Sorry. Sorry. I know. I'm sorry. I…fell asleep."

She made a choking sound. "Right. Figures. You fell asleep. I was up half the night worrying. Ever since Luke got the call. Wouldn't let me come, the rat bastard. Thinks he gets to call the shots now, since he planted this…this…parasite in my body."

"He was right. Too much smoke. You shouldn't breathe that stuff. Not in your…"

"Don't speak to me about my condition! Don't be taking his side!"

I breathed, choked when I couldn't push air in deep enough. Tried to think…

"You're not okay. I don't care what the rat bastard says, I'm on my way."

"No, Darce. I'm…" Another breath, easier this time. "I'm fine. Really. No harm done."

"But Luke said…"

"The corncrib's gone. And…oh, Darce. The clubhouse." My voice broke.

Hers went teary. "Luke said, but…I didn't want to believe it. I know it was a wreck, but…"

"It was. Probably would have fallen down on its own in another year." I swallowed my tears, tried to sound matter of fact. "Fire saved me the trouble."

I heard her swallow too, before her voice went Darcy-brisk. "Right. But you're really all right?"

"I am."

"So what's up with Whip?"

"He's…fine too… Last time I saw him."

Her voice climbed – in pitch and volume. "But he left you there? Alone? Men! Rat bastards, all of them."

"Not alone. Detective…Miller and the arson investigator…can't remember her name… They're here. Or were. I…need to…check… Yes. There's a squad car in the driveway. With an officer in it."

"Good. You can't be alone out there, Kat. Not now."

"No. I…I'll figure out something."

"I thought Whip had your back. What is up with that rat bastard?"

"We…had a…" What to call it? "A disagreement."

"Kat, you can't keep holding out on the guy. You'd be so good together. He's a man so he can't help being a rat bastard. But as rat bastards go, he's a good guy. You really should…"

"I did. We…did."

"You did? Hot diggety! Was it fabulous? Attagirl!" She paused. "Wait. Did he…? Was it bad, honey? Did that rat bastard hurt you?"

"No. no. It was…he was…wonderful." I carried the phone to the bathroom, splashed water on my face, tried to hold back a sob.

"But he left? Why? What…?"

My ears perked at the sound of tires. Whip? I pushed the curtain aside to look. Paul's SUV.

"Darce, I've got to go. Paul's here. I have to… I'll call you later."

WHIP

I was still staring when dark gave way to gray dawn. Sometime later my phone buzzed. I ignored it. Second time, I picked it up, saw it was Darcy again, declined. Third time – in the space of a minute – I sighed and answered.

"Whip, you've got to get over there. I would, but Luke is conked out and I have to… Never mind. You! Go to Kat's. Hurry!"

"Darcy…this is not…it's…it's between Kat and me. Okay? Stay out of it. Please."

"Listen, you. She's the best thing that could ever happen to you. And…oh, screw it. I don't give a flying fantail if the two of you work it out. Though you should. But that's for another time! Paul's there."

I was on my feet. "What?"

"You heard me. I just got off the phone with her. Paul. Is. There. Now. So get off your ass and get over there. Hurry!"

I was already halfway out the door.

I jammed my feet into my boots and grabbed a ball cap off a hook. "Stay," I said to the dogs. Then I changed my mind. We three stepped out before Paul opened his car door.

The officer stepped out of his car too. "Ma'am?"

"It's my brother. The one who set the fire. Probably."

"I'll call Detective Miller. He'll want to be here."

"Thank you," I said as I watched Paul open his car door. Leery at the dogs' angry welcome. As you should be, brother.

"Jesus, KP! Call off your mutts!"

To the officer, I said, "I have to talk to him."

"Not a good idea, ma'am. He could be dangerous. Wait till Milly gets here."

My heart broke a little, knowing I couldn't trust my own brother. I shook my head. "I need to do this. I'll keep the dogs close."

"Keep clear. Don't get between him and me."

I looked deep in his eyes and nodded. By the old sandbox, I thought, whistling for the dogs. "I mean it, you guys. Come!" They gave one last snarling bark apiece before trotting to my side. "Good dogs." I gave them both a rub. "Sit." No go. I took a collar in each hand as Paul came near.

"What the fuck, KP? What's with the cop?"

"The sheriff decided I needed protection after last night."

"Why? What happened?"

Nice try, Paul, I thought, not surprised. Bluffing his way out of trouble was what Paul did. His whole life. But I knew all his tells so I let it play out, let him believe I wasn't onto him. "You didn't notice anything when you drove in?"

"What?"

I raised an eyebrow, cocked my head toward the crib. Watched his face.

"Holy shit! What happened?" It was a convincing open-mouthed stare – if you didn't know Paul like I knew Paul.

"Smart money says...somebody..." I let the pause stretch. "Somebody...set fires." I cocked my head the other way. "First the chicken house. Then the corncrib."

He swiveled, mouth open again. But with a tiny twitch I knew. "Jesus! Two fires?"

"Two." A tiny corner of my brain marveled at how calm I felt. "But don't worry. Except for a raspy throat, I'm fine."

I had the satisfaction of seeing a flinch in his eyes. Not in genuine concern for me, I was sure. He never liked to miss a cue. To play a part – the doting big brother. "Thank God for that. I couldn't stand to lose you...too."

"Oh my yes, that would be sad. Why, that would leave you the last Patterson standing." I paused. "And the whole place would be yours. Sad indeed. Or quite...convenient."

"Jesus. What the hell's wrong with you? I'd never think that."

"No?"

"How could you even think it, KP? You're the only sister I've got. The only family I've got."

"Yes. Just us two. Since Scott died."

He blinked as if he hadn't heard the name in years. To be fair, perhaps he hadn't.

"You remember our brother Scott, don't you, Paul? In fact, weren't you there the night he died...too?"

"What are you talking about? You didn't die. You're fine. You said so." His voice rose in agitation. "You can't think I...wanted..."

He took a step forward but retreated at a growl from Dutch. I saw him take a breath, try to collect himself, plan a new tack. I waited.

"Thank God you're okay," he said. "And the house. It looks...fine."

I nodded. "It was touch and go. If the gas tank had blown..."

His face paled. Didn't think about that, brother mine? He turned to look at the rubble from the fires. "Jesus. What a mess. But no great loss, right? Better really. To get rid of those...relics."

I shrugged as best I could with two dogs itching to lunge at my brother. "No great loss." I let my eyebrows lift. "But questions... Why now? And...who?"

"Who?" His eyes came back to me. "What do you mean who?"

"Who set the fires."

"But...the chicken house, the crib...firetraps, both of them. No surprise they'd catch on fire surely."

I shrugged again. "No surprise for the arsonist." I heard another car arriving, glanced to see it was a squad car. "Detective Miller," I said, turning my eyes back to Paul. "He'll have the arson report."

"Arson? Report?" Incredulity itself. My brother the actor.

"The investigator found evidence...footprints, I think. Isn't it impressive how quickly they work?"

Whip's truck pulled in behind the detective's. And Paul's importance dimmed.

WHIP

I was relieved to see Milly pull in before me. I parked my truck next to his – blocking the driveway – making sure Paul couldn't get by. Cornered, he might turn vicious. But one way or another, he'd not get another crack at her. Not if I could help it.

Milly slowed his stride, so we stepped up together to flank Kat. I felt her eyes on me, but I wasn't ready to meet them. I reached to take Juno's collar. Her hand slid up my arm, held on as she asked Milly if he had the report.

"Preliminary. Elaine found a footprint behind the first fire. Male, size eleven. Another, same shoe behind the crib."

"Eleven. That's your size, isn't it, Paul?" Her voice was calm, but the hand tightened on my arm.

"What? No. You don't think I'd have anything to do with this? God, KP!"

"Smart money says you're the most likely candidate."

"You can't be serious!"

"Detective Miller? What do you think?"

"I think we'd like you to come down to the station, Mr. Patterson. Answer a few questions. Starting with where you were last night?"

Paul snorted. "You've got to be... I never heard a more ludicrous idea... Why would I set fires? Here?" He turned to Kat. "What is this, KP? Some elaborate scheme so you get your way? Keep the whole place? Huh? You probably set the fires yourself just so you could blame me."

"She was with me last night," I said. "We were together."

Her hand slid down to my wrist, squeezed. "We certainly were. As together as two people could be."

I couldn't help looking then, couldn't help getting lost in those smiling eyes.

"So you did it together. Trying to cut me out." Paul pointed at me. "He's supposed to be working for me," Paul claimed. "You tell the cops about our deal, Whip? Go ahead, you, ask him."

Milly said, "Whip?"

"I sketched out a housing development for Paul. West of the creek."

Kat smiled. "A good spot for it. Your land, Paul. Nothing to do with me." She shrugged. "But I suppose...about the fires...if Detective Miller thinks we should all go to the station... Is that what you think, Detective?"

Milly looked toward me. "What size shoes do you wear, Whip?"

"Twelve and a half."

"You did say it was a man's shoe, Detective?" Kat's voice was mild. Deceptively so.

"It was."

Paul exploded. "I can't believe you. I'm your brother, for God's sake. You want the cops to arrest your own brother?"

She cocked her head. I saw her shoulders square, her eyes narrow. Look out, Paul.

"Not if I had another choice, Paul. But since you played the family card, let me ask. Why would you set fire to your sister's home? Set up a camera to spy on her? Drug her dog to get in her house? Where you've always been welcome? Until now."

Now it was Paul's turn to open and close his mouth. Attagirl, Kat. He didn't take long to recover. "You're crazy! Why would I do any of that?"

"I can't imagine. But I think you did." She paused, holding his eyes a long moment. "Makes me wonder too – since you apparently don't care about your sister's well-being – whether you might have had...something to do with how your...our...brother died."

"I..." An accusing glance at me. "You *told* her? Son of a bitch!" He took a step toward me, and the dogs went nuts. He stepped back, eyes wild, profanity sputtering from his twisted mouth. "You...You promised!"

Kat squeezed my arm. "Whip didn't tell me, Paul. You did – just now."

"I didn't..."

"Stop lying!" She stepped forward with a firm "Stay" to the dogs. "What did you do? To Scott?"

"They're trying to frame me, the two of them! You going to stand there and let them do this? Some cop you are."

Milly shrugged. "Seems like a reasonable question. I've wondered myself."

"You can't believe I meant to do it! I was scared. I was only thirteen, for God's sake. I never meant to... He...slipped... It wasn't my fault...Tell her, Whip!"

I shook my head. "I...can't." I felt Kat turn to me, but I couldn't meet her eyes, didn't look at her till she focused back on Paul. Then I saw her eyes go to slits again.

"But you were there. And Scott fell. To his death. Did you push him, Paul?"

"No! I didn't mean to... I was scared. I... It was an accident... I only... You were never supposed to know. Scott never wanted..."

"Never wanted what?" She advanced again. "To die? I expect not."

"He..." pointing at me, "wasn't supposed to tell! He promised!"

"Whip promised to let you off the hook? Why, Paul? If it was an accident?"

"It was! I didn't mean...Scott...wanted...it was for the family! Don't you see? Tell her!"

I shook my head, no happier about it than he was. "I can't." I met her eyes then. Held them. Until I couldn't.

"I see," Kat said. "You promised Scott. Not to tell what Paul did." She turned on Paul. "And you let Whip take all the blame. All these years. While you went on your merry way."

"No. I..."

He never saw it coming. I didn't either. Kat moved too fast. She plowed her fist into Paul's gut with the force of a tornado on the plains. With comparable destruction.

Kat turned her back on the man sprawled on her driveway and said to Milly in a measured tone, "Take him with you, please. I'd like him off my land."

To me, she said, "I'll talk to you inside."

Kat

I paced the room, muttering obscenities. I was so pissed at Paul – for the fires, for his refusal to take responsibility ever. For letting Mother and Dad – and me – think Scott's death was all Whip's fault, letting us all think he was poison. "Let him rot in jail!"

I stopped mid-pace, chest heaving, hand to mouth as a sob escaped. It was me who pushed Whip away. Because Paul... I shook my head. It was me. I had to own it. Paul let it happen, let our parents brainwash me too. But later... I pushed him away. Because he scared me. Because of Justin. Again, I stopped. No. I had to own that too. Whip brought up feelings I never had for Justin. That's what scared me. My feelings. Scared me so much I pushed away my best chance at...

"But you don't believe in love," I muttered. "Don't trust it." Except for Gram, why would I? You couldn't call it love on our side of the house. Obsession maybe. Not genuine affection. Not trust. I put a hand to my mouth remembering all the times, all the ways I distrusted Whip

– while he proved himself completely and consistently worthy. No matter the cost.

The kitchen door opened. Whip. I stood, heart thumping, eyes searching his face. The burden he carried was there, in the slant of his brows, a wariness in his eyes. It was there all along. If I'd had enough compassion to look.

"Whip." I pushed aside my own fears – more complex and dire than before – and reached for his hand. "I…I'm sorry. We…all of us…I…blamed you. When all along it was Paul. We…I… It wasn't fair. To you."

He shook his head and my already racing heart accelerated.

"Please. Forgive me. I was wrong to push you, not to trust…" I stopped. Made myself take a breath. "Please, Whip."

"It doesn't matter."

"It does. We…I…treated you…badly. You deserved better."

He closed his eyes, shook his head again. "I shouldn't have come back. Shouldn't have…started with you." There went the hand through his hair. "I'll just…get Juno and…get out of your hair."

My hand went to my throat. A new fear more harrowing than before. "No…please…I… Is it too late? Did I mess it up? Our…chance?"

His eyes flashed once. And dimmed in the next second. "You…"

"Please, Whip! Give me another chance."

"You want…"

"I've been wrong. Pushed you away. Because I blamed you." I took a deep breath and made myself say the truth. "And because what I felt...feel...is...so...big."

"What? What do you feel about me, Kat?" He said it like it didn't matter, like he was tired – of me.

Don't blow this! "I...think...I might...do..." For the love of God. Say it! "Love you." I forced myself to meet his gaze, to push the words out from my desert of a soul. "I. Love. You."

His eyes closed. One hand scraped through his hair. While time stretched and I saw my shrouded hopes crash and burn like the corncrib.

"Thank God."

My heart jerked. "What? What did you say?"

"I said, thank God." His lips turned up in a shaky smile. "Because I love you too. Have since...feels like forever. And I thought...I never..."

"You...love me?" I stepped closer and watched barriers and burdens slide away.

"You don't sound convinced." He pulled me closer still.

Later, when I could breathe again, when I could bear to pull away far enough to see his face...I decided breathing was overrated.

WHIP

When we surfaced – who knows how long it took – I ran my hands, my eyes over Kat's face. Looking for truth, I suppose. It was there to see in shiny eyes. And the dark circles under them. She loved me. And she was hurting.

"What will you do about Paul?" I didn't want to bring him into the room with us. But he was already there.

Her smile dimmed, eyes dropped. "Paul who? I don't have a brother anymore. Not after what he did."

I slid my hands to her arms, put air between us. "We both know you're not built that way, sweetheart." I wiped a thumb under one moist eye.

"But…he… How can I ever forgive him? How can you?"

"I haven't. Not for how he tried to hurt you. But…Scott…" I took one step back, for distance, for strength to say what I never had. "I've had a long time to think about what happened, to…remember." I closed my eyes, saw it all again. Opened them to see her watching my face.

"It doesn't matter. You don't have to tell me. Paul's the problem. Always has been." She drew a ragged breath. "I'm done with him."

I put a hand to her cheek. "Sweetheart. He'll always be your brother. Can't change that. Or how you're made." I cupped her neck, pulled her close. Tell her the rest, I thought. "He...wasn't lying. About it being an accident. But..."

"Don't," she said. "Not for me."

"No. I should have told you before. The truth. Then maybe..."

"You think that would have changed things? That he wouldn't spy on me...on us? Not set the fires?"

I scrubbed at my hair. "No. But..." I took a step back. "I need to tell you now."

Her eyes searched my face a long moment. "You need to? Because...don't do it for me. It doesn't matter."

"It does. To me."

Again she studied me, nodded. "Okay. If you need to tell me...okay." She sank to the couch, tugged me with her. "But before you do, know this. You and me? We're good. Better than good. I love you. You love me. Whatever you say or don't say now, that doesn't change."

Kat

The way he looked at me then? I saw it for a gift I'd
unwrap the rest of my days. And my life's work stretched
out ahead – to earn that look in his eyes.

A long moment later he turned his eyes forward,
breathed deep, and began to talk.

"Scott was my best friend. The best anybody could ask
for." He stood, stared at the floor. "The first time we
climbed the water tower, it was my idea. After that, we
were both hooked. It was great up there, looking down
on Oakton, up at the sky. Quiet. Scott called it the place
where trouble couldn't find us." He paused. "Till that
night."

Another pause. Longer. "We'd been up awhile. Watching
the sun set, the lights come on in town. Hanging out. Till
we heard the voices below. Paul and his buddy Larry
Barnes. Drunk. Scott was mad, said we'd better head
down, keep them from climbing." His hand trembled as
it raked his hair. "We didn't get there in time."

I wanted to stop him, say again I didn't care. But his words spilled over themselves as he sped up the telling. As if he couldn't wait for it to be done and over.

"Paul got halfway up. And then he froze. The booze got him that far. Fake courage." Whip began to pace as if trying to outrun what happened next.

"Scott said we had to get him down, that he'd catch hell if anything happened to Paul." He shook his head. "Too stuck to talk him down, so…" Three steps, three more back. "It should have been easy. I'd swing Scott around Paul, below…where he could…" He stopped. "Should have worked. Both of us strong enough. Except Paul… I don't know…slipped…flailed…just when…"

His breath came fast. "I had Scott by the arm and then…I didn't. I…reached for him…, but…" I saw it all in his eyes, through his eyes. The lurch, the shock as Scott lurched into the dark, the terror…horror. I put a hand to my throat, tried to swallow, seeing those same rapid emotions in my brother's eyes, imagining Whip's nightmares, the awful sequence repeating itself again and again.

"Shh…" I don't remember how I got to his side. My only thought was to soothe. And to stop…seeing. I clasped Whip's outstretched hand, felt the taut muscles. Knew he tried again to reach…to keep his friend from falling. My hand circled slowly on his back. I felt his anguish seep into every finger.

"He was still alive. When I got Paul down. But I knew… He did too." I felt him swallow, the drum of his heartbeat. It was a long moment before he blinked, remembered I was there. "Nothing I could do. Except promise… And then he was gone." Whip put his head in his hands.

I gathered him close. Held on, held in my own feelings until I felt his heart slow. "Scott was wrong," I said. "To ask so much. Wrong to protect Paul."

"It wasn't...for Paul." The words came out stiff, as if his throat was rusty.

I kept going, needed to. "He never had to own up... All his life... Paul never had to take responsibility. Not even for the drinking that cost his brother's life."

Whip shook his head, blinked, shook his head again, as if the present were an alien world he stepped into. As if his ears didn't yet work here. "It wasn't for Paul," he said again. "It was for you. Scott said, 'Protect my family.' Your parents. You. Protect you from knowing, he meant. Scott said your mother would...fall apart..."

"She did."

"But worse if she knew Paul was...involved. 'Protect my family.' Scott said Paul was her favorite. It would kill her to know...to blame..."

I tightened my arms, too full of images and emotions for meager words. Too full for my big brothers, the wreck that was my family, this man.

WHIP

We didn't speak for a long time. And then we did. What happened after. The rumors, Dakota, the guilt that wouldn't go away.

She shook her head. "But you didn't do anything wrong."

I had to look away. "I didn't save him." A long breath. "I know. I couldn't." I shrugged. "My head knows it, but…."

She squeezed my hand and nodded. "Guilt is sneaky that way. Even when all the trouble Paul, my parents, Justin brought was theirs, not mine, the guilt can feel like mine. I feel it now. For all you gave up for my family."

I shook my head. "I was alive. Took me a while – and Jake kicking my ass – to appreciate it. To grow up enough not to pity party all the time." I shrugged. "I regretted a lot, that first trip up the water tower, not getting a firmer grip… But not the promise. How could I not do what he asked? For my friend." I leaned my forehead on hers. "I never questioned the promise I made. Till you. That's when the cost got too high."

Her smile went wistful. "I wish…"

"I know. I miss him every day."

She nodded. "Me too. But that's not what I meant." She seemed to search for words. "I know he tried to protect us. But it didn't work. There was a...hole...a hole where Scott used to be. My mother...drowned in that hole. Dad tried to fill it by blaming you." She shrugged. "Me too." She sighed once before leveling her eyes on me. "The point is none of it worked."

"I'm sorry."

She shook her head. "No. I just want... I want to remember Scott – not just the hole he left. We could have filled the hole by remembering, talking. We needed to talk about him and never did." She turned tearful eyes toward me. "You're the only one now, the only one who can help me remember."

I didn't know what to say. "You want me to... talk...about Scott?"

"Please, Whip. My memories are so hazy. Give me my brother back."

It hurt to hear her voice break. What could I tell her? To give him back. "You've got his eyes. Not just the color, the...same expressions. Your hair too." I tangled my fingers in it. "Only prettier. You're like him in other ways too. Smart, resourceful, loyal."

Stories came, halting at first because I'd packed them away too. But the more I talked, the more stories I found, like they wanted the light of day. How our friendship grew closer than brothers, the fun of playing on the team together, the way Scott stuck when I tried to push everyone away after Dad died, the goofy pranks we pulled. She told stories too. How he taught her to swim, the chem set he got for Christmas and the explosion behind the barn that singed his eyebrows. By the time we talked ourselves out, there was enough laughter to swallow a lot of the sad.

Eventually she laid her head on my shoulder and said, "I feel him now. Like he's here again."

I felt him too. I even felt like he'd be happy to know I loved his sister. I gripped her hands. "Kat. I need... You have to marry me. Will you? Please, say you will."

Kat

I blinked, opened my mouth, closed it, opened again. No sound. I couldn't get my voice to work. Marry! I looked away. Tried to think. Looked back. And saw his face shutter.

"Sorry," he said. "Bad timing."

I shook my head. "No." The shutters closed tighter. I grabbed for his hand. "Not bad timing." I swallowed hard. And blinked again, this time at the bright light as shutters cracked open. "Could we..." The light shimmered. "Shouldn't we...talk...about it?"

His kiss swamped me and any words I might say. No room for protest. Or rational thought. Only sensation. And something unfamiliar. Joy?

Much later, he asked again. "When? How soon can we get married?"

I put my hand on his chest, held him away, tried to get my heart to settle. A long shaky breath. A grin tugged on my lips as I swung a leg to straddle him. "What do you say…" I teased his lips. "Let's just…take that…slow," I said and fastened my mouth on his.

WHIP'S EPILOGUE

Five months later

"I'm going to ask for leniency."

Paul's trial was the next day. And though we'd been through it a dozen times, looked at all the angles, I said it again. "Your call, Kat. As long as you're safe."

"I can't be the one to send him to prison. Even if he gets the full sentence, he'll be out in three years. Madder than ever." She shook her head. "Leniency is better. He'll know I could have asked for more."

"And the land?"

"He made a lot with your development across the creek."

"He'll want more. You know Paul."

She shrugged. "He's got a hundred acres left." She angled her head to the east. "Whatever he wants to do there, I can't stop him."

I took a deep breath. Time to put my plan on the table. "I've been thinking about that parcel."

Her brow crinkled. "Another development?"

I shook my head. "I talked to Trav."

"Your brother?"

"Yeah. He needs more land. We talked to Harry, down at the bank. Between us, we qualify for a loan. Trav and me. We'll buy it."

"Trav and you?" The crinkle deepened.

"Kat. Hear me out. Okay?" No wonder I waited so long to bring it up. "Trav needs more land, to scale up his operation, make it more profitable."

"Can't he find land closer?"

"Hasn't yet. Besides, he can't swing it alone. He needs...an investor...a partner."

"Partner. You?"

"Silent partner. I'm no farmer. But it'll work, Kat. We buy it, Trav farms it. Like it is. No golf course, no overpriced houses crowding you. Us."

"But..."

"Hear me out." Time to say the rest. Quick, before I lost my nerve. "It's not just for you. I need to do this, Kat. I feel like a squatter here. Your place. I want to be an owner, not just a guy living under your roof."

She settled hands on her hips. "You contribute. Groceries, electric, office rent, for Pete's sake. Even though the room was just sitting there."

"Not enough. It's a good plan, Kat. For you, Trav, me."

"Paul won't sell cheap. He'll want more than farmland would bring."

"He won't get it. Not for the next five years, maybe ten." I held up a hand to stall more argument. "Stan told him. Between the Twin Creeks development and Rolling

Fields here, Oakton's housing market will be saturated a long time. Developers are all moving east. Paul won't find other buyers. We're his best shot for fast cash."

"Hmm. Sounds like you've got it all figured out."

I caught the warning tone, but... "There's more. Your part of the deal."

"Oh? I've got part of the deal?" Lifting brows signaled more warning.

"If you agree. Trav wants to rent your pasture, the barns. Move his flock here. Free up his land and the fields here for planting."

"That's what he wants, is it? What you want?" Clenched teeth? Oh boy.

"It's a good plan, Kat. You've got empty barns. Hills that'll be overrun with brush in a few years without animals on them."

"I see. So... You've been planning all this – with Trav, the bank, Stan. And didn't think to mention it to me?"

I lifted my hands. "Not planning. Thinking. Seeing how to make it work. Before I got your hopes up." My God, the woman could make me squirm. "Not trying to take over... I just... Oh hell. A surprise. I thought... A happy surprise."

Silence. A long, long silence.

And then her laugh rang out. "You shouldn't make it so easy to wind you up." She reached a hand to my face, her eyes dancing. "I might wish I'd been in on the thinking, but I can see it is a good plan." She dropped her hand. "If Paul will sell."

"He'll bite. Leniency and the promise of cash in one day? He'll bite. And with the land sold..."

"He won't venture away from the burbs to our hinterlands. Won't see a reason too."

"He'll miss out on a great sister, but…"

"He won't be breathing down our necks."

"Not quite so good as thinking of him rotting in a jail cell, but not bad, considering."

She laughed and looped her arms around my neck. "Not bad at all." Then, "I was going to wait till later, but… I've got a surprise for you too."

"You're finally ready to set the date?"

"No." Her laugh turned into a snort. "Well… Come upstairs. I want to show you something."

"Upstairs?" It was odd but we had so little need to go up there, I almost forgot there was an upstairs. "I thought you planned to work on other people's houses now you finished all the rooms down here."

She smiled. "Plans change. Come upstairs."

"Now?" I nuzzled at her neck. "Wouldn't you rather…"

"Later," she laughed and tugged me along. As if I wouldn't follow her anywhere.

"Huh." Fresh paint. The room that stretched the width of the house. "When'd you do this?"

"A week or two after you moved in. What do you think of the color?"

I rolled my eyes. "Um. Nice. What's it called? Sweet corn?"

"Morning sun. This will be our room. With a new bathroom here." She pulled me toward the small room to the east. "And closet." I looked at where she had the spaces framed. "Plumbers coming next week. Rain shower, tub, two sinks. Misty blue."

"Nice. So we're moving upstairs?"

"Got to." She smiled and pulled me through the large room to the small room to the west. "Because."

A brighter shade of yellow showed through the doorway, and I opened my mouth to ask its name. Except as she nudged me into the room, I didn't have enough spit to speak. A crib. My eyes sought hers.

"Surprise!" Her incandescence owed nothing to the late day sun coming in. She nodded and the gleam spread to warm me to the core. The baby's room.

My mouth opened and closed as I tried to push out sound. "When?"

"February." Her smile dazzled.

I reached for her. "A baby! Our baby."

"It's okay? You're happy?"

I kissed her. "Oh yeah. Stunned a little. But… Wow!"

Her eyes danced. "So…what do you say? Two weeks from Sunday? Ceremony on the front porch. Your family, Darcy and Luke, a few friends. The dogs. Champaign. A picnic."

Through the widest grin of my life, I said, "I see. So…you've been planning all this. And didn't think to mention it to me?"

She snorted. "It didn't come up." She pulled back, eyes searching my face. "You…you've never been just some guy living under my roof. You know that, right?"

I kissed her again. "Yeah. For sure now. Question."

"What?"

"Do we seriously have to wait two whole weeks?"

SALLY CROSIAR

Author's Note

My family still calls the land where five of our generations lived our Home Place – even though none of us has lived or set foot there in over forty years. Why does a place embed itself in one's psyche? Maybe it's the long legacy of my great- and great-great grandparents' aspirations that built our home. Maybe it's the land itself – farmland that fed our bodies, a playground of barns, hills, creek, and timber that fed our imaginations. Maybe for me it's because my roots were dug up at the tender age of fourteen. I did not transplant easily.

I still find fault with my great-grands' misguided belief that if they left the place we called home to their grandchildren, the house and land would forever remain in the Crosiar family. Those great-grands failed to anticipate the cantankerous greed of my uncles which made selling our Home Place the only option. And my roots never quite recovered.

Writing *Home Place* has been a sort of pay-back for the disruption of my roots, an attempt to re-write history – to let Kat hang onto her ancestral home when we could not. That's what I hoped for as I began this novel, but for a long time I couldn't see any practical way she could.

Kat's house was mine – the house my great-grands built to accommodate their passel of eleven children and aging parents. They built it in the mid-1800s, and it was every bit as big and impractical as Kat's house when I lived there a century later. My grandmother lived in the north half of the house while my parents, sibs, and I occupied the rooms to the south – fifteen rooms and two baths all told.

How could it make sense for Kat to live there? She'd have two of everything – kitchens, dining and living rooms. She'd have two back porches, two more in front, and still another across the north end of the house! Maybe she could run a B&B. But would it feel like her Home Place with strangers coming and going? I didn't think so.

Keeping the farm seemed just as impractical. Farm life is great. Making a living? Not so good, especially when half your land is the timber, creek, bluffs and untillable hills. But was I willing to let Kat live with the golf course that farm has in fact become? Not a chance. Kat and I are that much alike.

But here's where I have to stake my claim that *Home Place* is not an autobiographical story. The place is real – or as real as my birth-to-fourteen-year-old memories could make it. Kat's ancestors' did to her what mine did to me. Even Stupid Odd the cow was based on fact.

But Kat is not and never was me. She came to me as a full-blown character with fears and a backstory that were hers, not mine. Nor were other characters – except our mutually misguided ancestors – based on anyone I've ever known. Mine were kind, loving parents. I don't have a brother like Paul, one who died in a fall, or an ex-boyfriend who stalked me. While I have many feisty friends, none are by themselves quite like Darcy. And Whip? Like most authors, I have an active fantasy life.

Kat's not me, and her story is not mine. But I won't deny that she and I are alike in one important respect. We both hold our families' histories and the land that nurtured them in high regard. I happily bequeath my Home Place into Kat's hands, knowing she'll keep it safe and pass on our shared depth of feeling for the land, house, and history to new generations.

Appreciations

More than ever, I find the word 'acknowledgment' to be an insufficient and paltry word. It's certainly not up to the task of expressing my gratitude for the many who have helped shape this book and all my writing.

Where would I be without the encouraging nudges from my writers group? Not a novelist, that's for sure. These dear folks have listened to snips of this story over many months – when elapsed time had to make it tough to keep characters and story straight. I bless the enthusiasm – genuine or feigned – you've shared for this story. Mike Coyle, you get extra thanks for your early and insightful reading.

I clutch my heart in gratitude to my two book clubs who are the kind of readers every writer dreams of and the friends everyone wants!

Thank you, editor Christine LePorte and artist Nancy Lane for helping me polish and put a pretty face on my baby – and for making it look so like my own dear Home Place.

And always, always, to my clan, dear friends and the lovely men whom I've been lucky to travel alongside, please know I consider myself a tremendously lucky woman. Because of you.

And you, treasured readers make me a lucky woman too. Thank you for investing your precious time with my stories.

And now a favor. Pretty please. Add your honest review of *Home Place* on Amazon and help other readers find my work. I promise your review will do more than you know to lift the oft-slogging spirits of this author without a household name. And I thank you from the deepest part of my heart.

Read an excerpt from
Sally Crosiar's debut novel.

Chapter 1

Vi

The first place I stopped when I got back to Freedom was the cemetery. I suppose it might seem odd – not seeking out family who was still alive, but I always found the dead easier.

I parked under a towering tree and climbed out. Jeepers, I was stiff. Three-hours-on-the interstate-stiff. I stretched. Up, down, across, like I do before I step on stage or set. It didn't help and I knew why. Hell, I'd crammed myself into coach from JFK to LAX with fewer knots.

I scanned the ground on my way to the old Johansen plot. Once as a teen, I saw a rattlesnake curled at the base of my great-great grandfather's pillar-of-the-community marker. Figured that snake came to visit kin.

I didn't have evidence to suggest old Lars was the source of venom in subsequent generations – except for the fact that his stone towered over those of his two wives and maiden daughter. But the mean streak in our gene pool had to come from somebody. He seemed as likely a candidate as any.

I grew up under the steely gaze of ancestors in the house Lars built. Grim-faced and scary, the lot of them. Sadie said it was only that they had to hold so still. But I suspected the plain cussedness on those faces came down through the generations like the high foreheads and bushy eyebrows.

I had it myself, that streak of mean. I hoped kindness tempered the mean. If you judged by Sadie, my Hollis genes overflowed with sugar. Certainly, if I learned to be kind, it came from my sweet aunt. I practiced kindness at Sadie's. At home, the mean came in handy.

I wandered to a small stone near the edge of the hill, bent to pull a stray weed from Mama's grave. Did she get the kindness gene too? I wished I could remember. But my only memories were sagging shoulders, tired eyes, a disappointed cast to her mouth. And her casket sinking into the ground.

Tires on gravel made me jump. I ran my fingers under my eyes, pulled sunglasses off the top of my head. I let out my breath — hadn't realized I was holding it — when the car turned toward the Catholic side of the cemetery. No worries. They'd be too far away to recognize me.

No doubt half the town knew I was coming. But still. *My terms.* That was my plan. Blind them with Hollywood shimmer. Don't let them see what I've done when they weren't looking.

I turned back to the car, checked my make-up in the visor mirror, whipped out mascara, smoothed on lip-gloss. I gave myself a wink and turned my lips up in the saucy grin that's served me so well. It's the one thing I got from Mama that I – and praise hallelujah, the TV cameras – value.

It's all an act, I thought. But so what? It's a damn good act, and my old hometown is just another audience. I touched the amethyst drops in my ears for luck and turned the key.

As I eased back onto the blacktop, I cranked up the radio. My terms. My props. The rented Mustang, the mascara, the classic rock and roll. As loud as I pleased.

I cruised past the fire hall and the diner next door. Good old Pinewood Diner. Still running strong. I knew that from Sadie, of course, who still worked there a few days a week, but to see it standing there, ready to open for the breakfast crowd early tomorrow morning? I breathed deep and thought I detected the scent of bacon and maple syrup. My fake grin bloomed real. How many coloring books did Nate and I go through waiting for the lunch shift to end? How many dishes did I wash when I was finally old enough to earn a paycheck?

A softball game in progress pulled my attention to the elementary school – much changed from my days there. A few watchers hung out by the fence. No change there, I thought, and I had the urge to say Just ride it out. Life gets better. But what kid wants to hear how much spine that long ride might take?

Downtown – all two blocks of it – looked both familiar and different. The Community Center and a handful of storefronts looked more tired than ever alongside a bright café where the bank used to be and the splashes of color from the flower shop where the hardware was. Few people or even cars on the street.

The Baptist Church seemed as constant as my grim-faced ancestors. Likely its main mission remained – to starch and comb wayward kids like me into submission.

I slowed at River Road. Can I really slip into town without an audience? Unlikely, I thought as I spotted Mrs. Waters in her garden. Showtime. I smiled and waved as I made the left turn to Sadie and Harry's. Left, not right. Staying where I'm wanted. Not with Dad and Tammy at the old homestead. Not now, not ever again.

Want more? Find *Come Back* and all Sally's books at: www.amazon.com/Sally-Crosiar/e/B075SLLGN1

Made in the USA
Middletown, DE
15 November 2020

24120094R00241